THE LOST PAGE

ITALY

Rome

ATHENS

GREAT SEA

EGYPT

THE LOST PAGE

An Archaeological Thriller

JOE EDD MORRIS

Black Rose Writing | Texas

ISBN: 978-1-68433-770-5 (Paperback); 978-1-68433-812-2 (Hardcover)
PUBLISHED BY BLACK ROSE WRITING
www.blackrosewriting.com

Printed in the United States of America
Suggested Retail Price (SRP) $19.95 (Paperback); $24.95 (Hardcover)

The Lost Page is printed in Chaparral Pro

*As a planet-friendly publisher, Black Rose Writing does its best to eliminate unnecessary waste to reduce paper usage and energy costs, while never compromising the reading experience. As a result, the final word count vs. page count may not meet common expectations.

Map Artwork by Jan Cobb
Author Photo by Thomas Wells

For Max, Ellie Rose, Abbey Kate, Posey Claire, Millie, and Hallie Aven

In Memory of the Reverend Cathon Bowen Burt

Praise for

THE LOST PAGE

"*The Lost Page* expertly weaves past and present together in an electrifying story that imagines an answer to a two-thousand-year-old mystery."
–Joseph T. Reiff, Emeritus Professor of Religion at Emory & Henry College and author of *Born of Conviction: White Methodists and Mississippi's Closed Society*

"*The Lost Page* is an important novel laced with a refreshing sense of humor and filled with fascinating detail that could only have come from a writer with the credentials of Joe Edd Morris."
–Elaine Hussey, author of *The Sweetest Hallelujah*

"In *The Lost Page*, Joe Edd Morris transports readers to other realms and the engaging storytelling press-es them to contemplate what they really care about. A profoundly fas-cinating read."
–Michael Hartnett, author of *The Blue Rat* and *Generational Dementia*

"Any resemblance between *The Lost Page* and Dan Brown's blockbuster *The Da Vinci Code* is superficial. Morris is far more original than that. There are no bad guys here, no secret societies or cryptographic enigmas, just two innovative adventurers using their wits to navigate a chaotic environment amid a revolution in Syria."
–James E. Hutchingson, author of *Pandemonium Tremendum*

Antioch

LEBANON

SYRIA

Beirut

Baalbek

Maaloula

Mt. Hermon

Tyre

Caesarea Philippi

Damascus

Capernaum

Caesarea

Tiberias

Sea of Gennesaret

Scythopolis

River Jordan

Via Maris

Jericho

Kings Highway

Jerusalem

Bethany

Heshbon

Via Maris

Dead Sea

"Trembling and bewildered, the women went out and fled from the tomb. They said nothing to anyone, because they were afraid." (Mark 16:8)

CHAPTER ONE

Edinburgh, Scotland, October 29, 2011

The Boeing 787 rumbled over the western shore of Scotland. The pilot announced the final descent and the landing gears came down. Chris Jordan's heart revved. He hadn't been back to Edinburgh since he was a student there seventeen years earlier. He had mixed feelings at seeing the city again and what lay ahead. The message was brief: "Urgent. Come immediately. Need your help. Have artifact of great value. Can say no more. A. Stewart." His former New Testament professor would not summon him without reason. Chris glanced through the small oval window and suddenly, breaking through gray clouds, he saw the castle perched on the crag, Arthur's Seat, Carlton Hill, the endless church spires. Edinburgh, mist-shrouded city of mysteries. *Now, add another*, he thought.

When he had received the cable, he had been in a ravine near a village one hundred miles north of Mexico City. He had been there on temporary leave from his home base at the University of North Arizona in Flagstaff at the request of the Mexican university in Querétaro. Members of their antiquities staff had needed an archaeologist to assist in the recovery of a cache of ancient Aztec carvings a young boy had discovered while playing in the ravine. The place was isolated. There was a Methodist Mission with a medical clinic and a few houses scattered around one that had the only landline telephone in the village and it was out of order. Cell phone service was not available. He had wondered if something had been lost in the translation. The message had been brought to him from the antiquities department at the university in Querétaro, the address and phone number he'd left on his answer machine in Flagstaff.

Over the years, he had maintained contact with his former professor. They had corresponded and spoken by phone several times each year. Professor Stewart had been responsible for Chris taking a trip to Israel to assist in an archaeological dig that had turned his life in a different direction. Instead of saving souls, he would save the history of souls. His mentor had said, "Urgent!" But Chris had needed to know more.

He had driven into Querétaro for phone service. Professor Stewart's number was stored in his Blackberry. The phone had rung a long time, as trans-Atlantic calls do, before the familiar voice had answered.

"Laddie, good to hear from you."

"And you as well, Professor. I'm in the middle of nowhere in Mexico on a dig."

"Laddie, me boy, you could unearth a gold statue of Montezuma and it would not be worth more than what I have."

"You can't tell me?"

"No. Certainly not on the phone. Trust me, Chris. This is the find of a lifetime."

"For me, that would be forty-five years worth."

"I underestimated," the professor reconsidered. "It is the find of the millennium. Correction, of two millennia."

"You don't cut me much slack," Chris said. He looked at his watch. "Today is Thursday, October 27, my time. I can fly from Mexico City tomorrow."

"Excellent. That will put you here on Saturday morning. You will probably go through New York or Atlanta. Call me from there and give me flight details. Or e-mail my office. If you e-mail, give nothing more than your flight information. My assistant will meet you at the airport. Her name is Kate. She will know you. Pack for a fortnight, tourist clothes and something for exploring."

"Exploring?"

"Can say no more. Must be off. Cheerio."

"I'll be in touch," Chris closed, but the line had gone dead. *She will know you*, he thought as he hung up the phone. He hadn't seen Stewart in almost twenty years. What had his aging mentor told this woman about him? What kind of description had he given to her?

He looked at his watch. Eight-thirty a.m. He glanced again at the city as the plane swept its flank north toward the beginning of the Highlands. Dubbed the "Athens of the North," Edinburgh was also the capital of the Church of Scotland, the Jerusalem of Presbyterianism. The professor's discovery probably had something to do with John Knox and the Scottish Reformation, something local. Where else would the old man find anything? In his eighties and fond of saying he was "fightin' fit," Chris doubted he could travel far. He needed to stop thinking about the mystery and focus on getting off the plane. He was seated in the front. The flight was full and his carry-on had been stowed several rows back by a flight attendant.

Once off the plane, Chris headed for the baggage area. His two pieces of luggage came out quickly and he pulled them off the carousel. He'd followed Professor Stewart's instructions and packed for two weeks, clothes for one dress-up occasion, if that was in the cards, and the usual casual wear and "exploring" clothes: blue jeans and khaki shirts and hiking boots. What could possibly keep him in Scotland for two weeks?

He went through customs, procedures he'd done often when returning each semester from the States. In those days, he'd known why he was coming back and the set agenda for the next few months. He'd been greeted each time by the Scottish bride from St. Andrews he had married and divorced after ten years and two children. In contradiction to the reason she had wanted the divorce, homesickness for Scotland, Allyson had remained in the States to be with their sons. He sighed. This time around he didn't know who would be greeting him, only that it was a female, her name was Kate and she was the assistant to his former professor.

The airport had undergone renovations since his last visit and the memorized path through its corridors had changed. There was a new control tower and the arrival halls had been extended. The corridors had a polished look.

He ducked into a men's room. Washing his hands, he observed his image in the mirror. *She will know you.* He wondered again what the professor had told her. Chris studied his face. Forehead to chin, ear to ear, his skin was clear and smooth. The angular sharpness—raised cheek bones, deep-set eyes and cleft chin—was still there. His hair had thinned slightly across the front but the widow's peak remained a defining feature. The only change he could tell, that anyone from his Scottish years might notice, was the deep tan from the Mexican sun. Perhaps the professor mentioned his attire to his assistant. He still dressed the same, casual earth-tones. On this occasion, brown crew-neck sweater, suede jacket, khakis and Hush Puppies. He'd never been comfortable in a coat and tie. Professor Stewart once teased him that after becoming an archaeologist he looked like the earth he excavated. He finished washing his hands and dried them.

He followed the exit arrows, his eyes scanning left and right for someone searching for him, or holding up a sign with his name on it. He saw no one. He went through the automatic doors onto the sidewalk where the familiar and ubiquitous black taxis sat queued up.

"Dr. Jordan?"

The voice came from behind him. He turned and saw a tall, broad-shouldered woman, slim-waisted with long strong legs and dark red shoulder-length hair. She was wearing a navy double-breasted coat, a black turtleneck, tartan skirt and knee-length black boots with square heels. He began walking toward her, pulling his two bags on rollers awkwardly behind him, his carry-on swinging from a shoulder strap. Approaching her, he observed her triangular face with wide cheekbones, pointed chin, fine nose, eyes large and speculative. At first, he had thought late twenties. But as he got closer he could see the veins in her reddened cheeks, the beginning of wrinkles around her arched mouth and bright eyes. It was a face more striking than pretty, its character evidenced in the penetrating eyes and the refined angles of her face. His first thought—*distinguished*.

"Dr. Jordan, I'm Kate Ferguson, Professor Stewart's assistant." Her accent indicated Edinburgh or the Lowlands, the tone rising on the last syllable. It was almost British, sophisticated with less Scottish lilt and trill.

"Hello," he said, matter-of-factly. "Glad to meet you."

"And I, you," she said, hazel eyes sparkling cheerfully. Her handshake was firm, professional.

"How'd you know who I was?"

"I asked Professor Stewart for a photo and he gave me one."

"Good grief!" Chris exclaimed. "That was years ago. Out of curiosity, do you have it?"

Smiling, as though pleased with the request, she unsnapped a small purse that hung from her shoulder and handed the photo to him.

He held it up and immediately recalled the situation. The picture had been taken in Professor Stewart's office. The professor had just autographed his latest book and given it to him. Chris scrutinized himself in the black and white Polaroid. His hair was darker and thicker, the widow's peak more prominent. Standing beside the professor, he looked taller than his six-foot frame. He glanced up at her observing him then back at the photograph, wondering if she noticed other changes. *Not bad,* he thought and returned the photo to her. "At the expense of sounding narcissistic, guess I haven't changed that much."

"You haven't," she smiled. "My car is just across the way." She pointed toward the parking lot. "Do you need help with your luggage?"

"No. I can manage, thank you."

"Sure you do, here," and she grabbed the handle of one bag from him.

"So, how long have you been in Edinburgh?" he asked.

"Most of my life." She hesitated. "I don't live here, though. I recently moved to Dunbar, in East Lothian, about thirty miles east of Edinburgh. Do you know Dunbar?"

"Vaguely. It seems Mary Queen of Scots had a lover, the Earl of Bothwell, who would whisk her away to his castle there when she was in danger."

"You are very well-informed," she said, obviously impressed.

"I was a student here. I'm infatuated with Scottish history."

"I know. Professor Stewart told me," she said, striking a brisk pace ahead of him then glanced back. "I'm not your lover," she winked and smiled, "and I don't know that you're in any imminent danger, but I'm whisking you away there tonight." She stopped to let him catch up with her.

"Oh?"

"It's the International Storytelling Festival, one of Edinburgh's top events. It's the last days but there are no rooms in the city, at least none worthy of a distinguished guest," she said and flashed that bright smile again. "There's a beautiful old hotel in Dunbar overlooking the sea, The Bayswell. It's not far from my place. There's my car." She pointed to a white BMW, 128i Coupe.

He'd recently shopped for a BMW in Flagstaff. Professor Stewart was paying her well or she had a second job.

On the road into Edinburgh, she asked questions about his family, answers he felt she already knew. He told her he had been divorced and had two sons; one a computer programmer in L.A. and the second a psychologist in Colorado Springs. Yes, both were happily married. Yes, he got to see them when he was not in the field. He lived in Flagstaff, Arizona, and taught part-time at the University of North Arizona in their graduate anthropology program which took him on archaeological expeditions around the world.

His mention of Arizona expanded her face and drew a deep sigh. "Arizona. Home of the Grand Canyon."

"Yes! You are well-informed, too."

"It's something I've always wanted to see." It was not said as though fishing for an invitation but she made it clear with some additional comments it was a destination of her dreams.

"Why the Grand Canyon?" he asked.

"Not sure I have a reason," she said thoughtfully as she drove. "It's one of the seven natural wonders of the world. The pictures I've seen look fabulous. I cannot imagine how awesome it must be to see in person." She looked abruptly at him. "What are you doing now?"

He told her he didn't like the dig he was on; there was nothing exciting about unearthing Aztec carvings. He had been suckered into the project with the expectations of a much bigger find at the end of the carvings. At least it wasn't a hoax and the artifacts would benefit knowledge of the Aztecs.

"You might kiss it goodbye," she said with the flip of a hand.

"Why is that?"

"You'll see. Professor Stewart told me not to say anything. He wants to present his discovery to you himself."

End of that discussion. She'd asked questions about him so it was his turn. "What about you, your family?"

She drummed her fingers nervously on the steering wheel then the drumming stopped. "I have no family. Well, I do have a brother I rarely see. He works at the Dunbar Lifeboat Station." She was glancing back and forth at him and the highway, exceeding the speed limit and he noticed she'd never snapped on her seatbelt. "It's operated by the Royal Lifeboat Institution. That's it. My parents died last year. They were in their seventies. My brother, who's single, didn't want the home place so I moved back to take care of it."

"What did your parents do?" he asked.

"My father was a Scottish earl. My mother managed the estate and did volunteer work."

"How did your father become an earl?" he inquired curiously.

"His great-great-grandfather began stealing before everyone else did," she responded, casting a keen glance at him. "My mother worked at a bank, then spent the rest of her time trying to control me." She said it jokingly, but proudly, her head cocked back.

"Were you rebellious?" he probed, immediately wishing he could retract the personal question.

"I was independent. There's a difference. But you don't want to hear all about that."

So, she'd given him a psychological thimble's worth—wealthy, pedigreed, independent. He could probably add "spoiled" and only imagine the juvenile delinquent history. No wonder she was driving a BMW like a bat out of hell and defying seat belt laws.

"But you spent most of your life in Edinburgh," he said, changing the subject.

"I attended the University, got a degree, got a job, got married. Our home was in Edinburgh but our jobs required some traveling."

He'd noticed a pattern to her communication style: comments brief and to the point.

He was working on the delicate question in the brief delicate silence ...

"My husband is deceased." She offered the fact without emotion, her fingers drumming again.

"I am very sorry." He didn't know what else to say, as he sat there struggling for other words.

"We'd been married twelve years, no children. He was older. We had each other and our families. Suddenly, I was in a black hole."

Her voice betrayed a deeper self she was concealing. She was still in love with her husband. That was the most she'd said since she'd picked him up. Again, he worked the math. *Maybe in her late twenties.* She was hovering around forty, closer to his age, at least, maybe older, approaching fifty.

"I have an inkling about black holes," he offered. "But nothing comparable to yours. What got you through?"

"I still had my parents, of course, but my work has been my salvation."

"What type of work?"

"If I told you that, I might give away Professor Stewart's secret."

They were on A8 highway headed for the city center. Except for the spires and churches and street names which never change, some of the landscape had altered. She turned onto Shandwick Place which became Prince's Street, its colorful gardens streaming by on his right, the castle looming above them. Ahead was the Sir Walter Scott monument, Carlton Hill and Arthur's Seat, all of them places where he'd romanced Allyson. St. Andrews had a fine university but she'd always wanted to come to Edinburgh. They'd met at Greyfriars Bobby's, the pub made famous by the Disney movie about the dog who had gone there each day with his master and had continued going after his master had died and had slept on his grave at the Greyfriars Church behind the pub. Chris wondered if the pub was still there.

"I'll bet this brings back memories," she speculated, making the turn onto The Mound, an artificial hill connecting New Town and Old Town. Directly ahead, the gothic spires of New College where he'd attended class for three years.

"Yep, it does that," he responded, which was why he'd never returned; too many points of pain. He'd thought seventeen years would nullify, if not dull, the memories of that time with Allyson. Perhaps, if he'd never left. But now he was seeing them afresh, as though time had not lapsed.

"He is going to be so glad to see you," she said, smiling "You know you were one of his favorites."

"We were close," he confirmed, his thoughts still twenty years behind.

"He's wanted to get you here for a visit. He didn't think you'd come."

"If I hadn't hated where I was, I might not have," he said. "But when Professor Stewart said it was the find of the millennium, I couldn't resist. And if it's not, I can always turn around and go back."

"My, my, you're an edgy one," she clipped. "Don't get feisty, not just yet. Give Professor Stewart a chance."

He felt relieved as she pulled beneath the Gothic arch into the New College quadrangle, the statue of John Knox towering over them. He thought she'd just deposit him. He knew his way around. But she parked, cut the engine and got out. He noticed the flagstones were a different color, no longer dark slate but light honey. Park benches, which he did not recall, were also arranged in the shadow of the Knox statue, along with a row of bicycle racks.

"I wouldn't miss this for anything," she said excitedly. "You can just leave all your things in the car." The words were a command, not a suggestion, as she hit the lock button on her key fob.

He followed her to the entrance, watched as she used the swipe-card access and opened the door he'd opened for himself a thousand times. High tech security had arrived at ancient New College. Crossing the threshold, he immediately noticed the light colors of the foyer and a modern pale-wood desk facing the door.

"That is where the servitor sits," she pointed out as they ascended the steps. "Few students are here on Saturday, no classes as you recall. That was part of the logic in timing your arrival."

Up the steps, the change in décor continued. Gone were the dark oak panels; in were pastel walls with white trim, everything sunshine bright. The offices and classrooms they passed were modern and filled with computer technology. This was not the New College he had left. Ironically, it had literally become a *new* college.

"Professor Stewart's office has moved," she pointed up, as they climbed another flight of stairs. He asked for one on the top floor."

"At his age?"

"You'll understand."

Professor Stewart's office was a large rectangular room, tall draped windows along one side. His desk was at one end, a loaded bookshelf behind it and circular wall clock above the bookcase. As they entered, Chris saw the professor bent over a long table, his figure almost a shadow against the darkly curtained windows. The immediate image was that of an ancient scholar in deep study.

Professor Stewart did not look up until Kate cleared her throat. "My, my, laddie, it's been too long."

It had been too long, but, except for his white hair, the man looked as hale and fit as the last time Chris had seen him. He had that same patrician face, slender nose and strong jaw, bright intelligent eyes. He was wearing his usual black dress shirt and white clerical collar. "Yes sir, it has. Except for some coloration," Chris patted his head, "you haven't changed a bit."

"Nor have you," the professor said as he came around the table toward them, steadying himself at the corners with his fingertips. He pointed at Chris' waistline. "You're still lean and trim."

"I can thank climbing in and out of archaeological digs," he responded.

The embrace was firm and prolonged and then the professor held him at arm's length. "I told Kate she'd recognize you without the photo I gave to her—tall, rugged, handsome."

He blushed. She'd held out on him. "Thank you, sir. I believe the same could be said of a Scottish New Testament professor."

"Yes, yes. You are kind," he said, also embarrassed. "So, you have met Kate." He flipped his hand nervously. "Yes, yes, of course, you have."

"And your dear wife, how is she?" Chris inquired.

The professor's smile evaporated and his face was drawn. "She passed, laddie. Just last year. I haven't spoken with you since then. My apologies for not forwarding the sad news to you."

"How did she die?" he asked.

"She had a stroke. It was massive, took her instantly."

"I am so sorry. I know her loss has been difficult."

"All losses are, Chris," the professor said and glanced at Kate whose face was solemn. "But I submerged myself in my work and took a trip, which is why you are here. Please have a seat," and he pointed eagerly to a chair among others arranged in a semi-circle around an unlit gas wall heater.

"I've been sitting for hours on a plane, sir. I'd rather stand."

"By all means," the professor sympathized. "And you, Kate?"

"I'll stand, too. I think Dr. Jordan is interested in the reason he came. We can visit at lunch."

Professor Stewart turned and glanced at the large clock above his desk. "Excellent. We have a couple of hours. Kate, perhaps you have a place in mind for lunch?"

"Greyfriars," she responded. "It's a short walk. The weather's nice."

"It's the Storytelling Festival, you know," the professor cautioned. "The place will be crowded. We need privacy."

"They have a recessed dining area inside that's semi-private. I called and Ian, the assistant manager who knows me, reserved it for us."

"Splendid!" the professor beamed.

That question is settled, Chris thought. The pub was still there, apparently as popular as ever.

"Come, come," Professor Stewart motioned toward the table. "I've got it set up for you." He walked behind the long table, pulled the drapes and an explosion of bright morning sunlight filled the room.

Chris noted the view overlooked the Castle and parade grounds then lowered his eyes onto a display of, what appeared to be, ancient manuscripts or documents aligned on the table.

"As you, the archaeologist knows," Professor Stewart continued, "ancient documents must not be exposed long to light. That is also why the room has a slight chill and the heater is off. Moisture and humidity, change, are the worst enemies of old manuscripts. I try to keep the temp the same until I can get them into a controlled environment."

"However, ancient manuscripts have an amazing ability to survive," Chris interposed. "You may recall that Khalil Shahin, a.k.a. 'Kando,' the cobbler and part-time antique dealer of Dead Sea Scroll fame kept the Temple Scroll in Bethlehem in a Bata shoe box from nineteen fifty-six until the beginning of the Six Day War in nineteen sixty-seven, eleven years. If that scroll was able to survive beyond a controlled environment," he gestured toward the table, "your documents should have no problem. And there's no better controlled environment than your own British Museum."

Kate and the professor exchanged glances then she spoke quickly. "Right you are, Dr. Jordan. I'm sure you know the museum houses a number of famous New Testament manuscripts. By the way, I can now identify myself. I am Doctor Kate Ferguson, ancient manuscript expert and codicologist." She extended her hand to him and they shook again.

"Pleased to meet you, again," he said, and smiled at the awkwardness.

She glanced again at the professor. "If I'd told him on the way here, it would have spoiled your surprise."

The professor smiled in agreement. "Well, take a wee moment looking at them, Chris, then I'll close the drapes. You'll have more time later."

"I'm sure you're about to tell me what *they* are," Chris asserted, aware of a tone of annoyance in his voice, "the reason I flew thousands of miles at the drop of a hat."

"Aye," said the professor, embarrassed. "Please forgive me. This occasion should be more serious and formal, not rushed. They, or rather *it,*" he raised an emphatic finger, "may be the reason we have the gospels of Matthew and Luke, possibly John. *It,*" he raised a second finger, "is the oldest existing New Testament manuscript outside of Egypt and the Jordan basin. *It* is the oldest extant New Testament manuscript outside of anywhere," and he thrust an introductory palm toward the table. "May I introduce you, Chris, to Mark, the first Mark, the first Gospel According to Mark." He paused. "Or rather his first effort."

CHAPTER TWO

Jerusalem, August, 70 A.D.

The thuds and clashes of siege and battle fell heavily on John Mark's ears as he ran the maze of narrow streets. His sandals slapped loudly on the flagstones, but the heavy boots and clanking armor behind him echoed louder through the walled corridors of the city. Forty years ago he had run the same streets. Then, soldiers had taken his master and he had run for help to save him. Now they were taking his city, and he was running again to save his master. Not his life, for he had been crucified, but the story of his life. If he failed, the world might never know. If he could not escape the city, he would fail. They would all be doomed, he and every Jew, follower of Jesus the Christ or otherwise. The Romans did not know the difference and did not care. Soldiers would execute the Zealots and probably expel the rest, steal or destroy their property. The scroll, the master's story, would be lost forever.

For twenty years, he had labored on the story, the last four transferring his notes, weaving them, onto the master scroll. He had written what he had seen and heard himself. He had spent hours with Peter, putting into words everything the fisherman, the constant companion of Christ, had seen and heard. He had sought out witnesses and interviewed hundreds, pieced together strands of the oral tradition, stories of miracles and healings and religious confrontation still fresh from that time. He had revised and re-revised, edited and re-edited. He had entered each story and each time he had always emerged different, the words, the message shaping and molding him. At night, his mind was full of memories, sentences from the master that never changed. He had sensed everything with a third eye of salvation and was almost finished, down to the last days of the master, a few turns of the large scroll away. And he was trapped in the city where he had come to finish it.

He turned the corner onto the street where his mother lived, near Herod's palace and the Gennath Gate. The thoroughfare was usually busy, but tonight it was empty. He remembered that terrible day he had stood in his doorway, clutching his mother as they had watched the master trudge by, the heavy cross beam teetering on his shoulders. John Mark had moved to help him, but his mother had pulled him back: "You will be next." He wished now he had not listened to her. Yet, had he died with him, the written story would have died. That thought continually soothed his guilt.

He stopped a moment and leaned against a wall to catch his breath. He felt pain in his chest. He listened. He no longer heard the soldier behind him. The only reason a sixty-year-old man could outrun a soldier was the heavy armor the soldier wore. John Mark wondered how they won battles. He had outrun soldiers before. That was decades ago. But he was still lean and still had strong legs. He waited a while. Sweat ran into his beard he had recently clipped shorter along with his graying hair that had made him look older. The heavy odor of burning wood and decaying refuse hung in the August night air that glowed from the Temple flames. He had only a short distance to go. He must make it back. If he were caught, his mother would not know what to do with the scrolls. In his haste to survey the city and find a safe exit, he had neglected to tell her. He pushed off the wall and continued running, staying close to the walls of the buildings, in their shadows.

CHAPTER THREE

Edinburgh, New College, October 29, 2011

Chris stood as though nailed to the floor. All that moved were his heart and lungs as he beheld the ancient documents. He counted ten on the top row aligned with ten on the bottom. The professor and Kate had been working over them for months. He was seeing them for the first time. He should remove his shoes, get on his knees. His body trembled. He began sweating; he grew dizzy and faint. "I'll sit down now," he managed.

Kate quickly drew a chair to the table and he lowered himself into it.

Muted Scottish light fell on the pages. Scudding clouds caused a shuttering effect. Chris was looking at a manuscript from the first century C.E. It did not matter what it was or who wrote it; the fact that it existed was miraculous. Before the present 21st century, the oldest existing New Testament manuscript was the John Ryland's P-52 papyrus with a fragment of the Gospel of John dated 125 C.E. The oldest parts of the Gospel of Mark were in the Chester Beatty P-45 papyrus dated to the first half of the third century. If what he saw was the Gospel of Mark he was on holy ground. The room was suffused with spirit, *The* Spirit. He blinked away tears. "I think I'm going to cry," he whispered and buried his face in his hands.

Professor Stewart patted his back. "We understand, laddie. We've done our share of crying. It doesn't stop. Just touching one of those sheets sends shivers through us. One can get no closer to the historical Jesus."

"I've studied hundreds of ancient manuscripts," Kate added, "but nothing like this. Every time I touch it, every time, chills shoot through me."

Chris raised his head. "You said 'his first effort.'"

"We feel confident it was his first attempt," Kate injected.

"You are telling me this is the autograph?" Chris asked amazed.

"Yes! An autograph. We believe it is a rough draft," Kate repeated. "The author made so many errors he apparently decided to scrap his initial effort and start over but, like an artist's cartoon, kept the initial attempt. As you'll see, he composed on the front, the *recto,*" she reached over and gently touched the corner of one sheet as if to flip it, "and used the back, the *verso,* as a journal. It appears he was taking notes from interviews."

"Probably from Peter," Professor Stewart joined in. "By the time Mark wrote his Gospel, he had access to various independent units of tradition, a Passion Story in narrative form, and possibly some other substantial collections of sayings." He crossed the room to his desk and picked up a book. "Papias, a church Father of the early second century, not that far removed in time from Jesus' ministry, wrote that Mark was Peter's interpreter, that Peter gave him instruction to write things as he has recorded them, and that Mark wrote with great accuracy." The professor opened the book where it was marked, pulled out a pair of glasses from his shirt pocket, slipped them on and read, "'and he has not erred in anything.' This is a direct quote from Papias, cited in this book, Eusebius' *Ecclesiastical History.*" He shut the book, removed his glasses and returned to the table.

"And no one knows of this discovery?" Chris questioned, looking over the documents with astonishment.

"No one else," Kate responded. "You make three."

The comment rocked Chris back in his chair and a bolt of disbelief forced him upright.

"The British Museum is aware we have some ancient documents," the professor commented, "but not their identity. That has been kept sealed."

"My God!" Chris exclaimed. "My God, my God! Give me a moment to compose myself. I know the light cannot stay on them long, but I want to take this in a little at a time. Just seeing them is almost too much."

"Surely," the professor said. "Would you like some tea … or coffee?"

"Tea, please. Maybe scotch, if you have it."

"Not allowed on campus," Professor Stewart said, smiling. "We have Scottish tea."

Kate went to a table on the other side of the room where there were a microwave, a hot plate, bottled water and canister of tea bags.

"How did you get this?" Chris asked, waving a hand over the sheets.

The professor stepped behind the table, drew the drapes. They returned to the chairs around the unlit heater while Kate continued preparing the tea. The professor pulled his chair close to Chris and laid a hand on his arm. "It's long story, Christopher Jordan. I will try and be brief. In May of this year, I was invited to go to Syria, to the small village of Maaloula, about fifty-six kilometers northeast of Damascus. Isabel had died, and the idea was a compelling distraction. Maaloula is one of two villages in the vicinity that speak the Aramaic language similar to the dialect Jesus spoke."

"Actually, three, Professor," Kate interrupted above the soft roar of the microwave. "Maaloula, Jabadeen and Bakhaa."

The professor raised an annoyed brow. "Yes, three villages. All of them resisted the replacement of Aramaic with Arabic. The area is ideal for anthropological linguistic studies. Since the language, due to the inroads of Western technology and culture, is fading, this was an opportunity to study it and write a book about it in relation to the New Testament and the Aramaic translation into Greek."

"Amazing!" Chris expressed.

"Laddie, there's nothing really amazing about it. The villages have been isolated by geographic features for almost two thousand years."

"No, not the villages and survival of the Aramaic tongue. The survival of the Scottish fittest. That you, in your eighties I imagine ..."

"Eighty-six to be precise."

"... would venture to a foreign country, an Arab country in the midst of a revolution, to not only evaluate the ancient language of Jesus, but plan to write a book about it. That is absolutely phenomenal."

From Kate, "That's our phenomenal professor."

"Both of you tickle my narcissism," the professor said shyly. "On the day he was to die, Socrates began studying Hindu. One of his students asked why and he responded, 'Why not?'"

"Very well," Chris said, "Back to your project. I have heard of Maaloula."

"Oh! And how is that?" the professor asked, surprised.

"Caves there were used by Christians at the turn of the first century to escape persecution, especially during the reign of Domitian, then later Diocletian in the early fourth century. I've seen a journal article or two about some interesting artifacts found in them."

"Like what?" Kate inquired, her back to them preparing the tea.

"Not artifacts exactly," Chris explained, "but carvings of Christian symbols—the fish and Greek *chi rho*—on the wall of one along with part of the prologue of the Gospel of John, still legible, in Greek, not Aramaic."

"We're on the same page," the professor said, "but you're a wee bit ahead of me."

"Sorry, Professor" Chris said apologetically. "Please continue."

"We had been guests of the Orthodox Greek monastery of Mar Thecla, which reputedly has the remains of St. Thecla, one of Paul's students, another interesting story."

"'We?'" Chris asked.

"Three other New Testament scholars; one from Glasgow and two from Oxford. The details of the invitation are unimportant, but the Syrian government had sanctioned the study group as well as our place of residence. Assad's government, to some of its thin credit, protects Christians. All had been fine until the Arab spring, but more on that later."

Kate interrupted with cups of tea for each, then sat and joined them. "I've heard this several times, but it keeps getting better." She crossed her legs and raised a cup to her lips.

"I don't need to be lengthy," the professor began, taking a sip of tea. "I had been strolling in Maaloula one afternoon and came to an antique shop near the convent. I'd seen it before but saw nothing in the display window of interest. I entered and immediately to my right," he gestured with a hand as though reenacting, "were shelves filled with books. Many looked very old, not unlike those you see set out on the streets of Edinburgh by vendors." He was becoming more and more animated, his eyes flashing. "At the end of one shelf was something unusual. It was a scroll. I lifted it from the shelf and examined it, afraid to open it lest it crack, for it seemed brittle." He stopped briefly and sipped his tea again, his hand trembling slightly as the cup rattled back onto the saucer. "I asked the shopkeeper where he got it, and he pointed at the floor to a jar. He said the jar had been brought to him by a beggar who lives in one of the caves. The beggar was just trying to make an extra pound and had no idea what he had. Nor did the shopkeeper, whose name, you will need to know, is Walid, pronounced 'Waleed'."

"Why will *I* need to know?" Chris inquired, tasting the tea and nodding approvingly at Kate. He was beginning to suspect the reason for his being summoned.

"Because, there are several antique shops in Maaloula," the professor resumed. "It is a tourist town. Only one has a shopkeeper named Walid. So, the shopkeeper, wanting to be generous, he thought, paid the beggar two hundred-fifty Syrian pounds, the equivalent of about three British pounds or, based on current rates, less than five American dollars. Then the shopkeeper proceeded to break the jar's seal, retrieve the scroll and put it on the shelf. He had no idea what he had."

"This sounds almost like the story of the discovery of the fourth century Siniaticus Codex," Kate said. "You two know the story. Professor Constantine von Tischendorf saw the monks in the Greek Monastery of St. Catherine's at Mount Sinai stoking their fires with the papyrus leaves. There is no telling how much ancient scripture went up in flames."

"When did he purchase the jar?" Chris pursued. "How long before you bought the scroll?"

"Thank God, only a few days," the professor said. "Otherwise, someone else would have snatched it up."

"What did you pay him?" Chris questioned, "If I might ask," aware he might be prying.

"I don't mind telling you. I gave him five pounds," the professor answered.

Chris slapped a hand on his forehead and looked at the professor. "You bought the autograph of Mark for five pounds, a few dollars?"

"Correction!" Kate said. "As we have tried to emphasize, it is not the original full gospel but the author's attempt, a rough draft. Based upon what we know about writing at that time, probably not his first attempt."

"Quite frankly, laddie," the professor said, "neither the shopkeeper nor I knew what was in the scroll. On the surface, the price seemed fair. Old scrolls are sold every day in the Middle East. But the description of where and how this one was found suggested a major artifact. Walid seemed a wee dense, but I didn't need to make him think he'd sold the pearl of great price."

"Where and how did the beggar find it?" Chris persisted.

"The shopkeeper asked the beggar," the professor continued, "and he said he was drunk and fell against the wall of his cave, part of it crumbled and there was another cave. When he sobered up the next morning he saw the jar. He brought it into the shop saying his mother was seriously ill and he needed money for medicine."

"Someone had sealed it into the wall of the cave," Chris surmised.

"That's what we think," Kate concurred, still chuckling about the man's story. "We also think the master copy is still there somewhere."

"Did this beggar say there were other jars?" Chris asked, mindful of his excessive questions, but no one was telling him to back off.

"Walid was not of the presence of mind to ask the beggar," Kate said sarcastically.

Chris looked at the professor. "Didn't you get a chance to track this beggar down, get more information?" he asked with disbelief.

"Unfortunately not," the professor said. "The Syrian revolt, which had started in April, was gaining momentum. Riots were breaking out, especially north of us in Homs." His voice quavered with a slight rasp and he took another sip of tea. "The British Embassy in Damascus, which, incidentally, helped us get to Maaloula safely, strongly recommended we leave as soon as possible." He paused, took a deep breath. "Kate, may I have some water please. The tea hits the spot but my throat is dry. I'm afraid I'm talking too much."

"Certainly," she responded and stepped to the utility table near them, poured a glass from an enamel pitcher, returned and handed it to the professor.

"Thank you." He downed several swallows. "Forgive me. I will continue. The embassy staff offered to help evacuate us, and we did not decline. Whatever I had in my possession, and I still didn't know at that time, I was not about to try and open, not in those circumstances and in those conditions. As you can see," he waved a hand toward the table behind them, "the papyrus pages were dry but amazingly intact. Kate's expertise is responsible for unrolling the scroll and separating the sheets."

Kate gave the professor a single nod of thanks.

"Whoever sealed that jar did a yeoman's job," Chris commented.

"More than a yeoman's job," Kate agreed enthusiastically. "I haven't seen the jar, but that manuscript is in miraculously good condition."

"From the mind of a secular archaeologist who spent three years here in seminary," Chris said, "I'd say a divine hand was involved."

"We've had similar thoughts, laddie," the professor added.

"How and when did you know what you had?" Chris asked. "How can you be sure it's not a forgery? They surface all the time. No!" He raised a hand.

"First question is how did you get out of Syria and into Scotland with it? I don't care how much the Syrian government protects Christians, if it knew you had this," he thumbed over his shoulder to the long table behind them, "it might start a war."

"I cannot answer that question now," the professor said, his voice slightly hoarse. "I will at some point."

"We can answer your first question," Kate offered.

"It's a long answer," warned the professor, "but you will not be bored. It's also one of the reasons Kate is involved. She obtained her doctorate and wrote her thesis on ancient New Testament manuscripts. She can spot a forgery before it's opened." He glanced at her. "I could give examples, but it would take up time."

"Thank you, Professor," she said. "You've now tickled *my* narcissism."

The professor turned his eyes back on Chris. "The possibility of forgery is also one of the reasons we've not told anyone. We wanted to be absolutely sure. Another reason," he leaned over and tapped Chris' knee, "is that we waited until now to contact you. This manuscript is the first attempt. The author, we presume John Mark, obviously became disappointed and started over. The final effort is probably not far away, in that cave or near it. Another reason we've kept it under wraps is obvious. If we told the story," he said, fluttering his hands wildly, "there would be a manuscript rush to Maaloula that would make the gold rush in your Wild West look like a church parlor game."

"The research has taken several months," Kate said. "As you well know, Dr. Jordan, all ancient artifacts contain information that helps us estimate their age, where they originated, and something about their travel history. We have used the latest scientific techniques available to us: video spectral comparator, stereo microscope, carbon dating and thirty-nine-megapixel color digital camera. Carbon tests on a tiny manuscript fragment place it from the first century of the pre-Christian era to the end of the first century C. E. That's within the time frame most scholars believe Mark's gospel was written."

The mention of carbon tests piqued Chris's interest. At the expense of offending them, he risked the question. "How can the British Museum not know about this if you used carbon testing?"

Kate pitched a doubtful look at the professor, who nodded she could answer. "We didn't use them," she said, her tone defensive. "We used an independent source, sent them only a fragment and did not reveal or identify the piece."

"What about the multispectral camera?" Chris risked again.

"I didn't say multispectral camera," she bristled. "I said video spectral comparator. You can buy them on e-bay. As you know, the multispectral camera is very sophisticated and we'll have to wait until the documents are sent to the British Museum. Any further questions about our methodology, Dr. Jordan?" she said, her eyes lacerating him over the top of her tea cup.

Chris realized he needed to repair some damage but unsure how to go about it. "I must hand it to you, Dr. Ferguson. You've done a superb job. You are also absolutely right about what one can learn from ancient artifacts. It's astonishing what can be gleaned from a strand of hair or a particle of dust. The stains from a spill can speak volumes, not to mention the parchment type, age, origin as well as the ink, style of writing, vocabulary and syntax."

"Yes, but these documents were written on papyrus, not parchment." She made the comment in a softer voice.

"Thanks for that heads up," Chris countered. "Now that we've convinced each other we know our business, let's take a look at the real star of the show." By the smile on Professor Stewart's face, Chris felt he was on point.

They left their semi-circle of chairs and returned to the long table. Once more, the professor stepped behind it. He pulled the drapes again and again light poured over the documents, eliciting a comment from him. "Not our usual dirty gray Edinburgh light. Better use this Scottish sun while we can," then turned to Kate. "This is Kate's area of expertise. She'll take over at this point."

Kate walked to the table, her boots clomping on the wooden floor. Behind the table to her right was a wipe board on a tripod. Standing militarily erect, she picked up a long pointer from the tray of the wipe board, slapped it lightly a couple of times in her palm. "First of all, a word about the scroll itself," she commenced, her accent taking on a more British intonation. "I will not go into the details of how it was unrolled and disassembled and the pages separated. I will say that due to its high quality leather casing and the flawless sealing of the jar, the process was not as lengthy or detailed as we had anticipated."

She'd performed one Herculean task, Chris reflected.

She gently slapped the pointer in her hand again. "Let's begin first with why we think this is the work of Mark or John Mark, as he is referred to several times in Acts, the only book in the New Testament that mentions him. You will note two smaller fragments of papyrus off to the side." She pointed to each. "The smaller one I'll get to later, but the other is a personal note. The message is brief: 'Be safe on your journey, my son. My love to you.' It is signed *Matera*, or "mother" in Greek." She picked up a magic marker and hastily wrote on the wipe board. "That could be anyone's mother," she continued. "But it is addressed to IM at the top, the initials for *Ioannis Markov* or, in English, 'John Mark.'" She wrote the initials I M on the wipe board and below them Ἰωάννου Μάρκου—the uncial Greek for John Mark—below the uncial Greek for "mother."

Chris was impressed. Her Greek pronunciation was flawless. He looked at the professor. "This is absolutely fascinating. You suppose the note was something the author of the note handed to John Mark or—"

"—Or," Professor Stewart interrupted, "she placed it in the scroll unbeknownst to the recipient who would see it on his journey when he opened it to begin writing. If she handed it to him, he would have read it and discarded it. That's my theory." He eyed Kate. "But then I'm not very sentimental. Kate thinks he kept it as a memento for his journey. Regardless, it is the most significant evidence of authorship associated with the scroll."

For some reason, Chris didn't perceive Kate as very sentimental, but she definitely had his attention. "Where was he going?" he asked.

"That's as important as where he was," said the professor. "I'm interrupting too much but after all," he glanced at Kate again, "this is my territory. According to Acts, John Mark's mother, whose name was Mary, had a home in Jerusalem. It was probably a large home, one of the early church-houses where a hundred or so could congregate. If our speculations are correct, John Mark was in Jerusalem when the note was written." He tipped his hand to Kate.

She picked up the thread. "Another piece of evidence identifying the author is the smaller fragment. There is a magnifying glass for your benefit, Dr. Jordan."

He picked up the magnifying glass, leaned over and held it over the small scrap of writing.

As he focused the glass, she continued in her lecturing tone. "It is a receipt for twenty sheets of papyrus. Papyrus was sold in rolls of twenty sheets. The standard size ran forty-seven centimeters in length and twenty-two centimeters wide which fits the dimension of these sheets. Twenty sheets, according to some historians, cost about four drachmas." She held up four fingers revealing her well-manicured and painted fingernails. "That's roughly three British pounds, five U.S. dollars. This papyrus, however, was not paid for in drachmas but Tyrian shekels or Tetradrachmas of Tyre."

Chris straightened up in his chair. "The evidence is beginning to have a cumulative effect," he remarked. "This is an impressive array of documentation."

"And it continues," she said, her voice rising. "At the beginning and final margins of the scroll, a strip of papyrus would be glued along the ends of the roll which, in some cases, wound around a stick called an *umbicus*. Usually, there was identifying information on the first strip indicating the variety and size of the papyrus as well as comments honoring emperors or other officials. On the strip attached to the last page the author is usually identified. The info on the first strip attached to the first leaf was called a protocol and included place of manufacture. Generally, the protocol was cut off before use but in this case," she leaned across the table and pointed to the first sheet, "the author left it intact. The information on it is a gold mine. Of course, with this truncated rough draft, there is no end strip, thus no signature."

Chris exhaled a deep breath. "Incredible! Next you're going to tell me you obtained the date."

The professor and Kate looked at each other and exchanged smiles.

"Go ahead and tell him, Kate," the professor encouraged, "about the names of the consulars on the protocol."

Self-confident but not overbearing, Kate proceeded. She was on a roll and enjoying it. "The Romans named years for the two consulars, the *Counsule Ordinariis* who took office in that year. Years were named in this manner until the last consular was appointed in five hundred forty-one C.E. One of the names is illegible." She pointed to a smudge on the document. "It appears the writer possibly spilled some ink and attempted to blot it which smeared the name." She looked up. "Incidentally, this happens in several places in the manuscript, another reason, we believe, he decided to abandon it and start over. We have no idea how long he was at work on the project, probably years, or how much papyrus he used to get to this point."

The professor jumped in again. "Chris, you'll have time to examine the scroll more closely this afternoon, you will see the smudges and, in some places, entire sentences slashed and begun anew."

Kate picked up. "The name of the other consular is legible: M. Aurelius Lepidus. The place of manufacture is Tyre. We looked up M. Aurelius Lepidus. He was consular in sixty-six C.E., thus our date for the document, at least the date it was manufactured. Again, the time frame fits."

"My apologies, Kate," the professor intervened again, "but this is important. By the second century C.E., there was a bishopric in Tyre. Tyre is a key," and he nodded for emphasis.

Kate resumed. seeming slightly annoyed at the interruptions. "You will also see on the reverse side a new handwriting, only a few sentences. The handwriting is definitely not that of I.M.," she said pointing at the initials on the board

Chris raised a brow. "This is getting intriguing," he said. "So now we have two authors, one we probably know and one we don't."

"We think it is a woman," the professor said conspiratorially. "The letters are refined and delicate, not as dark and bold as the author's as though lighter pressure was applied. Without sounding chauvinistic ..." He cast a wary glance at Kate. "I would say the handwriting is definitely feminine."

Chris looked at one then the other. "What are your theories about this mysterious addition on the reverse side?"

The professor went first. "I think it was someone, perhaps his mother, when she inserted the note, began copying a part of the manuscript she liked, then had to abort or for some reason stop." The professor paused when Kate drew a low but sharp breath. "As usual, Kate has an alternate theory."

Capturing Chris' attention, she eagerly conveyed her thoughts on the subject. "We are together on one thing. It was a female copying the first few lines of the beginning. Then we part ways. I do not think the effort was aborted. The three sentences, in the same column, are complete. They are the first sentences of the manuscript. I think it was some type of test. The author came across someone who could help him copy. He wanted to see her penmanship and *voila.* For all we know, there were manuscripts floating around in that ancient world copied by this same hand." Her eyes sparkled as she seemed to roll that thought over in her mind for what could have been the thousandth time.

"My counter to the feminine hand theory," Chris stated, "would be the unlikely event of a female with the ability. All due respects, Dr. Ferguson, we know the literacy rate in the Roman Empire was about sixteen percent and most of that percentage was men. The possibility drops further when it is a Jewish female, which, given the circumstances, this would likely have been." He could see her anger rising but needed to finish his thought. "Jewish women were considered second-rate citizens and received no formal education. Jewish men began formal education at age five and were learning Jewish law by age ten. Young girls learned at home from their mothers or other women."

Kate had laid the pointer on the table. She was tapping her foot, arms crossed, waiting for him to finish. Tightening her lips around her words, she pounced. "Your premise is pure poppycock," her Scottish accent back curtly popping the p's. "I would like your sources for such blather. I have studied first century Judaism and found that women were not second-rate citizens. They did hold traditional roles, but they also held power. Need I remind you who financed the disciples and much of Paul's ministry? They were women of means."

"Now, now, Kate," the professor said, raising and lowering his hands in a calming gesture. "I don't think Chris meant to attack women, just stating his knowledge. We obviously have different sets of opinions."

"My apologies, Dr. Ferguson" Chris offered. "I was just formulating a counter theory, that's all."

"Very well," she said, still ruffled. "We can discuss it more later. I'll wrap up my thoughts. The scroll comprised these twenty pages when the author decided to stop and start over."

The professor turned to Chris. "He had finished the episode of the healing of the blind man at Bethsaida."

"If the narrative follows the gospel as we know it today," Chris replied, "next would be Peter's confession of the Christ."

"Exactly, laddie," the professor expressed.

Pacing, popping the pointer in her hand again, Kate waited for any further interruptions in what was supposed to be her presentation. There were none. She emitted a "Thank God, at last," sigh and recommenced. "On the last page—she pointed to the sheet far right on the bottom— "the final sentence trails off as though ending in frustration. We don't know why it stops abruptly. If he was going to stop because of his mistakes, the author would have halted progress back on the eleventh page," she pointed to the first page in the bottom row, "where, as you will see later, there are several corrections and a couple of ink smudges. But he keeps going with only a minor error," she pointed to the fifteenth page, "and stops in this passage."

He then began to teach them that the Son of Man must suffer many things and be rejected by the elders, chief priests and teachers of the law, and that he must be killed and after three days rise again. He spoke plainly about this and ...

"Your theories?" Chris asked.

"I can assure you, they are theories," said the professor humbly. "We simply do not know."

Kate commented: "We've wondered if perhaps it had something to do with the last page and the resurrection, the author's struggle with the concept."

"Because the next paragraph in our contemporary gospel," the professor noted, "has Jesus telling Peter to 'Get behind me Satan' and the well-known 'take up his cross and follow me' passage. The original, if we can find it, should shed some light."

"Professor, you take it from here." Exasperated, Kate handed him the pointer and sat down, pumping one leg crossed over the other.

CHAPTER FOUR

Jerusalem, August, 70 A.D.

John Mark looked both ways before he opened the outer door at the gatehouse where Rhoda, their servant, lived. She was probably awake, but he moved quietly, crossing a narrow courtyard to the main entrance. His father had been successful. Their home was bigger and nicer than most in Jerusalem. A large living area with a kitchen and three smaller rooms comprised the downstairs area and above that, a spacious upper room for entertainment and relaxation. Few homes of the followers of Jesus were as large, which was why it became a gathering place.

He slipped quietly into the ground floor living area. His mother was sitting on the raised hearth where he had left her, in front of a good fire that was now burning low. She had not heard him enter. Her head was tilted back and her head cover had slipped and gathered above her shoulders. He observed her looking out the window at the flames and billowing smoke engulfing the night sky. An oil lamp flickered in a niche in the wall behind her, its light casting her nervous shadow onto the wall in front of her. Others burned on shelves around the large room, throwing intermittent pools of amber light onto the stone floor.

He took a step toward her and she turned, alarmed.

"John Mark?" His name flew from her mouth as a question whispered in doubt that he had made it back alive.

"Yes, Mother, it is I, but barely." He crossed the room and stood beside her. She was a small, wiry woman, in her eighties, her smallness magnified by the oversized robe wrapped around her. "Twice, I had to run to evade soldiers. The Third Wall to the north has fallen. The soldiers were battering the northwest Second Wall and then turned their attention to the Antonia Fortress where the Zealots had rallied."

She raised a shaky hand and pointed at the window. "That is what I see burning."

"No. What you see burning is the Temple. The fortress fell and the Zealots retreated to the Temple. The fire is out of control."

"It will reach us soon," she gasped.

"Not soon," he replied, "But the city may fall by daybreak."

She dropped her face into her hands and began weeping.

He put an arm around her, affectionately patted her shoulder. "The master had predicted this would happen and he wept, too." He thought that memory might console her.

She raised her head and looked up at him, tears streaming down her cheeks. "The master … " she said, her voice low and tremulous. "It seems only yesterday he was here, in this room with his disciples. They came often. It was a happy room, filled with joy and homecoming. Jesus always sat across from me, at the other end of the hearth," she motioned with an open hand. "The others scattered around on the cushions, laughing and joking. Then they would adjourn upstairs and eat, sleep on the pallets we provided. Peter came here when he escaped from prison to leave a message for James. We were praying for him when he burst through the door … "

"I was here, Mother," he reminded her. "Do you not remember?" Her memory had been failing, at times to the point he wondered if he was hearing fact or fiction, something contrived to cover her embarrassment. "Everyone was here—John, James, Andrew—"

"Oh yes," she exclaimed recapturing the thread and continuing, "Phillip, Matthew and Mary the mother of Jesus. Peter was in great haste. He told how the Lord had delivered him from prison. He said tell James and his brothers about it. Then he quickly departed. That was the last time we were all together. Now they are gone." She sniffled and wiped away tears. "It is a sad empty room."

"But Peter returned," John Mark prompted her again.

"That is true, for a few visits, but I had little time with him. You and he gathered in the corner there," she said sulking and pointed as though accusing the place. "He talked, and you listened and wrote."

"It was his idea," John Mark retorted, feeling defensive. "The end had not come. Eyewitnesses were dying. Everything should be put in writing, Peter said. But he could not write, in Aramaic or in Greek."

"Oh, I know," she sighed, looking into the hearth where a fire barely flamed. "He was an uneducated fisherman. Your father would be as proud as I that we sent you to the finest schools where you learned Greek and Latin. But Peter was wise. He was concerned, too, that others were writing. That man named Saul or Paul. He changed his name." She tossed a flippant hand into the air. "My nephew Barnabas introduced you to him. You traveled to Antioch with them."

"I also left them, south of Antioch, at Perga."

"And, later, you rejoined them. From the beginning, I did not have good thoughts about the man," she expressed with derision. "He claimed to be an apostle, that he saw the master in a bright light on the way to Damascus to persecute followers of Jesus. But that does not make him an apostle." She placed a hand on his arm and looked into his eyes. "What you write, my son, is not what Paul is writing."

"Not entirely, Mother. Paul is trying to solve problems that arise within groups of believers he has visited. He is trying to spread the faith to the Gentiles. In that, we share a common goal. But I am writing the story of the master, his life, his last days and passion and what it means to be his disciple."

She withdrew her hand from his arm. "I must confess, John Mark. Please do not be upset with me, but, while you were away, I looked at one of your scrolls, the smaller one," she said, her head down, a hand covering her mouth.

"I am not angry." He reached over, withdrew her hand from her mouth and held it a moment for assurance. "I know you handled it with care."

"With great care," she emphasized. "But I read only Aramaic and very little Greek, the *koinē* or common language. You are, indeed, trying to spread the master's teachings to the Gentiles, to all people."

"And his life," he added. "His life is the epitome of his teachings." From the window he could see the distant flames. He needed to go before it was too late but his mother needed him. He could tarry a little longer.

"And when you were traveling, you could write this story in the rooms provided you?" she questioned.

"I could, and I did. But writing is difficult. The work is hard as labor. Because of it, my back is bowed. My eyesight has been affected. A scroll is tedious, constantly unwinding it to see what I had written, then back to where I had stopped and to begin again. One cannot make a mistake. My first attempt had many errors. I had to start anew."

"Surely, you did not discard your work," she reprimanded, scolding him before she had reason.

"I do not discard papyrus, Mother," he responded curtly. "It is expensive; the Egyptians control the market. I use the reverse sides of my draft, the one you opened, to make notes, sketch and practice my final pages."

"The first time you left Barnabus and Paul, you came here to Jerusalem," she said.

"Yes." He sensed where she was going with the stray comment. She may have memory problems but her mind could still weave a devious plan.

"And here in this house," she palmed an open hand around her, "there are good places to write. There is a bench upstairs you used as a desk and adequate light from early morning until dusk. At times, you wrote at night with an oil lamp."

He nodded. She was true to form. "But, Mother, Jerusalem is burning. We must leave."

"You did not stay long," she persisted, oblivious to his comment or the impending danger. "I have always wondered why Tyre and not Jerusalem for a place to write."

"I went to Tyre for several reasons." She was testing his patience. He began pacing back and forth, looking out the window, looking at her but her eyes were averted. "Jesus had been there. Tyre had a small congregation of his followers. It was also a cultural center with libraries and a steady supply of papyrus from Egypt. It has a fine port. Once I finished, I could go immediately to Rome, have the gospel copied and distributed." He stopped pacing and waited.

She finally looked up into his eyes. "Now, you are back in Jerusalem," she said, a slight lilt in her voice, a hopeful gleam in her eyes.

Like the other comments, this one, he knew, was also one of design. It came from loneliness and neglect. "Mother, I came to see you. I missed you. But there were gaps in the narrative. There are still eyewitnesses living here. You are one. I had hoped to finish the scroll here," he gestured at the floor, his voice calming to a whisper. "I had hoped to speak with any who had seen the resurrected Jesus. But that, now, is impossible. The city is falling to the Romans. I may have written all I can write. I need to get the scroll to a safe place where it can be copied and passed on for others to read."

"Unfinished!" she expressed with a look of dismay. "Without the story of the resurrection? Jesus rose from the dead. Many spoke of it."

"Yes, that is what others have said. The story, as it happened and unfolded, has other explanations. Jesus may not have been dead. He may have been taken by Joseph of Arimathea and resuscitated. We do not know. The master did not want people believing in him because of his miracles. He wanted people to believe in miracles because of their faith. That is why I say I may have reached the end. Would you still believe in the master, his teachings, if you had heard nothing more than a young man dressed in white saying he had risen. That could mean anything."

She did not respond immediately. Her face was that of one struck by something suddenly and strangely out of the dark. She looked at him as though stupefied. "John Mark, the stories are too many not to believe. Not long after his resurrection, which I believe, Jesus appeared to many in Galilee, including the disciples. On the day of Pentecost the master's spirit struck hundreds, maybe thousands. One cannot dismiss the multiple evidences of his presence. Whether or not you remain in Jerusalem, you would do well to finish the master's story."

"Dear Mother, all of what you say, I have heard. I have also heard from Peter himself that many doubted after witnessing the risen Lord in Galilee. Some did not believe the women who saw the empty tomb. There were many who saw the risen Christ and did not believe."

"Perhaps," she said, still composed by the fire with little show of emotion. "I will not argue with Peter. As you well know, he is a man of ups and downs. I know how I feel, how I believe. I am *not* up and down, but constant. There are many like me."

She might be more up and down than she thought, but John Mark would not convince his mother otherwise. "I do not doubt your faith, dear Mother, or what you tell me. Except for my remaining in Jerusalem, your comments and advice are well taken. But I must leave. I must preserve what I have and, if it is God's will, complete the ending, if there is another besides the one I have now. I desperately need to get to a place where I can make copies." He glanced again out the window. "But I am trapped. Three legions are swarming over the Third and Second walls; the Temple is in flames." As he spoke, they could hear the cracking and popping of burning wood, debris falling. "I could try one of the gates along the eastern wall. In the confused dark, foragers are slipping out to find provisions and returning. They cannot go far. Titus also placed a legion on the Mount of Olives."

She reached up and grabbed his arm. "The tunnel!" she exclaimed.

CHAPTER FIVE

Edinburgh, New College, October 29, 2011

The professor stood, picked up the pointer where Kate had left it on the table, and walked to a map of the ancient New Testament world thumb-tacked to the wall beside the windows. "Some New Testament scholars, including my old friend William Barclay, God rest his soul, have concluded that the Gospel of Mark was written in Rome for a Roman audience." He pointed at the ancient capital.

Chris raised his hand as though he were back in the professor's class. "There's another variation on that history, professor," he expressed. "Some ancient authorities, Eusebius of Caesarea among them, whose book you've already noted, contend Mark traveled to Alexandria ten years after Christ's ascension, became the first bishop there, and was responsible for establishing Christianity in Africa. Coptic tradition says he was martyred in sixty-eight C. E. If that were true, he could hardly have spent much time in Rome or even written this document, dated around sixty-six C. E."

"I know, I know," the professor said, flicking a hand as though shooing a fly. "Those are legends, a dime a dozen. Rome, so Barclay's theory goes, had a large, number of house churches, each wanting a copy. Once the original was complete, several copies were made for these churches. Other churches heard about it and asked for copies or sent scribes to make copies. Rome had a wonderful system of roads." He circled the pointer around the Mediterranean area. "And the book spread quickly outward from the center of the empire."

"What I've heard this morning changes all that," Chris said. "Earlier comments about Tyre are resonating."

Kate was nodding in agreement.

"I agree," the professor confessed. "This document changes everything. Most scholars agree that Mark was written between sixty-five and seventy C.E. The author, if it was John Mark, who was a young man probably in his twenties during the ministry of Jesus, would have been about sixty years of age when he wrote it. Nero persecuted Christians during his reign, fifty-four to sixty-eight C.E., so sensible devotees would have left Rome." He began walking toward the table to sit down. "Some scholars believe the Gospel of Mark—it was not called gospel until the mid-second century—was written in Tyre or Sidon, a city north of Tyre." He turned around, walked back to the map and pointed to Sidon then Tyre. "Scripture does tell us—Mark, chapter seven, verse twenty-four—that Jesus went to Tyre."

"The name Tyre keeps popping up," Kate interjected. "According to Acts, following the death of Stephen, a congregation was founded in Tyre. Paul visited there on his way to Jerusalem and spent a week conversing with the disciples."

The professor was still at the map and as she spoke, pointed again at the city on the map. "It would also fit the time frame for John Mark to write there." He moved the pointer southeast, "before returning here, to Jerusalem. In other words, the gospel was not written in one place, though most of it was probably composed in Tyre."

"Why would he go to Jerusalem?" Chris asked. "If I know my history, about that time the city was under siege by Titus's war machine to put down the Jewish revolt."

"That's the reason, Chris," Kate explained. "He was going to check on his mother, possibly others, and get them out of the city to safety."

For the first time, she addressed him by his first name. Maybe his damage control was working. She was softening ... or he was. Perhaps both were.

Professor Stewart cleared his throat.

Kate heaved a sigh of pseudo-frustration. "Once again, our good professor has a different opinion."

"I don't disagree that he went to Jerusalem out of concerns for his mother, the professor said tactfully. But, and I draw your attention to the gospel itself and the missing last page, it is plausible he went for another reason."

"The missing last page?" Chris asked, puzzled.

"Laddie, surely now," the professor said in playful reprimand, stepping from the map and tapping the table in front of Chris with the pointer. "We spent several days in class on the last verses of Mark, how the gospel ends abruptly at chapter sixteen, verse eight and the attempts by editors in the following centuries to fill in the gap and make sense of it. Scribes, over time, created five different endings to provide a more satisfying conclusion to the gospel."

"Yes! Now, I remember," he professed, embarrassed. "How could I forget?"

"No one contests the early abrupt ending," Kate inserted. "What is contested are the endings we have today. Are they real endings or contrived? I am one who believes the ending as we have at chapter sixteen, verse eight, is what the author intended."

"What supports that theory?" Chris questioned.

She stood to emphasize her points, ticking them off one by one on her fingers. "The last twelve verses of Mark are missing in parchment codices B and Sinaiticus. They are missing in the old Latin manuscript k, the Sinaitic Syriac, etc. Also, Clement of Alexandria, Origin and Ammonius show no knowledge of the existence of these verses. Jerome noted it was missing in Greek copies known to him. Almost all the Greek copies do not have this concluding portion." Out of fingers, she sat down.

"She has us both there, laddie," the professor admitted. "But I contend the five current endings we have now, especially the long version in the King James Version, are not what Mark intended. A last page is missing. I think the apostle reached a stopping point in Tyre and the author needed to interview witnesses of the resurrection that were still alive." He returned to his chair and sat down. "They would have been in Jerusalem. His mother was possibly one, along with Mary Magdalene, Mary the mother of James, other disciples. Paul said Jesus had seventy-two other disciples and over five hundred by the time the master finished his ministry. Some would still be living in Jerusalem."

"By the notes on the verso, we do know he was interviewing people," Kate indicated.

"How do you think the author ended it?" Chris asked, turning to the professor.

"I am not sure," the professor responded. "He did not end it in Jerusalem. The city was being destroyed and he had to flee, possibly with his mother, though that is insignificant for our purposes. At some point, he did finish it, I think, and the page disappeared, detached and fell off like the torn end leafs of scrolls were prone to do." He glanced at Kate. "As she has said, Kate thinks the abrupt ending was intentional, that it was consistent with Mark's Messianic Secret. But there is only one way to find out how it ended," the professor said, rapping a knuckle on the table.

"Now I know why I'm here," Chris uttered, squirming in his chair. "The original scroll, the autograph."

"Yes," the professor revealed, his eyes averted. "It's there, in Maaloula, probably in a cave."

"And you want an archaeologist to find it," Chris said, apprehensively, "the only one of that profession in present company."

"Not just an archaeologist," the professor expanded, swiveling his eyes toward Kate—"but an archaeologist and an ancient manuscript expert"— then back on Chris.

Both were looking at him for his reaction. The professor telling him the name of the shopkeeper was the first hint why he'd been summoned. Second hint—Kate said the manuscript was the first attempt. Number three popped up when the professor said the, "master copy is still there somewhere." Chris had already been thinking it over. The prospects were exciting, even for going into a country near the full bloom of revolution and with a dictator killing dissidents left and right.

Now, those prospects suddenly dimmed. He would be going into the midst of an Arab uprising with someone he'd just met, barely knew. *Thanks, but no thanks*, he was thinking. But there was the scroll on the table before him. He could put up with a lot to become the most famous archaeologist of the twenty-first century, a flesh and blood Indiana Jones. He was sure he and Kate would get to know each other better, and in short order. But, if he was going into the heart of Arab spring with Dr. Kate Ferguson as his companion, he needed to know more about her, which meant figuring a way to speak with the professor out of her presence. "Let me think about it."

Kate's eyes rolled back. "Think about it?" She heaved a deep sigh. "This is a no-brainer, the chance of a lifetime, and you're going to *think* about it." Her cheeks, rosy from blasts of Scottish winds, turned red. Her hazel eyes pulsed with anger. But Chris thought he detected something else, deeper emotions beneath the histrionic mix: anxiety.

The professor eyed her sympathetically but said nothing.

Chris sat up straight. His eyes leveled out and he shot her a stern look. "Dr. Ferguson, I believe you are over-reacting."

The professor entered the fray. "I believe, Chris, what you perceive as her overreaction is my fault."

Chris swung his eyes on the professor. "How so?"

"I took some liberties," the professor said looking down into his lap. "Even though it's been almost twenty years, we've stayed in touch." He looked up nervously at Chris. "I felt I knew you. So I ... "

"What he's trying to tell you is the trip's a done deal," Kate disclosed, calmer. "And I apologize for my reaction."

"A done deal?" Chris exclaimed, coming out of his seat.

The professor, obviously embarrassed, sat back with his hands steepled beneath his chin and looked at Chris. "I'm afraid I have already ordered plane tickets and made provisions for your stay in Maaloula. I'm sorry, Chris, but the situation in Syria is deteriorating. The dictator, al-Assad, could close the border at any time. Turkey has sided with the dissidents. Our British Ambassador speaks out against Assad in his blog." He wiped a trembling hand across his brow. "The revolution has not yet reached Damascus, but there are demonstrations daily in the capital. Only yesterday, forty were killed across the country. Maaloula is not yet caught up in it. For the sake of the New Testament and Christians everywhere, we have a brief window of opportunity."

Chris lowered himself back into his chair and said nothing, just sat there dumbfounded. He observed the professor was sweating.

The professor waited briefly for a response and then continued. "If you decline, I will certainly respect and accept your decision, though with profound regrets. We can make cancellations; nothing is in stone. Kate can go alone. She has gone solo before. In fact, that was the original plan."

Kate was waiting for Chris' reaction. He noticed her legs jiggling.

"With all due respects, Dr. Jordan," she said, "you told me earlier on the drive in if it was not the find of the millennium, you would turn around and go back to Mexico."

"I did say that."

"So, you accept?" the professor asked eagerly.

"I wouldn't go this far and turn it down. Besides, I have ultimate confidence and faith in you, Professor Stewart. I had just wanted to think about it a little more. That's all. Didn't mean to cause such a stir."

"Och aye!" the professor said with a grand smile and slight clap of his hands, his bright eyes beaming.

Kate's knees stopped pumping. Her face relaxed. She closed her eyes and sighed. She opened her eyes, looked at him and smiled. "More than you'll ever know, Chris, thank you." Her tone was conciliatory and sincere.

He nodded and thought he detected her eyes misting. She was back to his first name. He needed to work up to hers. Where they were going, both were going to need a friend.

The professor patted him on the knee.

"That decided, we can move on," Chris pressed. "Our manuscript stopped at Jerusalem." He looked at the map on the wall. "How did it get to Damascus?"

"Let's discuss that over lunch," suggested the professor. "I'm famished. You say Greyfriars, Kate?

"Aye!"

"We will have privacy?" the professor confirmed. "After all, we'll be discussing highly sensitive material."

"Not to mention plans bordering on illegal," she added.

"Illegal!" Chris exclaimed.

"A mere overstatement, laddie," the professor commented and winked.

"Yes! Privacy is assured," Kate added.

"Jolly good," the professor said.

CHAPTER SIX

Jerusalem, August, 70 A.D.

The tunnel. As a boy, John Mark had gone through Hezekiah's tunnel, built by the great king seven hundred years ago to bring water from the Gihon spring outside the city walls to the pool of Siloam. "Why did I not think of that?"

"You left too quickly to assess the city for me to tell you," his mother said critically. She stood. "There are other tunnels and many are escaping through them, but this is the main outlet. You would, of course, emerge in the valley Kidron. If Titus has soldiers on Olivet, you must follow the valley south and circle behind the mount."

"I would need to take great care with the scrolls," he said. "They are wrapped and tied securely in leather but the water gets shoulder high in places. When I was a child, it was over my head and I had to turn back."

"In places, it is not two meters high," she reminded. "You would have to bend to make your way. You will need dry clothes at the end."

"I would not take time to change. The Gihon spring is beneath the city walls. At night I would not be seen but need to take no chances. By the time I reach Bethany, I will be dry."

"Lazarus and Martha are dead," his mother said matter-of-factly, her hands hanging at her side. "You know that." She was always one step ahead of him.

"Yes, but Mary, I presume, is still living. She would welcome me. If not, there are others of kindred faith in Bethany who would shelter me."

"You could finish the scroll and make a copy there," she suggested.

"Bethany is too close," he cautioned. "Jericho is too close. I could return to Tyre, where I wrote most of it, but even Tyre, I think, is too close. I need to get further away. Christians are in danger."

"Antioch?" she said, knowing his fondness for the place.

"To Damascus."

"Why Damascus?" she exclaimed, her eyes alarmed. "Just a few years ago Jews were murdered by gentiles there."

"Damascus is far away," he said confidently. "The faith spread rapidly to Damascus. Many gentiles converted with Paul. Aside from having a strong community of believers, the city has a large library and access to the writing materials I will need for copying the master's gospel. The massacres were against Jews not Christians. I think I will be safe."

"There are Roman legions in Syria as well," she warned.

"But they are preoccupied defending the Parthian border. Damascus is a strategic distribution center. Once I am finished, I can make copies then send or take them to Caesarea Philippi, Caesarea Maritime, Alexandria, Antioch, Ephesus, eventually to Rome. Ah, Rome! The ultimate destination. There are several communities of followers in Rome, each with its own scribes. I will supply a master copy. From that, copies will multiply. Many people will read the gospel. It will cover the empire."

"This will take time. I may never see you again," she said sadly. "You are all the family I have."

The words hit him in his heart. She knew how to affect him. But she was right. His father had died twenty years before. One brother became a zealot and was killed shortly after the crucifixion of Jesus. Another died of leprosy. His sister disappeared about the time her friend Mary of Magdala vanished and was never heard from again. People speculated. "Once I finish, I will return to you," he assured her. "We can thank the empire for good roads. If imperial letters can travel over one hundred miles in a day, surely I can go fifteen. When I was with Paul, we traveled twenty miles in a day's time." He walked over and again put his arm around her. "But I have a better idea. Come, go with me."

She cast a sharp, doubtful glance at him.

"I will take care of you," he said, assuringly.

She turned her face away from him, arose and walked to the window, as if to see better the devastation, then turned around. "I am an old woman and … "

"Old women are leaving Jerusalem nightly. You are a strong old woman. The Lord will protect us."

She sighed and with a tired, slow hand wiped a strand of hair from a serious eye. "The Lord cannot protect us from everything. He wants us to be strong but he does not want us to be unwise. Making that kind of journey would be unwise. I could not get through the tunnel. You know how I hate enclosed places. That is why I remained outside while you entered the Herodium where Jesus was on trial before Pilate."

"But if you stay, the house will be destroyed. You will die in a fire or be killed."

"I am too smart," she smiled faintly with light sarcasm, "to stay here and die in a fire. And I do not think they will hurt an old woman. Yosef ben Mattitiyahu, Joseph son of Mattathias, the Jewish teacher, they call him Josephus, is with Titus. He has been negotiating."

"And he was struck by an arrow, a Zealot arrow," he retorted.

"That was the first effort," she reminded him. "He tried again. Granted, he was unsuccessful, but Titus does not want to destroy this city."

He pointed angrily at the window. "He does not want to destroy the city yet, look, the Temple is on fire."

"We do not know how that happened," she remarked calmly, "perhaps an accident. The soldiers are throwing their flaming sticks everywhere. I believe once the fighting is over, the Zealots, not old women minding their own business, will be executed and the Romans will rebuild the city, a city that will bring you home." She crossed her hand over her heart.

"You are surely right about the Romans rebuilding," he agreed. "They are builders. But it will no longer be a city of the Jews. The Romans will expel the Jews, even old women, and make it a Roman city. You and I will be dispersed."

"I hope you are wrong, but we will see. Regardless, I cannot accompany you, not even to Bethany, even if we did not go through the tunnel.

CHAPTER SEVEN

Edinburgh, Greyfriars Bobby, October 29, 2011

Greyfriars Bobby's Bar was in the same location on Candlemaker's Row. The statue of the little Skye Terrier named Bobby still sat on the round pedestal on the street island in front of the pub. But Chris noted changes. Outside tables with decorated barriers shielded customers from pedestrians. Following Kate and the professor inside, he observed there was still an upper and lower bar, but gone was the separation between the classes, allowing only the lower class in one side and the upper class in the other. They had entered the lower bar. Chris noted the interior had not changed significantly from the traditional décor of wood paneling and old leather seats. He and Allyson had always sat in one by the window. It was still there.

A young male waiter dressed in black, white napkin over his arm, signaled to Kate and he led them to a recessed booth toward the back, away from the bars and lunch traffic. Chris sat on one side facing the professor and Kate. Immediately, another waiter came. They ordered drinks, he and the professor a pint of ale and Kate a scotch, Glenfiddich, on the rocks.

"Now, where were we with John Mark?" Professor Stewart asked.

"He was in Jerusalem," Chris responded. "Damascus was next."

"He did not go immediately to Damascus," Kate said. "On the reverse side of the scroll, where he recorded interviews, there is one, fairly lengthy, that is unmistakably with Mary, as in Mary and Martha."

"It could have been any Mary in the New Testament," Chris suggested.

"No!" she quickly countered. "The person he is interviewing references Lazarus as her brother. They lived in Bethany which would have been his first stop after leaving Jerusalem."

The professor joined the discussion. "The notes on the verso indicate he is trying to finish the work, trying to tie up the resurrection which, apparently, became a major loose end."

"I would like to read the entire manuscript," Chris stated.

"You will," said the professor. "We blocked out the entire afternoon for you to review it, front and back. Of course, it's in Greek, the *koine*. I take it you read *koine*."

"I had two years of *koine* in college, two here in seminary. I took your New Testament Greek course."

"Yes, yes. Of course, you did." The professor's face turned red. "Well, back to where I was ... where was I?"

"You blocked out the afternoon for me."

"Yes. It's only twenty pages," the professor continued, "forty including both sides. We know John Mark bought a roll of papyrus in Tyre. Based upon the date on the receipt, sixty-six C.E. it was probably a fresh roll, purchased four years before he headed for Jerusalem. We must assume he had purchased other rolls and probably from the same source."

"How long was he in Tyre?" Chris asked.

"We don't know," the professor maintained, "At least four years but probably longer. We have no idea how long it took him to write what we have. His gospel is the shortest, but it is also the most compact, indicating he gave considerable thought to its structure and narrative."

"We get glimpses of his mind at work in this manuscript," Kate said, returning to the parley. "He makes comments in the margin. For example, incidents which appear in early pages, such as the transfiguration and story of the rich young man, he notes should be placed later." A waiter walked by and Kate lowered her voice. "He may not have been a professional scribe but he knew what he was doing. You can detect pinpricks in the corners of the papyrus leafs. These served as a guide for left- and right-hand justification." She picked up her paper napkin and spread it on the table. "Looking closely, you can see guidelines. Like the scribes of his day, John Mark drew horizontal lines and marked the margins for the two columns on each page." With her knife, she drew invisible lines on the napkin. "His letters hang from faint ruled lines. They are well-stroked, evenly spaced." She looked directly at Chris. "As you know, in their earliest form, the scriptures had no chapters and verses. You are an archaeologist. You have ample knowledge of ancient texts."

He nodded. "I know that the earliest New Testament texts were written in Greek uncial," he said, "large square type letters, in continuous script, no spaces or breaks between the letters or words."

"This is true of most manuscripts of the early church," she remarked critically, "but spacing and punctuation, contractions, began to appear in some manuscripts around the third century."

Chris smiled and stroked an imaginary point in the air for her.

An ironic smile crossed her lips but she continued unperturbed. "After Bethany, we are unsure where Mark went. We've looked at some first century maps of Palestine." She nodded toward the professor. "There were several routes from Jerusalem to Damascus. One road from Jerusalem tracked near Bethany, passed through Jericho, and then turned north paralleling the Jordan River to Scythopolis, contemporary Beit She'an. Just a minute." She reached for her purse on the seat beside her, unsnapped it and pulled out a ballpoint pen. "This will work better." On the napkin she sketched a rough map of Palestine, oval Sea of Galilee in the north, Jordan River running due south emptying into the Dead Sea. With rounded dots, she dropped in key cities—Jerusalem, Bethany, Jericho, Heshbon, Scythopolis, Damascus—calling out their names as she went. She drew a continuous line from Jerusalem to Jericho then due north to Scythopolis. "This is the road I was talking about," she said, pausing, her pen still stopped on Scythopolis. "There it crossed the Jordan southeast of the Sea of Galilee and went directly to Damascus." She continued the line accordingly and stopped at Damascus. She sat back and observed her artwork as though in admiration. "Another route led due east from Jerusalem through Jericho to Heshbon," she continued, drawing a second road across the Jordan, "and intersected with the King's Way, another major route from Egypt to Damascus." She paused again, then added thoughtfully, "He may have had a problem going to Jericho. Vespasian had a garrison there." She put the pen down to signal she was finished.

Chris mused at the napkin turned map. *Not bad.*

"Kate believes John Mark took the first route," the professor injected, without referring to the map on the napkin. "There were more communities with Christians along that road, which meant steady provisions. I believe he took the second, speedier route through Heshbon in the Trans-Jordan then up the King's Way."

The waiter brought their drinks and took their orders. Chris and the professor ordered a sandwich. Kate ordered haggis. Chris had had haggis only once in his life, at a Robbie Burns dinner in Edinburgh. He'd thought he was going to throw up before he tried the first bite.

"You are assuming, of course, that John Mark went to Damascus," Chris said. "Just because you found his manuscript, or part of one, in that location doesn't mean he was actually there. We know of numerous instances of manuscripts uncovered far from where they were probably written. The Ryland fragment of the Gospel of John is one. It was found in the Egyptian desert, far from its original composition in Ephesus."

Kate was chomping at the bit to interrupt him. "But the Ryland was a copy," she said, "not the autograph. Here we have, by all the evidence, a first draft autograph."

The professor, sensing an argument developing, jumped in. "Chris, we are confident he was in Damascus from internal evidence on the scroll. On the verso, next-to-last page, notes seem to indicate a publishing plan." He raised his pint and drank, smacked deliciously as though the ale was a needed distraction. "You will need to turn the pages over carefully—"

"—We've provided some padded tweezers for that," Kate interrupted. "You lift the sheets at the corners and slowly turn them over. I can show you."

He nodded appreciation and then turned back to the professor.

"But you will see all of this," the professor continued unruffled. "You will see the word Damascus, then an arrow to Caesarea Philippi, another arrow to Caesarea Maritime, then a final arrow toward Rome, that one bolded with extra strokes. It was as though the writer was thinking to himself, scratching out his thoughts much in the way someone might make a shopping list."

"His plan," Kate said after sipping her scotch, "was to get it written, make one or more copies, get it distributed and read to the congregations, which he could have done himself. It was common practice for the author of a piece to read it to others. The literacy rate in the empire, as you correctly mentioned earlier, Chris, was quite low."

"The key question," Chris noted, "the reason I'm here, relates to Mark's original. Right?"

"Well, that's not the *key* question," she said. "We presume it's in one of the caves near Maaloula, but which one?"

Chris raised a finger and moved to the edge of his seat, a signal he was about to say something profound. "Here's where we are at this point. There are several key questions, answers to which we may never know. Given: John Mark made a master copy, presumably the one he began working on in Tyre. Given: he transported it to Damascus." He raised his pint, took a swallow and grinned at the professor, as if to say 'good stuff.'

The professor smiled and raised his glass in response.

"Partially given," Chris continued, "he departed Damascus at some point, taking a copy or copies with him to the cities indicated on the verso of the truncated manuscript, terminating in Rome. Not given: What happened to him after that? Conjecture: he returned to Damascus and deposited the manuscripts in a cave." With his finger, he drew an imaginary line on the napkin from Rome to Damascus. "Conjecture: he deposited them in a cave before he departed. But the key question for me is why are the manuscripts in a cave outside of an ancient village whose inhabitants spoke Aramaic and not in Damascus? In other words, how did the manuscripts get from Damascus to Maaloula, who transported them, and why internment in a cave outside of Maaloula? Was Maaloula even there then?"

"Here's to you, laddie," the professor said, raising his glass. "That is not an area we have explored. The reason the manuscripts were put in a secure place is simple logic. Either Mark or someone else put the master copy in a safe place like we do manuscripts we have completed and submitted to publishers who require we place copies in a safe deposit box. His safe deposit box was in a cave off the beaten path. How the manuscripts got to Maaloula is sheer conjecture at this point. By the drunken beggar's description, John Mark or someone jury-rigged, as you Americans are fond of saying, a safe within a cave that stood the test of time until a drunk careened into it. Why Maaloula? We do not know. Perhaps you two will find out."

"Why Maaloula?" Chris said, echoing the professor's question. "If memory serves, that part of Syria doesn't hold a monopoly on caves. There are the natural grottos of Dara'a, south of Damascus near the Jordanian border." He pointed to the approximate place on the map that was still spread before them. "I've been to the volcanic caves at Sweide." He glanced at Kate to ensure she was listening. "A large cave was discovered there in

December of two thousand and nine. Then, in the opposite direction, north of Maaloula is the Aldwayat cave at Masta el-Helou. The significance of that discovery relates to the story of your scroll. It was discovered when a large boulder was removed blocking its entrance. It is a limestone cavity, much like the caves of Maaloula, dating back to the Paleolithic age."

"The hidden treasures that are beneath our nose," mused the professor. "A wall crashed by a drunk, a boulder moved, a shepherd boy throwing a rock into a cave. Who knows what you might find when you get there? Perhaps one of those human secrets that baffle probability will come into play."

Kate had been quiet for the past few minutes. Her smile was gone and she didn't toast when he and the professor raised their glasses. She did seem interested in his knowledge and expertise. He wondered how long until it would be just the two of them. "When do we leave?" he asked.

The professor leaned sheepishly across the table, his eyes resigned. "Tomorrow."

"Tomorrow! I just got here."

Kate rejoined the discussion. "Time is of essence. The situation in Syria is deteriorating daily."

"We have a small window where we can get in and out within thirty-six to forty-eight hours," the professor added. "There's a revolution going on. Kate is right. Once you told me when you would arrive, I had the University travel office arrange roundtrip flights to Beirut."

"Why Beirut?" Chris asked. "Damascus has a good airport."

"It does today," Kate said ironically. "It might not tomorrow. Maaloula is near the Lebanese border. The main road from Beirut to Damascus intersects a good road north to Maaloula, circumventing Damascus."

"I've notified people along the way," the professor divulged. "You will have contacts in Beirut, Damascus and Maaloula. You will stay in Maaloula at the same monastery where I stayed, St. Thecla. They are expecting you. They are the only ones in Maaloula who know you are coming. All they know is that you work for me and are there to conduct linguistic research and explore ancient graphics on the walls of caves, plus some sightseeing."

"I guess you're just going to whisk us into Syria under a cloak without a visa," Chris said, mildly sarcastic.

"This is another practical reason for flying into Beirut," the professor emphasized. "The only way to obtain a visa at the Syrian border is if you have a visa for Lebanon, which you can get at the airport in Beirut. They make it easy. Tourism means money."

The operation was beginning to sound like the beginning of a James Bond movie, Chris thought. Jean Connery had attended the University of Edinburgh. Perhaps some of 007 had rubbed off on the school of theology. "Professor, with all due respects, did you know Sean Connery when he was a student here?"

The professor's face reddened, his brow furrowed. "No, but I wish I had. He'd love a trip like this."

"It's beginning to sound like espionage," Chris added.

"Laddie, it is espionage of the highest order, the highest and noblest quest, nobler than King Arthur's Knights of the Round Table quest for the Holy Grail. At stake, possibly, is the future of the New Testament."

Chris thought his mentor had overstated the case, but finding the autograph of the Gospel of Mark would be the greatest find in the history of the New Testament, possibly the greatest archaeological discovery of the century, second only to the one already in the professor's office. He raised a glass and toasted the professor. "Skoll."

"If you gentlemen will excuse me, I need to visit the lady's room," said Kate and she left abruptly.

CHAPTER EIGHT

Jerusalem, August, 70 A.D.

John Mark waited another hour, past midnight and then prepared to leave. The tumult in the city still raged. It would draw attention. Soldiers on Olivet, except for sentries, would be asleep.

"Let me feed you," his mother urged. "You do not look like a man of sixty. You are still lean with your broad shoulders and muscular arms but if you do not eat you will look old when next I see you."

"There is no time, Mother. I must go."

She pushed some bread and a calf-skin of water into his hands.

"I cannot accept this," and handed them back.

"But ..."

"There is little water and food in the city," he replied. "Every drop and crumb are precious. Once beyond the walls, I will find nurturance."

He pulled out a small leather pouch from his waist. "I have some money." He opened the pouch, pulled out two coins and pressed them into her unsteady hand. "Here are two drachmas, about four days wages. You will make it last months."

"How do you have money when all you do is write?"

"In Tyre, I gained a reputation as a scribe. People hired me to write receipts, contracts. Some needed secretarial service. I kept records and wrote annals and letters, as much as two drachmas for one letter." He reopened the pouch and retrieved another coin. "This is a half-letter."

She smiled faintly and accepted the extra coin.

"One more time," he pleaded, "come with me."

She nodded her refusal and hugged him. "I fear this will be the last time I touch you, my child. The last time I will feel your strong arms, look into those dark eyes." With unsteady hands she stroked his beard, the sides of his face, and moved them through his graying hair. Then she pulled him down to her face and kissed him on the cheek. "Give my love to Mary, if she is still there."

He could feel her trembling in his embrace then realized he was the one trembling. "I love you, Mother. I will return. I must complete the master's work. The world must know."

He looked around before quietly shutting the outer gate. He wanted to bid farewell to Rhoda but her gate house was quiet and dark. Above him, the sky to the east was clear. Like a smile twisted in spirals of smoke, a crescent moon hung over the orange glow from the Temple fire. The pool of Siloam was a rock-cut cistern in the southeastern corner of the original city of David. Most of the conflict was in the northern quadrant, around the fortress and Temple. If he was careful and did not encounter difficulty, it would not take him long to cross the city to the pool.

He was surprised to find the area around the cistern quiet. Surely, others had similar plans. His footsteps echoed as he descended the short stairway to the pool. It was a source of water for the city and the tunnel was well known. Originally, the pool had been outside of the walls of old Jerusalem and later sealed within the walls by Hezekiah. Reportedly, Jesus had healed a man born blind here. The story came to him second hand, so he did not report it.

He found the tunnel entrance and made his way in darkness. At first the water was around his ankles but it began to rise as he continued, feeling his way in the dark. He recalled it was five hundred meters long and very curvy. The dark was the darkest he had ever known, but the narrow walls channeled his careful, forward movement.

Midway he saw a faint light ahead and heard something in the water.

A man's voice called out. "Who comes?" the voice inquired loudly.

Was this a soldier? Had the tunnel been discovered? "Someone to get water," John Mark responded.

The light neared, and John Mark saw dimly a man holding a candle, a sack of grain over his shoulder. The man spoke again, harshly: "Back up or step aside. I bring food for the city."

Above them in the city, foragers were slipping through the defenses amid the chaos and now this one was wisely using the tunnel. John Mark had just passed a spot where the walls seemed wider. Gripping his bag tightly and holding it above his head, he back-stepped to the place made more visible by the man's candlelight. John Mark turned, pressed his back against the tunnel wall, and caught a kinder look of gratitude in the man's eyes as he breathed, "Shalom," and pushed by him. John Mark moved forward, counting his paces in case he had to back track again. But he encountered no further obstacles, only the water that rose to his shoulders mid-way then began receding.

At the mouth of the tunnel, he paused, listened. The city seemed quieter. Did it mean the battle was over, the Zealots captured or killed? Or was it a lull before a final assault, by either side? It did not matter. At last, he was free of the city.

Dripping wet, he stepped from the tunnel into the chilled air. He wanted to shake himself, but the noise would alert Roman guards on the walls directly above him. In the distance, hundreds of campfires burned on Olivet. Forty years ago, there was only one. Jesus asked them to sit and pray then went further up the garden slope with Peter, James and John. He asked them to stay and keep watch. Jesus walked on further. The night was quiet and his words very clear: "Abba, Father, with you everything is possible. Let this cup pass from me, yet not my will but yours." He returned to find everyone asleep. He left again and found everyone again asleep. He left again, a third time, and a third time they all were asleep. Then the master was arrested. The soldiers were about to arrest John Mark, also. They grabbed him, ripped his linen garment from his body; he ran naked into the night into the same valley, the Kidron.

John Mark knew the valley by heart. As a child, he had played on its slopes and in its ravines, built small cities with its rocks. The brilliant chip of moon plus flames from the Temple provided ample light for him to clamber down the valley's incline and then hasten southward through its basin. He stopped and took one last look at the city. Jerusalem, the city where he was born, the mother of us all. Jerusalem, once capital of a kingdom that stretched from Mesopotamia in the north to the Red Sea in the south, from the Great Sea to the trans-Jordan. Jerusalem, now a vassal of Rome and under destruction. All because of Zealots, delusional fanatics. In his bag, he carried the words that had predicted the devastation.

Jerusalem was not supposed to end this way.

CHAPTER NINE

Edinburgh, Greyfriars Bobby, October 29, 2011

"This is fortuitous," Chris said leaning across the table and speaking *sotto voce*. "I needed to talk with you about her."

"Is there something wrong?" the professor asked. "I thought you would be pleased with her. She's been a jolly good worker ... and attractive," he raised his brows and winked.

"Where did you get her?"

"She is on loan to me from the British Museum. She is their top ancient manuscript expert."

"I'm sure she's not the only one they have," Chris said. "I imagine the University here has one."

"Yes, but Kate's the best. Her knowledge is more than just the technical aspects of ancient manuscripts. She has a good feel about history and psychology, why people do what they do. She fascinates me with her ability to intuit the mindset of a culture within any given historic timeframe."

"On the drive from the airport, she made comments suggesting she was a bit rebellious in her youth, but she preferred the term 'independent.'"

"My dear, Christopher, she is one independent individual. I've never worked with anyone quite like her. She can be abrasive and come across as controlling, but she is extremely well-informed. And if she respects and likes you, one could not have a better friend. Also, she, like you, is no stranger to the Middle East. Also, like you, she has no family obligations that could distract her."

"She told me she was a widow. I didn't pry."

"Her husband was killed in Syria," the professor confided. "He was a military observer, part of UNTSO, the United Nations Troop Supervision Organization. It was founded for peacekeeping purposes in the Middle East. He was in the mission called Observer Group Golan based in Damascus, Syria." He looked up to ensure she was not coming. "He carried out fortnightly observations to ensure both sides kept troop levels and military equipment within the agreed upon limits of the disengagement treaty put into force in nineteen seventy-four following the Yom Kipper war of seventy three."

"How was he killed?"

"He was shot manning an observation outpost, sniper fire in the neck," the professor pointed to the lower back of his head, "where he had no protection. It happened in two thousand five."

"That had to be devastating to her."

"Of course, it was," the professor said. "She was escorted there to claim his body and return with it. She puts up a good front, masks the loss well, but she's never gotten over it. It is never mentioned in our discussions."

Chris now understood the anger he'd felt, the tough mental exterior. "How did they meet?" he asked.

"The army, special forces."

"Special forces?" He was expecting to be told next she was a top agent.

"Apparently, and I don't know the details," the professor continued, "the secrecy goes with the nature of the beast. She speaks little of that part of her life, but they met within that framework."

"Was she in the army or special forces?"

"He was in the army, one of the branches, there are several. She was a language specialist in the special forces."

"That could mean several different areas," Chris said.

"She was involved in translating raw intelligence in different languages, from both written and spoken sources. Besides being an ancient manuscript expert, she can speak several languages including Arabic in several dialects."

"She's an impressive lady," Chris acceded. "All the Arabic I know is 'Hello,' 'How much?' and 'Which way?'"

"She's also been in and out of Israel several times, Beirut, Bagdad and Tehran, Cairo during the overthrow." He looked up. "Button up, here she comes."

Kate smoothed her skirt as she sat down.

The server brought their food. Kate immediately began attacking the haggis with her knife and fork, cutting it into multiple pieces. She had drifted again out of the discussion, a drift that seemed self-induced. She would return. Chris could count on that.

"I didn't pack for a trip into the heart of Arab spring," Chris said.

"Wear nothing that makes you look like an archaeologist," Kate advised. "No khakis or Indiana Jones hats. Beside our ancient graphics mission, we're supposed to be tourists traveling to Maaloula to see the sights."

Chris glanced at the professor who'd told him khaki shirts.

The professor deflected the look. "Believe it or not, there are sights to see in Maaloula," he said. "It's an oasis and tourist mecca. People go to see Saint Takla Convent and Saint Sergius Monastery. They go to see the caves. Go online, Chris, you'll see. Some of the canyons resemble the siq at Petra."

"Back to the dress code," Kate said. "Daytime temps will be in the sixties and seventies, forties and mid thirties in the evening, minimum chance of rain. Think layered clothing, sweater weather. Everything needs to fit in a carry-on."

What Chris had packed for Scotland would work in Beirut and Maaloula. He could easily pare two bags down to his carry-on. He'd done it often. "I guess then we go to Dunbar tonight, Kate picks me up in the morning, and we're off to the airport. What time does our flight leave?"

The professor waggled an urgent finger and quickly swallowed a bite of food. "I forgot to tell you, Kate. We've had Chris on a wait list with the University tour office. A room became available at The Balmoral, just down the way."

Kate looked disappointed. "And I was looking forward to showing him my home."

"Sorry," the professor said. "I was thinking of logistics, not aesthetics." He looked at Chris. "She lives in a manor, a step-down from a castle."

She gave the professor a reprimanding frown.

"Maybe some other time," Chris said. "I was looking forward to seeing where the good Earl took Queen Mary ... and the Bayswell Hotel."

"To answer your question," the professor commented, looking at Chris, "Your flight, an Air France, leaves in the morning ten after six. You'll need to be there fourish. There's a connection in Paris. From there, it's a six and a half hour flight to Beirut." He downed the rest of his pint. "You'll arrive about five o'clock Mid-east time. Your contact is Dr. Radwan Krekorian, who runs a small Armenian hospital. He's arranged auto travel to Damascus then to Maaloula. Depending on the situation in Syria, the route could change. Kate has the details."

The waiter brought the check. Chris reached for it, but the professor picked it up.

"Who's funding this?" Chris asked.

Professor Stewart pointed a finger at himself. "Up front, I am," he responded.

"Up front?" Chris exclaimed.

"Enough said, laddie. I will be repaid. I don't have that many more years left so why shouldn't I invest part of my retirement on the stakes of a lifetime. Your question reminds me, do you have ample cash? I've set aside some for you. You'll need it for the visas."

"Customs won't detain me for bringing more than ten thousand dollars into the country, will they?" Chris asked and grinned at his joke. "I have plenty. I planned for a two-week stay. Consider it a contribution to the cause. It's all in dollars."

"Good!" the professor exclaimed. "They'll take dollars in Lebanon, but you'll want to change some to Syrian pounds at the Beirut airport. As a seasoned traveler, you know that."

"One question before we go," Chris said. "You were going to tell me how you got the manuscript back to Edinburgh."

"It was really quite simple," the professor said. "I rolled it up in a newspaper, put a thick rubber band around it and carried it under my arm. Who would trouble an old man about his newspaper?"

Chris shook his head. "Amazing! Simply amazing."

"Another reason we've not gone public," the professor said, "is all the problems they had with the Dead Sea Scrolls, charges of illegal excavation and such. I excavated nothing, only purchased an old scroll in an antique store. You will have to be more careful. If you are successful and find the other scroll, you will have excavated."

"What's that plan?" Chris enquired.

"It's in the works," Kate said.

"I guess that's about right for a mission in progress on Halloween," Chris said.

With a raised finger, the professor corrected him. "All Saint's Eve, laddie. It bodes well."

CHAPTER TEN

Bethany, August, 70 A.D.

John Mark made his way down the familiar rocky slopes from the Gihon Spring. He descended the mount obliquely, cut a diagonal path to maximize his distance between the troops on the wall, and on Olivet. He did not know how far their sentries extended then he heard, "Halt! Who goes there?" It came not from the Olivet but from the wall above him. They could do nothing to him from there, but they might have sentries on the ground.

The call came again: "Halt! Who goes?"

John Mark did not respond but quickened his pace until his movement suddenly leveled at the base of the mount where the Kidron and Hinnon Valleys converged. He did not hear the voice again. Perhaps the sentry had called for help. John Mark kept listening for the familiar sound of clanging metal chasing him but heard only the tumult of the city and voices on Olivet fading behind him, his own footfalls growing louder on the rocky soil as he continued running along the southern base of the mount.

The night air was cool. He was shivering in his wet clothes, but he kept on until he no longer saw the walled city and the flames licking from its dark shape. He felt safe, at least for the moment. He was like one moving through a dark house where he had once lived and was now, after years, revisiting and moving by instinct. The moon still shone over the black shoulder of Olivet, his only point of reference. But he had a sense for distance and knew how far he must go to begin his ascent to Bethany. He had been to the small village several times with his mother to visit Mary and her sister and brother but they always followed the road from Jerusalem. That route was short; the route he was now taking was longer.

In the faint moonlight, judging from the shape of the mount against the sky, he had reached mid-point along its base and began his ascent. It was past midnight and most of the village was asleep. But he could see scattered lights, oil lamps still burning from the day, and headed toward them. The moon was behind him, the same that now seemed to smile. He kept thinking about his mother, how she would survive. Maybe he should have stayed. If he had, the master's word would have vanished. He would ask Mary to check on her ... if Mary was even there.

He recalled the house was on the main street through the village. He opened the gate, crossed a small courtyard and lightly knocked once on the small door. He did not want to startle her. He waited. He knocked a second time. The door cracked.

"This is John Mark, son of Mary."

The door opened.

"John Mark!" a woman's voice cried out excitedly. "Praise to God! Enter," and her arms pulled him through the low doorway and embraced him.

He had not seen Mary in almost twenty years. Then she was a middle-aged, dark-haired woman. Now, in the dim flickering light of a nearby oil lamp, she looked younger than the seventy years he had estimated her age to be, but her face looked pallid with dark areas beneath her eyes.

She held him at arms' length. "John Mark," she said his name again to dispel her disbelief. "After many years, you come to my house in the middle of the night. I must see you better." She moved him closer to the lamp. "You have aged well, John Mark. You have your mother's high cheeks and forward, dark eyes." She fluffed his hair with her hand. "Your hair looks shorter than I recall, some gray in it, in your beard, too." She pulled on it teasingly then stood back. "You are wet! You are breathing hard! There is something wrong."

"I came through the Hezekiah tunnel." He was still trying to catch his breath from the long and difficult climb. "The Romans are destroying Jerusalem. Mother would not come with me. She sends her love to you."

"Your dear mother." Her hands were still on his shoulders, her eyes intense. "I have not seen her in several years. I no longer go into the city. It is too dangerous. How is she?"

"She is healthy and as strong as you remember her. She will survive. The city I am afraid will not. She told me your sister and brother had died. I grieved when I heard this sad news. What happened?"

"They were older than I," she said. "They had physical problems. Martha could not walk from this room to the kitchen where she loved spending time. I would help her, but she could not stand. Lazarus developed a breathing problem." They still stood near the lamp and she was fussily brushing his wet clothes with her hands. "One night he became ill with much fever and could not swallow. He was dead before the dawn." She held his cheeks between her hands. "You have left the city. I hear many others, too, are leaving."

"You are correct on both counts. But I left to save this," he said, pointing to the leather bag looped around his shoulder.

She withdrew her hands from his face and touched the bag, eyed it curiously. Her brows raised. "What is in the bag that could cause you to abandon your mother to the Romans?"

The words cut. "I implored her to join me, but you know my mother. What I carry is more precious than all of our lives."

She glanced again at the bag and then back into his eyes. "I cannot imagine something that valuable."

"The master."

Her eyes widened. "He is not in the bag," she said in a tone of sarcastic wonder.

"No. His life and teachings. I traveled with my cousin Barnabas and the man Paul to Antioch. I left them, returned to Jerusalem, the last time I saw you at my mother's, and then went to Tyre to write the master's story so his good news will live."

A hand flew to her mouth, and she sighed deeply. "That truly *is* more valuable than our lives."

"Jesus said, 'Whoever loses his life for me and for the gospel will save it.'"

"How long have you been writing?" she inquired. "Here, please sit down." She pointed to the hearth where a fire had been banked, the coals glowing bright orange through the gray ash.

He removed the satchel and set it on the floor near his feet. "I have been working on the project for almost twenty years, since I last saw you.

Witnesses were dying. Time was moving on. Peter was concerned the story would die if not preserved. Most of that time has been used interviewing people, gathering information. As you know, we have been taught to memorize what we hear. Most of what I hear—about his teachings and miracles—agrees with my memory. When it does not, I take note but do not include it in the main scroll. Most of what I know has come from Peter."

"Peter, God bless him. He is gone."

"Those returning from Rome say he was crucified in reverse position," he said sadly. "But I was able to be with him before he went to Rome and record his memories of the master, the teachings and events as he remembered them. I covet knowing what you know, what you have seen with your own eyes and heard with your own ears."

She, the calm one, sat with her hands folded in her lap and, at first, did not respond. She had turned her head, and her face in the shadows concealed her emotions. Mary, always the listener, said little. Perhaps that was the reason for her silence. He waited.

Finally, she spoke. "I doubt what I know would be helpful. I know so little."

"But you were close friends with Jesus. He came to your home often. You saw and heard things."

"This is true. I was there when he brought my brother, Lazarus, back to life."

John Mark felt embarrassed. He was almost finished with the scroll and had not included her brother's resurrection in the narrative. There were reasons. He did not witness the event and, for whatever reason, Peter did not reveal it to him. One cannot think of everything, but there was another, stronger, reason. The story of Lazarus' resurrection was inconsistent with Jesus' theme of faith, of belief. His Kingdom was near. The resurrection of Jesus was different from the resurrection of Lazarus. John Mark was more interested in the final chapter. "My mother and I received that news with great joy. Did you see Jesus, the resurrected Christ, after his crucifixion?"

Again she hesitated, lifted a fire rod and stirred the ashes as if to bring them to life or something else deeply buried in her thoughts. "Is this a good time?" she asked. "It is still dark. Can you write?"

Looking around the room, he eyed the oil lamp on the window ledge beside the door. "We can move the lamp here," he patted a spot beside him on the hearth. "I have little time. I need to travel while it is dark."

"Where are you going?"

"Damascus. You will probably ask me the same question my mother asked. Why Damascus?"

"You are correct. Why that far away?"

"Damascus has a strong community of believers. It is safe. There, I can finish his story, the gospel of Jesus Christ and Son of God."

She said nothing more, got up and moved the lamp, set it on the hearth beside him.

He retrieved his bag from the floor and removed the shorter scroll. Next, he pulled out a small inkhorn, blackened around the edges, and a long narrow box. He was concerned the ink might have leaked. He had secured the lid and bound it in heavy cloth he would use to blot his letters and clean the pen when he was finished. He removed the top of the inkhorn and from the box took a long reed sharpened to a point with a slit in the middle. "Writing is not an easy task, especially when one is traveling," he commented. He untied the scroll and began unrolling it. Before stopping, a fragment of papyrus slipped out and floated to the floor. He reached down, picked it up and held it close to the lamp. "Be safe on your journey, my son. My love to you." It was signed, "Mother." She was always, somehow, wanting to be part of his safety. She must have slipped the note in when she opened and perused the scroll. He replaced the note, continued unscrolling and at a certain point stopped. Then he looked at Mary. "When was the last time you saw Jesus?"

"At the house of Simon the Leper who lives nearby. I went to anoint him."

"To anoint Jesus?" He dipped his pen in the ink jar and wrote. "Were you invited?"

"No. I had heard he was dining there with his disciples. Simon was one of the lepers he healed. Earlier, he had left from here, this house, and entered Jerusalem on a donkey." A flame appeared in the stirred coals and she added two sticks of wood. "There was much fanfare. A crowd was waving palm branches and shouting hosannas: 'Blessed is he who comes in the name of the Lord. Blessed is the coming kingdom.'" She moved away from the renewed flames and closer to him. "He and his twelve disciples returned to Bethany and stayed here. As you can see, this is not a large house. They slept in this very room. Am I speaking too fast?" and paused for him to finish what she had said.

He stopped writing and she resumed. "Next, he created a disturbance in the Temple and drove out the money changers. He allowed no one to carry merchandise through the Temple courts. He told them it had been written that the Temple—only he called it 'my house'—and said, "will be called a house of prayer for all nations, but you have made it a den of robbers.'"

He stopped again and looked at her. "Were you there?"

"Yes, this I witnessed with my own eyes. Martha and Lazarus were with me. Jesus had stayed here and, after breakfast, we went with him and the twelve into Jerusalem and the Temple. He went to the Temple every morning when he stayed here or in Jerusalem."

"What did you see or hear next?" John Mark probed further.

"We heard people talking. The chief priests and scribes were looking for a way to kill Jesus. The air was filled with tension. I felt great harm was coming to the master. That evening, we returned to Bethany, and the next day we were back in Jerusalem. The chief priests and scribes challenged Jesus' authority. Jesus told a story, a parable, about tenants. The chief priests and scribes did not like the message within the story. They let it be known they were looking for ways to arrest him. I will stop a moment and let your writing come to the point."

He nodded his appreciation, continued writing, dipping his pen, scratching out the words with great haste, then nodded for her to begin again.

"We were back in Jerusalem at the Temple the next day. You could tell the tension was building. Jesus spoke of the signs of the end of the age. I do not recall all he said, but we were to be cautious, watch. No one but the Father in heaven knew the time, but there would be great upheaval, many bad things happening, the sky would go dark and the moon would give no light." She noticed John Mark was having trouble seeing and she reached over and moved the oil lamp closer to him.

"Thank you. That is much better." He finished writing her last words. "You were speaking of the sky and the moon."

"Yes. Jesus said the Son of Man would come on clouds. He kept saying, over and over, 'Watch!' I felt the end was near, that Jesus was about to be arrested and killed. So, I did the only thing I could do, I went to Simon the Leper's house with an alabaster jar of nard, broke the neck of the jar and poured the perfume over his head. I was rebuked, told I had wasted three hundred denarii."

"Rebuked by Jesus?"

"No, by some of his disciples," she exclaimed. "They said the perfume could have been sold for more than a year's wages and the money given to the poor. He said they would always have the poor but they would not always have him."

He continued writing as she spoke and stopped. "That was a brave thing you did," he said.

"It was a far braver thing Jesus did. Shortly after, he was arrested, and you know the rest."

He laid his pen on the hearth, the tip hanging over the edge. "He was arrested after he supped with his disciples at the home of my mother in the upper room then taken to the Sanhedrin, then Pilate, and then ... his crucifixion. You did not answer my question before; perhaps you were distracted. Did you see the risen Christ?"

"I saw my brother he raised from the dead. I did not see Jesus, alive or otherwise, after I anointed him at Simon the Leper's. Everything happened so quickly. The last I heard, he was captured by soldiers in the garden called Gethsemane."

"Yes, I was there."

"Oh, my! What happened?"

"It was horrible. A crowd sent from the chief priests and elders invaded the garden. They were armed with swords and clubs. Judas, the betrayer, kissed the master. Then men in the crowd seized and arrested him. Peter drew his sword and severed the ear of the high priest's servant, but Jesus calmed him. They tried to arrest me, pulled off my linen. Naked, I ran through the night back to the city. Everyone deserted the master and fled. That is how it happened. That is how I wrote it. Were you there when they crucified him?"

"I did not witness the crucifixion." Moisture gathered in her eyes. "Mary Magdalene and Mary, the mother of James, told me about it. They went to the tomb. It was empty. But that is all I know personally. Others I have heard saw Jesus after his crucifixion. They touched him, ate with him, but I did not. I already believed. I saw my brother rise. Even that did not cause my faith. Before that occurrence, I believed." She reached a hand to her eyes, bushed away tears before they fell. "There were those who saw Lazarus when he was dying and saw him walk from the tomb, and they did not believe. It would not matter to me if Jesus did not rise from the dead." The flames had died down and she pulled her robe around her, clutched it at her neck. "It would not matter to me if they found his body in the tomb. I heard of some who saw him after his resurrection and still doubted. I know others believe very differently than I, but it would be of no consequence if the master did not bring back my brother or rise himself from the grave." She reached across the hearth and laid a hand on John Mark's shoulder, patted it for emphasis. "I would believe his teachings." Then looked straight into his eyes. "They are from God. He was from God." She looked down. "I know at first I did not answer your question. I did not want to disappoint you."

"Believe me, dear friend, you have not disappointed me. And you may not believe as differently from me as you think. The master, throughout his ministry, cautioned us and others about believing because he performed miracles. He instructed the disciples not to speak of them."

"Thank you for sharing, John Mark. Your words are consoling."

"In this scroll," he pointed to the near finished work in the bag on the floor, "I emphasize Jesus' focus on faith. I am now near the end of the work including the resurrection. This was one of the reasons I returned to Jerusalem, to speak with witnesses, including you."

"What will you write?"

"I do not know. At the moment, the women—Mary Magdalene, Mary, mother of James, and Salome—have brought spices to anoint Jesus' body. They find the tomb empty. A young man dressed in white robe tells them to not be alarmed that Jesus of Nazareth has risen and to go and tell his disciples and Peter that he has gone ahead of them to Galilee. They leave the empty tomb quickly but say nothing to anyone because they are afraid."

"And that is the end?" she asked with disbelief.

"At this point, yes."

"Perhaps I will think of more, so it will not end in fear."

"Please, yes," he encouraged her. "You can tell me before I leave."

"Where do you go next? What route do you take to Damascus?"

"To Jericho where there are friends. From there, I will follow the road beside the Jordan to Scythopolis. Just north of there, at Gesher, one can cross the Jordan. Roads east of the Lake of Gennesaret lead to Ashtaroth where a major road goes to Damascus."

"That is a great distance," she exclaimed, her hand over her mouth.

"About one hundred and fifty miles. Caravans cover the distance in six days. Of concern to me is Scythopolis. People say the city has sided with the Romans against the Jewish insurgents, so I must be careful. Jesus was crucified as an insurrectionist. His followers have been identified. I was one and, as I told you, almost arrested with him. Another, shorter route, would be to cross the Jordan east of Jericho, go to Heshbon and take the King's Way from Egypt. But then I would miss seeing friends and other followers I know."

"Either way, there is danger," she cautioned. "There is surely danger if you take the Jericho road at night. Even in daylight, it is treacherous. You are surely tired." She moved closer to him and placed an arm around his shoulder. "Stay and rest. Remove your clothes and let me dry them." She picked up the iron rod, stirred the fire again, added more sticks and the flames returned.

He would not argue with her. His eyes were heavy. His clothes had dried some as he sat on the hearth but traveling with dry clothes would lighten his load and allow a faster pace.

"I will get you an extra robe," she said, leaving the room and quickly returning. "This belonged to Lazarus. He was wearing it the day he died the second death, and I have never discarded it. I will get you a bed," and she left again.

He disrobed while she was gone and slipped into the dry robe, his thoughts on the original owner of the garment. Lazarus was a good man. He never married in order to care for his sisters.

She returned with a pallet, one that looked unused, and a blanket. He watched as she prepared it for him, placing it near the fire so he would be warm. Some had accused her of being lazy and letting Martha perform most of the chores but he was observing a whirlwind of caring energy. He re-rolled the scroll where he had written on the reverse side what she had said, retied it. He capped the inkhorn securely, picked up the pen, wiped it, placed it in the box and returned the items to the bag.

. . .

He arose before dawn. His outer and under garments were dry, as well as his sandals which he had forgotten to remove when he had entered the tunnel. Mary had prepared a small breakfast and provided some bread and dried meat for him to take with him. These he did not refuse. Bethany was beyond the city and the siege and had access to provisions.

She walked him to the outer gate, embraced him and whispered into his ear, "Be careful, John Mark. You carry a great future."

"You were going to give thought to my final page," he reminded her.

"Yes, I apologize for not remembering to tell you. I did give much thought to the resurrection and words you should leave for posterity."

"And?"

"You impressed me with your words about faith. Faith triumphs over fear. That is all I need to say. Let that thought, and God's spirit, go with you."

He thanked her and embraced her again.

As he stepped through the outer gate, the edge of the horizon beyond the Jordan was burning with the sun's early rays. Jericho was about eighteen miles down the mount. He had friends there and knew of a community of the faithful. His chances of connecting with anyone were minimal. He knew people in Damascus, which lay six days ahead. He second-guessed himself. He would probably not stop in Jericho. He would continue up the road by the Jordan to Galilee and Scythopolis, cross the Jordan east of there then on to Damascus, no wiser or knowledgeable than when he left Jerusalem.

CHAPTER ELEVEN

Beirut, October 31, 2011

Chris and Kate sat beside each other at the rear of the business class section, their backs to the bulkhead. The seating was by design. Kate only liked arrangements where she could see everything before her. Of course. Her husband had been shot from behind, the bullet entering the rear of his neck where he had had no protection. Unless the professor had told her, she did not know Chris knew her husband had been killed, just that he was deceased. The professor had said it had happened in 2005.

She had said very little since the flight left Edinburgh and nothing when they were in Paris at the Orly Airport. Paris, the city of lovers. The layover had been a couple of hours, time enough for him to sit at the gate and reminisce, reflect on all the long weekend jaunts he and Allyson had made to Paris from Edinburgh. His mind had skimmed across old conversations. Precious moments had turned like screws inside of him.

Based upon what Professor Stewart had told him, Kate probably had similar memories of her husband. Both had been in the military. Paris had intersected their lives frequently. She had said she'd been married twelve years. He had worked the math again. She had married in 1993. He had thought of all the collective, cumulative pain in those two chairs at the gate of an airport in Paris and had considered the irony. He was back in Paris with a woman who had married the year he had married and had been widowed in 2005, the year he had been divorced.

On the second leg of their flight, he continued wondering about the enigma seated beside him. The bright effervescent personality that had met him at the airport in Edinburgh had disappeared. Had she been back to the

Middle East since she had claimed her husband's body? If not, this was *déjà vu*, the old wounds reopened, the reason for her glum silence and the dark wraparound sunglasses.

Her hair was pulled back in a pony tail revealing the fuller features of her face. For her age, she looked incredibly younger. That she dressed chic and stylish was a mixed bag. She would attract, as well as distract, attention. Heads would turn. Western women received attention in the mid-East, most of it unwanted, especially if they were blonde or red-headed. Politically safe dress for women was sleeves to the elbows, no revealing cleavage and head cover or scarf in religious rites. Blue jeans and T-shirts were acceptable. She'd been there, done that, but he thought she was a bit overdressed. Gray cowl-neck sweater, suede jacket and leggings tucked into trendy boots projected rich tourist. She had warned him about looking like an archaeologist. For the flight, he had decided on something casual—black turtleneck, tweed jacket, corduroy slacks and Hush Puppy shoes. She was bordering on more than just a touch of aristocracy. He bet, at some point, there'd be a discussion about wardrobe. Her oversized carry-on suggested she had one. It was longer and wider than most. He had had concerns it wouldn't pass muster and had made a remark at the Edinburgh airport to that effect.

"They've always let me through. I know it looks big, but the dimensions are perfect regulation, to the millimeter," she had responded, gesturing with her forefinger and thumb. "It was specially made, in Paris."

Despite her moodiness, if he was going to Syria in the midst of a civil war, he would surely be safe with a woman who had been in the British Special Forces, drank Glenfiddich on the rocks, ate haggis, spoke Arabic and had a slush fund of anger from an old war. She would not unravel on him. He could count on her, a definite plus in the overall scheme of things. But they were half-way to Beirut. If she was going to be his partner, it was time to loosen things up. She was obviously not going to take the initiative. He waited while she opened her purse and took out a compact and lipstick, made a few passes at her face, looked into the mirror and redefined her lipstick. She returned the items to her purse and snapped it shut.

"May I buy you a drink?" he asked.

"You may order me one," she responded with a tight smile.

"What's your pleasure? No, let me guess. Glenfiddich on the rocks."

"You are very observant," she said without emotion, "but I doubt Air France has Glenfiddich."

"We'll see." He pushed the service button.

Shortly, a male flight attendant appeared and Chris ordered a Glenfiddich which they did not have. "Your best scotch, on the rocks, then," he requested. "Two of them."

"I thought you were a beer connoisseur," she quipped.

"I am in Arizona. I lived in Scotland seven years. I've missed the scotch."

"I thought you were only there three years in seminary," she probed.

"After seminary, I enrolled in the school of archaeology, completed my master's and doctorate in four years, and then moved back to the states with a Scottish bride who loved Scotland and hated every square inch of Arizona."

The flight attendant brought their drinks.

Chris toasted, "Here's to Scotland."

She lifted her glass with him. "So, where is she now? You said you were divorced."

"In Arizona. She decided she wanted to be close to the two sons." He remembered Kate had no children.

"When was your divorce?"

"Two thousand and five." He watched her blink, a slight mist bloom in her eyes. She took a long sip from her drink. The lines around her eyes tightened briefly.

"That's when my husband died," she said, a slight tremble in her voice. She looked into her drink, turned the glass slowly, meditatively in her hand and then looked up. "He was killed ... in Syria."

"I know. Professor Stewart told me. I am truly sorry. I know it had to be devastating."

"There are no words." She wiped back a tear.

He pulled a handkerchief from his inside pocket and handed it to her.

"Thank you," she said gratefully, sincerely.

"I don't know how I would deal with a loss like that, of someone I loved deeply."

"I withdrew from the special forces unit," she revealed. "They understood. I immersed myself in research, in analyzing ancient documents, a different, safer world of adventure. For a long time, I had no social life. In my retreat, I discovered a different, softer side of myself." With his handkerchief, she flicked a tear from a corner of an eye, as if to treat the show of emotion lightly.

"This is your first time back, to the Middle East, I mean."

"Yes, my only trip back since claiming his body. He was killed on the Golan Heights, but the United Nations flew me to Beirut and then had me escorted overland by U.N. jeep to Damascus. I thought I was over it, the bereavement complete." She took a long sip of scotch. "I've dreaded going back but knew it was something I needed to do. It was going to be easier with someone else, a distraction to buffer the pain."

"That's why you got upset when I said I'd 'think about it.'"

She nodded. "I was terrified when you said that and then relieved when you accepted."

He'd read correctly the flash of disappointment in her eyes, the submerged fear. "I can relate. I was apprehensive about returning to Edinburgh. I thought the pain of a broken marriage was over until I set foot on Scottish soil and saw the old places of romance. Suddenly, the memories came rushing back. Allyson and I met at Greyfriar's."

"I apologize. You should have said something."

"Your choice was fortuitous," he responded, tilting his glass toward her. "I wasn't even sure the place still existed. I'd thought if it did, I needed to face it, put it behind me. But divorce is not the same as losing a spouse. I sensed you were quiet because of this history. Again, I am sorry. If there's anything I can do to help."

"I feel your sincerity. And, yes, you can help." She looked at him and forced a smile.

"How?" he said, surprised at the call for help, at the revelation of this soft underside of her personality.

"Distract me."

She smirked when she said it, a gesture that could have been a flirt, but he tossed it aside as part of her struggle to break out of her strong exterior. He considered how he might distract her and his answer was close at hand. "I've given a lot of thought to our friend John Mark and the suggested route he might have taken from Jerusalem and Bethany to Damascus."

"Another besides the two Professor Stewart and I mentioned?"

"Yes. I had an opportunity to study those same maps of first century Palestine in the professor's office yesterday after lunch. There was a

Gideon's Bible in my hotel room. Following my evening devotion, I reread the Gospel of Mark, not word for word, but scanned Jesus' movements as recorded by the author."

"Devotion?" She looked surprised. "You are devout?"

He winced at the question but thought it was fair. After all, they were strangers probing, searching for common ground. "I'm not Joe religion jumping up and down and shouting, but I'm a believer. If I weren't, I might not be here. I probably wouldn't care if there was an autograph of any gospel or not. After all, I studied the New Testament for three years and have a divinity degree. This is the kind of mission I live for. And you?"

"My husband's death, his name was Geoffery, set me back religiously. But I attend a small Methodist church in Dunbar. It's actually the oldest Methodist church in Scotland. John Wesley founded it."

"But you were not born Methodist."

"No. My parents were fervid Church of Scotland. Geoffery was Methodist. I never went back to my parents' church. And you, your denomination, if any?"

He raised his glass and smiled at her. "Methodist. United Methodist."

The scotch was working its magic. She responded, touched her glass against his, and returned the smile, the one he'd seen when she met him at the airport. Her animation was coming back. She shifted sideways in her seat so she was facing him. "The alternative route," she raised a brow. "You've piqued my interest," her lips curling into that smirk again.

"You and Professor Stewart were right," Chris began. "John Mark could have taken either route you suggested but in his gospel, as well as other gospels, Jesus spent most of his life in Galilee. If Mark's gospel is a work in progress, I would think our author would want, perhaps need, to connect with as many points in Jesus' life as possible. If he were a good reporter, he would have sought out witnesses to get the facts. Depth, not speed and safety, may have been more important to him."

Her elbow was propped on the armrest, her eyes peering over her raised glass, looking directly and steadily into his as if everything he was saying came from them.

He continued. "With that presupposition in mind, I agree he would have gone from Bethany to Jericho first, near the Mount of Temptation. Based on your theory, he then took the northern road from Jericho, one that roughly parallels the River Jordan to Scythopolis. At Scythopolis, he had a decision to make."

"I said he crossed the Jordan north of there," she commented, "near Gesher, took an eastern route through Ashtaroth, then a road north to Damascus."

He nodded. "My counter to that is that the year was seventy C.E. There were still people alive on the western shore of the Sea of Galilee, particularly around Capernaum where Jesus spent most of his ministry. John Mark knew more people on that side of the sea than the eastern mountainous side. He was probably still writing, gathering research, composing." He lifted his glass and took a sip. "These people would have been invaluable to him. They could provide places of shelter and rest and food. Capernaum also lay on the Via Maris, the other great highway from Egypt to Damascus. At Capernaum, the route is a direct shot to Caesarea Philippi, another key city in Jesus' ministry with a strong Christian following. It's also indicated on the reverse of the manuscript." He stopped and looked at her for the response she seemed ready to make.

"Please proceed," she encouraged.

He set his drink down on the tray in front of him, turned his napkin over on the wide arm rest between them and drew his pen from his shirt pocket. "I doubt I can duplicate your fine artistry of yesterday, but here goes."

Amused, she leaned back and watched.

Quickly, he sketched a map of the same area with the same key features, oval Sea of Galilee, Jordan River due south to the Dead Sea. He pointed at the Sea of Galilee. "The Jews called this the Sea of Genneraset in the times of Jesus. Along its western shore are Magdala, Capernaum, Chorazin, Bethsaida," he said, placing dots as he called out their names. He glanced up at her. "You know all of this, so consider this a refresher."

She smiled as though she was being entertained.

"Early in his ministry, Jesus taught at Capernaum. The synagogue there now is fourth century Hellenistic architecture and design but probably sits on the same spot." He checked her face again, concerned he might be talking over her, doing to her what he'd perceived she'd done to him in the professor's study. Her eyes were on him, not the map he was drawing. She seemed genuinely interested. "In Capernaum, Jesus healed many, cleansed the man of unclean spirits, a leper and a paralytic lowered through a roof.

He visited in the house of Simon Peter, which has been unearthed by archaeologists and reconstructed. This would be a place where John Mark could stop, as well as the house of Levi where he also dined. People came from distant points to hear Jesus—Tyre, Sidon, Jerusalem and Idumea in trans-Jordan." He looked up again. "How am I doing?"

She nodded. "So far, so good," and returned the stroke in the air he'd given her the day before.

"In Galilee, Jesus ordained the twelve. At Bethsaida, he walked on water. If the author were near the end of his gospel, and indicators suggest he was, he would head straight for the home of the gospel. He would go to Capernaum." He stopped because she had raised a finger to make a comment.

"It would be wonderful if we could transport ourselves back into time," she said dreamily, "and be there when these events happened. I had forgotten how much of Mark's gospel took place in Galilee. You do know your New Testament history."

"What I've just covered is in the first six chapters of Mark's gospel," he said. "The miracle of loaves and feeding of the four thousand, an event that takes place in all four gospels and also in Galilee, covers the first part of the eighth chapter. So far, that's half of the book of Mark."

"You make a strong case," she said, her tone complimentary. "I'm impressed. Of course, we have no way of knowing."

"We might if we find the autograph. If he was carrying a draft, no telling what else might be involved."

The announcement was made that the plane was beginning its descent to Beirut. They finished their drinks, handed the glasses to the attendant and buckled their seat belts. She seemed to be withdrawing again.

"Once we're in Beirut, what's the procedure?" he asked.

"The first thing we do is get Lebanese visas at the airport." She opened a small purse and retrieved a sheet of paper and unfolded it. "We take a taxi to a small Armenian hospital called only the C.M.C. An address is provided."

"This is the hospital the professor's doctor friend runs."

"Yes. Doctor Krekorian, who graduated from the medical school at the University of Edinburgh. He is the same individual who arranged transportation for the professor to Damascus and Maaloula."

"We presume he is going to do the same for us."

"Yes." She looked at her watch. "We are arriving at about five o'clock. It will take an hour to get through customs and purchase our visas."

"At least," he murmured.

"Perhaps the good doctor will have food for us or recommendations before we depart," she said.

"We're not spending the night?"

"No. Time is of essence on this trip, always." She was speaking again in her authoritative voice, back to profile, and then began telling him facts he knew as if he had no inkling. "The distance from Beirut to Damascus is eighty six kilometers or fifty-three American miles." She referenced his map still lying on the armrest and, with her finger, drew an imaginary line from the Mediterranean coast line to Damascus. "By car, if we did not have to stop at the border and get Syrian visas, the driving time is about an hour. That depends on the weight of the driver's foot. The distance from Damascus to Maaloula is only about thirty minutes."

"We should arrive between eight and nine o'clock," he conjectured.

"Let's hope," she responded optimistically.

• • •

The official in the passport booth was a man of medium weight with a heavy sagging face, puffed eyes and a fat upper lip. He quickly processed Kate's visa, handed it to her and she stepped aside..

The official looked at Chris and shook his head. "I cannot grant you visa."

"I don't understand," Chris said. "I've been in your country before and had no problems."

"When was this you were in Lebanon?" the official questioned.

"About ten years ago. I was granted one immediately and paid about thirty-five dollars American money."

"The tourist visa costs nothing now," the official said. "Since two thousand six, it cost nothing. But the problem is here," and he pointed to a page in his passport. "You have been in Israel. We cannot grant visas to people who have been to Israel. What kind of doctor are you?"

Kate reached over and tugged at his arm, but Chris didn't understand the signal.

"It is for an academic degree. I am an archaeologist, not a medical doctor."

Kate jerked on his sleeve again. He didn't respond.

She then intervened and said something to the official in Arabic, flashed Chris a conspiratorial smile, draped an arm around his shoulder and said, "Isn't that right darling?" and then kept speaking Arabic to the official. When she finished, whatever she said was effective. She beamed dramatically at the passport official who smiled grandly back at her. He picked up Chris' passport, flipped some pages back and forth perfunctorily, placed a stamp on one page, and smacked it loudly with a blotter. "Okey dokey," he said, continuing to smile. He looked at Kate. "Congratulations," then at Chris, "You are lucky man. Enjoy your stay," and he motioned for them to pass on.

She gripped his hand until they had turned a corner out of sight then let go and clamped hers over her mouth.

"For crying out loud, what did you say to the man?" Chris asked, exasperated.

She was still throttling laughter then removed her hand from her mouth. "I told him we were engaged to get married, that we had both worked in Lebanon before and fell in love with the country, adding 'isn't that right, darling?' That's when I put my arm around you. I told him our dream was to wed beneath the beautiful pillars of Jupiter at Baalbek and, here's the clincher, that the wedding is tomorrow."

He could feel the blush. His face felt warm.

"That's the best distraction I've had," she said and patted him on the back.

"Don't give me credit. You created it. All I can think of right now is life in a Lebanese prison. What if he'd asked for our marriage license?"

"I was prepared to tell him that was our next stop."

He shifted his carry-on to the other shoulder and continued shaking his head in disbelief. "We've got the Syrian border officials to encounter next. Wonder what they'll say. I was only in Israel two days to make a presentation, that's all."

"The Syrians will probably say nothing," she said confidently. "If you have a Lebanese visa, they will usually issue one for Syria."

"And the Israeli stamp?"

"You've already passed muster. They probably won't flip that far in your passport."

"It's on the second page," he exclaimed.

After changing their money into Syrian pounds at an exchange kiosk, they walked outside to get a taxi. A young man standing by a white, older model Mercedes with a TAXI light on top motioned them over and asked in broken English if they were looking for a ride. He was short and thin, boney face, clean cut and wearing a white shirt and white slacks. A distinguishing feature was the mop of hair that looked incongruently larger than his head.

"Yes, we are going to the C.M.C. Hospital," Kate stated.

"I know the place," he said before she could show him the address. "Get in," he motioned with his hand. "I take you. No problem."

He drove cockily with swerving panache, reminding Chris of New York City cabbies. He said he knew the place, but if he did, he was taking a circuitous route. Chris leaned forward and spoke as though the man were deaf. "C.M.C. Hospital. You know? We have the address."

"Yes, yes. I know. Not to worry. No problem."

Eventually, when it seemed the street would dead end in a residential area, an unlikely place for a hospital, the driver came to a screeching halt in front of a gray concrete double-deck structure that looked more like an office building than a hospital, its windows square moons in the dark night. Kate paid the driver, and he drove off.

"How much was it?" Chris asked.

"A few dollars. Gas is cheap here, less than a quid a gallon, little over a dollar in your currency."

"Did you tip him?"

"Yes. It was a ghastly ride, but we may see him again. It happens. The world of travelers is small, especially in Beirut."

Upon entering the building, the carbolic smell clearly defined hospital. The receptionist paged Dr. Krekorian and he quickly appeared. He was a handsome-looking older man in his sixties, tall and lean, aquiline face with groomed salt and pepper hair, dark eyes. He was wearing a white coat with the proverbial stethoscope looped around his neck. "Dr. Ferguson, so good to see you," he said, taking her hand in both of his. "Professor Stewart speaks highly of you. And the gentleman with you is ...?"

"Chris Jordan," Chris said, reaching to shake the doctor's hand, which was strong and friendly.

"Radwan Krekorian. Dr. Jordan, of course. Professor Stewart also speaks well of you. I think you studied under him at one time."

Chris nodded. *Also speaks well of you.* He guessed he was the tag along.

"So," he brought his hands together in a soft sultanic clap, "I take it our taxi driver found you okay."

"The taxi who brought us was your driver?"

"We sent one for you, gave the description to him that Dr. Stewart gave to us. He knew your plane's arrival time."

Chris and Kate looked at each other and then back at the doctor.

"We do not know," Kate said. "We just took the first taxi we saw. He asked if we were looking for a ride and here we are."

"It is of no importance," Dr. Krekorian said. "You are here. You must be famished. My staff has arranged some food for you if you will follow me please."

For a small hospital that seemed in the middle of nowhere in Beirut, the place was busy. Threading their way through a continuous stream of nurses and orderlies, they came to a room at the end of a long hallway where a table had been set and food prepared.

"Please sit," Dr. Krekorian said, pointing to three chairs around the small square table. "I will join you. Would you like tea to drink? Perhaps just water?"

They both said tea. Dr. Krekorian stuck his head outside the door and shouted down the hall, "Rashida, please bring us three teas," and then he joined them at the table.

Chris decided to open the discussion. "Professor Stewart told us you had been helpful getting him to Damascus and Syria and could do the same for us."

"Absolutely," the doctor affirmed. "It is arranged. A taxi will take you after we eat."

"A taxi or a private car?" Chris asked.

"Taxi. It is a taxi we use," Dr. Krekorian responded. "We could get a private car for you, but border officials are accustomed to taxis transporting tourists, and Professor Stewart said … just a moment." He got up and closed the door. "I arranged for this room to eat. It is quieter, and we can speak more privately. Professor Stewart said you were traveling as tourists. I understand your purpose is different. I do not know the reason and do not need to know. I am a Christian. This is a Christian hospital. We are here to help. We do not ask questions. I must tell you, however." He made full rotation with his finger. "This is a Hezbollah neighborhood. We must mind our manners."

"We understand, Dr. Krekorian," Kate said. "We are doing nothing wrong, only research which, for the moment, cannot be revealed for reasons I am sure you would understand."

"Say no more. I trust Dr. Stewart," Dr. Krekorian said.

"How do you know him?" Chris inquired.

"The first year of my medical studies I lived in a room in his house in Edinburgh."

"When will our ride arrive?" Chris continued. Kate gave him the kind of look his wife used to give when he was asking too many questions.

"When you finish eating," Dr. Krekorian said, noting the sharp glance from Kate.

A young woman arrived with a tray of tea and condiments. She was tall and stately with elegant features, about Kate's size but slimmer. She was the only one they'd seen who was in civilian, not hospital, attire. In perfect English with a British accent she inquired if they needed anything else and named some options. Dr. Krekorian looked at the two for a response. They were fine with the tea, they said, and the young woman departed.

"Please, a blessing," the doctor said and extended his hands.

They held hands around the table while he said a brief prayer that ended with a Trinitarian benediction. He swept a hand over the table. "We have for you a meze, typical Lebanese dinner of pita bread and hummus, broiled fish, olives, salad, yogurt, eggs, and, of course, escargots," pointing to each as he identified them before passing the small dishes.

Predictably, Kate reached for the snails and placed several on her plate. "Here," she said motioning to Chris. "You should try these."

They looked worse than haggis, if sheep's heart, liver and lungs, could be made to look edible.

"They are especially tasty in late autumn," Dr. Kerkorian added.

"You don't know what you're missing," Kate urged, eying Chris.

He did not want to sound rude or be impolite. "Thank you, I'll pass."

The doctor was observing them as if he detected tension. "As we eat, I believe I should provide you an update on the situation in Syria and a possible alternative route around the capital."

"We appreciate any information you can give us, Dr. Kerkorian," Kate replied.

"As you know, the situation is deteriorating rapidly, a reason we want to get you to Maaloula without delay. Last week, your ambassador, Robert Ford," he looked at Chris, "had to leave Syria after receiving personal threats. Syria responded by withdrawing their ambassador from Washington. The breach between the U.S. and Syria is growing. A Mr. Haynes Mahoney is the *chargé d' affaires*."

"This is important information, Dr. Kerkorian," Chris said. "We were aware of the diplomat situation but not the name of the *chargé d' affaires*. That's a name we must remember. At some point, we may need to contact him."

The doctor continued. "Three days ago, forty were killed across Syria, most in Homs and Hama, north of Maaloula. Security forces were shooting randomly at people. The same day, Turkey announced its support of the dissidents. Today, my country's police accused Syria of orchestrating abductions of Syrian dissidents in Lebanon. So far, Damascus and Aleppo have been uninvolved but there are daily demonstrations in Damascus and the tension is high."

"Do you think we should stay on A5 and drive through the city?" Chris asked.

"If there are just demonstrations, we should have no problems," Kate said with assurance.

Dr. Kerkorian was listening seriously to them. "I would not advise this," he said, looking first at Kate and then at Chris. "The situation is too fragile. It could erupt any moment within any demonstration. If that happens, you could be trapped. There is an alternate route which connects around Damascus and goes to Maaloula. There is another through Baalbek. You might have less difficulty crossing the border there, but it is a longer route."

"We'll take the shorter route and monitor the situation," Kate maintained.

"Yes, of course," Dr. Krekorian said. "You can check with me. He pulled a slip of paper from his white coat and handed it to Kate. "The service is erratic, but I have jotted down my phone numbers for you. The second is my cell phone. I assume you both have phones that will work in Lebanon and Syria."

They nodded.

"Excellent. You could also text, which is more efficient."

Dr. Kerkorian excused himself and opened the door. "Rashida! Call Muhammed," he shouted down the hall, then returned and sat down.

"Besides being the great prophet, who, might I inquire, is Muhammed?" Kate asked.

"There are several million Muhammeds in the Arab world, but I assure you, this Muhammed is one of the best. He is your taxi driver, the same who transported Dr. Stewart to and from Maaloula. Stewart gave him the highest praise."

"I hope he's better than the last one," Chris said.

"Oh, it was not good?" Dr. Kerkorian questioned.

"He drove like a bat out of hell," Chris declared.

"Our Muhammed is Christian, Dr. Jordan. I can assure you, he knows no bats in hell," Dr. Kerkorian joked and smiled broadly.

They finished eating and followed Dr. Kerkorian down the hall back to the entrance foyer.

"Please, wait," Dr. Kerkorian said. "I almost forgot."

He stepped into an office down the hall and returned with something wrapped in brown paper. "Per your request through Dr. Stewart," he said and handed the package to Kate.

"Many thanks," she said gratefully. "I will take good care of it."

The inside secrets continued. Sooner or later, Chris would be let in on this one.

The taxi pulled up in front of the hospital, and Dr. Kerkorian escorted his guests down the steps. The driver got out. Chris and Kate looked at each other and tried to show no emotion.

"Muhammed, come and meet your passengers for Maaloula."

Muhammed stepped around the cab and gave the usual Arab greeting, "*As-salamu-alakum*," with a big smile. "We meet again."

CHAPTER TWELVE

Galilee, August, 70 A.D.

Not long after John Mark stepped through Mary's gate, the sun was a blazing disc rising over the plateau beyond the Jordan. The descent from Jerusalem to Jericho was always harder than the ascent. Mary was right about the road. Following the deep valley Nahal Prat, in places it was steep and narrow with twists and turns. He had to step more carefully lest his feet slip from beneath him and he fall. If he slipped, the fall could mean death.

He thought of his mother. Amid the noise of war and devastation, she would be stirring the fire, putting on a pot of water to boil. Rhoda would come in, and they would begin the day together as they always did. Thank God for Rhoda. She was faithful and loyal. They would speak of him, of their concerns and love for him. They would kneel and pray to their resurrected Christ. He prayed, too, but his prayer was different. He prayed to a Christ of unknown power and transcendence, one less reachable, less touchable. This was the Jesus he had known, the Christ Peter had described to him, the Christ who preferred a shroud of mystery around him, the Christ that evoked faith.

The trek down the road took him all day. John Mark decided to stop and stay at an inn at the end of the valley Nahal Prat and before the road reached Jericho. A story had been passed on to him, a parable told by Jesus, of a traveller who had been beaten and robbed and left for dead. A priest and Levite passed by the poor man without helping, but a Samaritan stopped, put the man on his donkey, took him to an inn and cared for him. John Mark had not included the story in his gospel but thought it worthy of investigation. He inquired at the inn if anyone there, the owners or clerks, had heard of this story and none had. He made a notation on the verso of his draft and decided to give it more thought.

Jericho was still asleep when he entered the outskirts, its red clay houses just beginning to glow with the first rays of dawn. Roosters were crowing and a few dogs barking. One trotted by with a squealing rabbit in his mouth. But John Mark saw no one moving about. It looked deserted, like a ghost city. Above, loomed the mount where Jesus had been tempted. He came to a well and stopped, sat down and reflected. He pulled the scroll from his bag, opened it, unrolled to that place in his narrative, and reread what he had written. He scanned past the temptation story, read what he had written about Jesus walking on water, the feeding of the four thousand, Peter's confession, on past the transfiguration to the story of the healing of a boy with an unclean spirit then read the following line, "They left that place and passed through Galilee."

He rolled the scroll back up, retied it and replaced it in the bag. He was pleased he had looked at the mount and thought to reread the story as Peter had related it to him and what followed. He knew the work by heart and mind now, every word and sentence, but rereading stimulated his thinking, turned it in different directions. He would go to Scythopolis, but he would not cross the Jordan north of there and go to Ashtaroth, as he had planned. He would not take the shorter route to Damascus. *They left that place and passed through Galilee.* He would visit the places he had written about, where the stories had occurred, the sites of miracles and teachings, the resurrection appearances, and his unresolved final page. Mary Magdalene, Jesus' mother and Salome said the man at the tomb told them to tell the disciples and Peter, *"He is going ahead of you into Galilee. There you will see him."*

The route would take him longer, but perhaps he would learn more, as he had learned from Mary in Bethany, her anointing of Jesus which should be added. Amending a scroll was difficult, but it could be accomplished. Working carefully with a damp cloth and glue, he had done it before, detached and added papyrus leaves. He had ample ink in the inkhorn he carried on his belt but was low on the soot and Arabic gum he mixed with water to make his ink. He only had two writing reeds. He could replenish his supplies in Caesarea Philippi or Damascus. He had the extra scroll and sufficient space remaining on the verso for taking notes to amend his narrative. People did not understand the meticulousness, the cautious discipline in writing a story where sentences must flow together, every detail fit, the key themes interlock. The gospel of his master must be as complete as he could accomplish, which included the resurrection, still dangling.

He would remain briefly in Jericho, perhaps see a couple of his friends, but not impose on them. They would argue and encourage him to stay longer. Galilee was ahead of him and Galilee was where Jesus spent most of his ministry. He reflected momentarily on his lack of good sense, that he'd even considered bypassing the best parts of the story.

A little further into the city, he saw a man step from a small house. He was wearing a colorful robe and sat on a bench beside the entrance of the house. As he neared, the man looked familiar. Could it be, John Mark wondered? Was the man even still alive?

He approached the man and spoke. "*Shalom alichem*, friend."

"And *shalom alichem* to you."

"You are the first to rise in your city, for I have seen no one else," John Mark said cheerfully.

"I rise to see the world, as much of it as possible," the man replied with equal good cheer.

He *was* still alive. "Are you not Bartimaeus, son of Timaeus?"

"I am he."

"The one healed of blindness by Jesus the Christ?" John Mark queried.

"The same beholding you. Who inquires?" Bartimaeus asked.

"I am John Mark, son of Benjamin and Mary of Jerusalem. I was with Jesus the day you were healed." He remembered the spot beside the road earlier when he passed it. The tree and the wall behind it were still there. Jesus and a large crowd were leaving the city and a blind man, sitting by the road side called out, "Jesus, Son of David, have mercy on me." Peter was upset with the man and cautioned him to be silent, but the man would not stop and shouted again. When Jesus called to the man, he jumped up, threw his cloak aside and went to Jesus. Everyone was astonished at Jesus' question to the man: "What do you want me to do for you?" as if he could not see the man was blind. Of course, the man said he wanted to see and immediately received sight because of his faith.

"I am sorry," the man named Bartemaeus apologized. "I followed Jesus that day but do not remember you. I did not see. Then, suddenly, I saw everyone but remember no one but Jesus. My eyes were on him. Please come, sit," he said and pointed to the spot next to him.

"For a moment only, for I must not tarry."

"And this great urgency?" Bartemaeus inquired.

"The story of the Christ." John Mark patted the bag hanging from his shoulder. "Your story and many others, too. I must move beyond harm's way to complete it."

"Jerusalem is burning," Bartemaeus said dolefully.

"Tragically, this is true."

"Vespasian and his soldiers came here. Many people fled to the mountains. Some stayed. Vespasian built a garrison. Soldiers walk the streets."

"You remained," John Mark said.

"Had I been blind, I might have run. But now I see, thanks to Jesus, Son of David. I run from no one, surely not Romans."

"Your healing has given you faith."

"I believed before I was healed," the man responded emphatically.

"Bartemaeus, you know better than I, the one writing the gospel. Over and over, Jesus said that miracles did not produce faith, faith produces miracles." John Mark placed a hand on the man's shoulder and rose to bid farewell.

"They will come here next, the Zealots," Bartemaeus predicted. "Then the Romans will destroy Jericho. Be careful, my friend. Stay clear of the garrison on the hillside."

John Mark thanked Bartemaeus and continued on his way, reflecting on the event.

The experience with Bartemaeus was all the more reason he should go to Galilee. There were others still living who had been touched by the master and become his voice.

He walked on through the vacant streets of the oasis that produced and exported balsam, the place Mark Anthony once gave to Cleopatra as a gift. Then Herod leased it from her. Some dogs he'd heard barking came out to investigate, sniff out his presence. A few people were stirring around their domiciles. It was the first day of the week and shopkeepers would be soon opening their stalls. He stopped and looked around. Somewhere there was a large sycamore tree. He wondered if it was the same one he was approaching.

He had heard only fragments of the story, how a local superintendent of customs or tax collector named Zaccheus climbed the tree in order to see Jesus as he passed through the town on his way to Jerusalem. It was reported that the master saw him and called him to come down, that he would visit in his home. Whether or not Jesus did visit him, John Mark did not know. That was all the story he knew. The outcome might have had something to do with the man's name. In Hebrew, Zaccheus meant "righteous one." Perhaps someone in Jericho would know.

He stopped at one house he knew, opened the patio gate and knocked on the door. A woman opened the door, a woman he did not know. She had a long hawkish face, beaked nose, with inquisitive dark eyes.

"Yes, who are you?" Her voice was abrasive.

"Please accept my apologies, but I thought Efraim son of Eli lived here."

"No! He is not here."

"Might I inquire where he lives?"

"You may, but I do not know," the woman replied, irked. "He left when Vespasian and his soldiers came."

"Did he take his family with him?" John Mark questioned further.

"Yes. Everyone. Now excuse me," she said and she closed the door.

He walked on and tried one other place, further away from the mountain slope, but when he arrived it had been demolished, possibly the work of the Romans or Herodians. Up in the mountains, at the entrance to the canyon that stretched to Jerusalem, was evidence of aristocratic splendor: Herod's palaces, the aqueduct, the hippodrome. Jericho was where the wealthy came to relax and play. Years ago, before Jesus was born, Aristobulus III, the last scion of the Hasmonean royal house, drowned mysteriously here in Jericho in a swimming pool.

Jericho was a place where Jesus could have spent more time. It was also, perhaps, one of those places where he advised his disciples to "shake the dust off your feet when you leave." Did he record that? He wasn't sure. He thought he knew his own work by heart. He couldn't record everything. Peter, who disliked boorish folk, had particularly liked that command. That may be what John Mark should do now in Jericho, shake the dust and not waste his time tracking down the rest of a story. He had one good story from Jericho. The city, which Jesus passed through and never stayed, did not deserve better. Galilee was friendlier territory.

He traveled almost twenty miles a day. There were only two towns along the road, Archelais, built by Herod's son to house workers for his date plantation, and Phasaelis, built by Herod and named for his brother. At Phasaelis the road forked, and he took the eastern branch. The weather was clear, days warm and the evenings cool. He stopped only to sleep and slept off the roadside beneath trees for shelter. He encountered no signs of communal life until the second day when he reached the outskirts of Scythopolis, the juncture of several main roads and also the location of a major Roman garrison. Taking no chances that he might be stopped and interrogated, he skirted the city.

In the early morning of the third day, he reached the southern shore of the Sea of Gennesaret. He took a mountain path and followed a high ridge. The lake below pressed into the hills like a mirror and reflected a cloudless sky. The scent of white and pink almond tree blossoms hung in the air. Yellow daisies and violet anemone danced in the occasional breeze. He could see from one end of the sea to the other, where the Jordan entered in the north and emptied in the south, the rocky plateau of Gamla to the east and the snow covered Mount Hermon in the far north. Following the rim of the lake, his eyes tracked half of the land he'd mentioned in his scroll—Tiberius, Magdala, Capernaum, Bethsaida. These places were where the master spent most of the three years of his short ministry. He climbed these hills, walked the shores below, moved in and out of the villages and called his disciples here. Some were men who fished, like those in the tiny boats he saw below that appeared as specks dotting the deep blue. Though he grew up in Nazareth, not far away, it was here Jesus spent most of his time.

It was here also that John Mark's father loved to come. Galilee was his favorite place. His father had done well as a potter making oil lamps. He began crafting simple earthenware vessels then expanded to terra cotta and bronze, decorating them with designs. Lamps used olive oil and he branched into that trade. When customers came to his shop they could purchase all they needed to light their homes—lamps, oil and wicks. His business was good. He could afford time off with his family. At every chance, he took the road north from Jerusalem to Shechem, then to Sepphoris and finally due east to Gennesaret. His family usually traveled in the spring, but at times in the autumn. They often journeyed down these same hills to Bethsaida, where many went for the same reason, to rest and play and to enjoy the balmy weather and warm waters of the sea away from the noise, heat and smell of the city.

Following a path others had made, he walked a few miles. Tiberias was directly below. He thought of descending. This city was safe. Its inhabitants had sided with Rome in the early stages of the revolt. Vespasian had shown mercy and spared it. John Mark had heard the Sanhedrin had escaped Jerusalem during the siege and were headed to Tiberius, but that report was not confirmed. From his lofty vantage point, he could see the fortress Herod Antipater had built, the stadium and the forum. Because the city had been built on a necropolis, pious Jews refused to live there. The affluent, however, were attracted because of the springs; the poor because of the promise of land and housing. Was that a reason Jesus had never gone there? Were there other reasons? John Mark did not know. There was no reason for him to visit the place, so he did not mention it in the gospel. He cupped a hand over his eyes. In the distance, he could see Capernaum. He remembered words he had written, "When Jesus again entered Capernaum, the people heard that he had come home."

John Mark continued on.

He could understand why Jesus considered Capernaum to be home. Located on the northern shore of Gennesaret, the town had no particular advantages over any other, but it was the home of Peter, Andrew, James and John as well as the tax collector, Levi, also called Matthew. Capernaum was a quiet place with a good synagogue where Jesus could teach unmolested. On a mountain side near Capernaum, he appointed his twelve disciples. Off the shore of the town he calmed a storm. Around Capernaum, he healed many. They were recorded in his book: Simon's mother-in-law, the demon possessed, a man with leprosy, a paralytic, a woman with a bleeding disease who merely touched his robe. There he raised the daughter of Jairus, the synagogue ruler, from the dead.

He stopped. That event was a resurrection. It was a short story toward the beginning of the scroll, embedded between the healing of the woman who touched Jesus' robe and his infamous journey to Nazareth, his hometown. He remembered now why he had placed it there. It was a resurrection, the ultimate miracle, and capped a series of lesser healing miracles. The event had been followed by Jesus' visit to a place where he was without honor and could perform no miracles, except laying his hands on a few who were ill and healed. Then the words, "He was amazed at their lack of faith." The healing of Jairus' daughter was a resurrection, yet *He was amazed at their lack of faith.*

He thought again of the last leaf in the scroll, the master's message, his emphasis on faith, his insistence on its mystery. Surely it would come to him, a vision or revelation, about how to end the great story. Could he leave it hanging with women leaving an empty tomb and fearing? Possibly. But he also thought the conclusion needed more. Mary's parting thoughts had helped.

As the gospel stood, Peter does not see the resurrected Christ, but is told to wait for him in Galilee. "There you will see him." Why, in all their discussions, had Peter not spoken of seeing the resurrected Christ? As with other miracles, was it because of something Christ said to him? *Tell no one.* John Mark felt something would come to him in Galilee.

Perhaps, in Capernaum, at Peter's house he would learn more. Peter was gone, crucified in Rome. His mother and mother-in-law, who had lived with the family, were surely dead. But Peter had brothers and sisters, a wife. He spoke rarely of them, but his mother said he spoke of his children when he came to their home. His brother Andrew might still be alive. Any of them might have some knowledge, or shed some light on the resurrection if Peter spoke of it and if not, why?

Approaching the town below, he took a shorter path that angled downward toward the city. The bright green of the slope ahead of him and the deep blue of the lake diminished as he descended. Capernaum had not been involved in the revolt against the Romans and was spared by Vespasian and his troops in their southward march to cleanse the area of Zealots. It looked the same as John Mark remembered on his last visit over forty years ago before the master was crucified himself as a rebel, an insurrectionist. A main street ran north and south. On both sides were small districts bordered by cross-sectional streets and no-exit side streets. The blonde building stones of the synagogue contrasted with the smaller plain blocks of black basalt used for the houses and the town's other buildings.

He completed his descent and looked both ways before entering the main road. The sun was now overhead. He was hungry and had some food remaining in his travel bag but would keep going. There were friends in Capernaum, people who would remember him and feed him.

He remembered Peter's house. Located between the synagogue and the sea, it was one of four basalt houses grouped around two large courtyards. Like most of the other houses, it was made with coarse basalt blocks reinforced with stone and mud. Stone stairs led to the roof, which was constructed of light wooden beams and thatch mixed with mud.

People in nearby houses observed him with curiosity as he stepped through the courtyard gate and knocked on the door. A lady in the next house called to him, "You must call loudly to her, she does not hear well."

"What is her name?" he inquired.

"Miriam!" the lady shouted.

He thanked the woman, knocked again, louder, and then called through an open window: "Miriam!" He waited then called again, "Miriam?"

He heard a weak voice, "Yes?" It came from behind him.

He turned and saw a woman clutching her headdress at the neck. She wore a white tunic embroidered around the edge. She must have come from behind him through another courtyard entrance or was visiting in one of the other houses. Her face was recessed in her scarf, but he could see it had attractive features. He spoke loudly, "You are Miriam?"

She gave a slight bow and motioned with an extended hand for him to open the door and enter. He opened it but waited for her to pass ahead of him. It was a gloomy room. Little light came from a window facing the narrow street. The cobbled floor and hearth and other familiar features— the circular oven in the corner by the hearth and the basalt mill beside it— evoked sudden sadness. He looked up. The ceiling had not changed. The large square of uneven beams and re-thatched roof where the paralytic was lowered for Jesus to heal were still evident. The healing happened here, in this room, along with many memorable moments of fellowship.

The woman named Miriam held up a hand for him to stop in the doorway. She removed his sandals. From a small bowl beside the door, she drew a cloth and washed his feet.

She stood and he spoke loudly to her. "I am John Mark, son of Benjamin and Mary of Jerusalem."

She nodded she heard him, as if to say, you speak loudly enough. "My neighbor exaggerates my hearing problem. Yes. I remember you. I was young then, you were older," her voice warm and friendly.

He wondered how she could remember him. That was forty years ago. He was about to ask her—

"You spent much time with my father," she interrupted his thought.

"Peter, the fisherman?"

"Yes," she said softly. "That is how I remember you, *one* of the reasons. Please sit down. You must be tired."

He sat on a stool near the oven, leaving the only chair on the other side of the hearth for her. He moved his stool closer to her so she could hear. "There were other reasons?" he inquired curiously.

"Yes," she responded.

Did he dare probe further? "I cannot think what others there might be."

A shy smile blossomed. "There was one other, but it is now unimportant. I was young then, you were older."

She had liked me, he concluded. His interests had been different in those days. He was so involved in the master and his message, the new wave of reform he brought to Judaism, he had never noticed her. He would not ask if she was married. He looked around. Evidence of a man filled the room— fish nets, striker pins, weaving bobbins—but no man was present, just the woman named Miriam, the daughter of Peter.

"I was saddened about your father," he commented with concern.

"Thank you. It was almost twenty years ago, but it seems like yesterday. You know what happened," she stated.

"He was crucified in Rome, like the master, only upside down."

She nodded. "He did not deserve the dignity of dying like the Christ. At least, that was the word brought to me."

"And Andrew, his brother?" John Mark asked.

"Andrew went north to Bythnia to establish a church. I heard he was also martyred by crucifixion at the city of Patras in Achaea, in Greece, on an X-shaped cross for the reason similar as my father's. My uncle did not consider himself worthy to be crucified on the same kind of cross as Jesus." Her face was downcast, her eyes misting.

"And your father and uncle's friends, James and John, the sons of Zebedee?"

"As you may know," she responded, "because of their tempers, the brothers were called *Boanerges*, 'sons of thunder.' James' fiery temper angered Herod, and he was executed. We are told this by people who speak the truth. Some say he went to Spain. I think he was martyred, the first disciple to die for the faith." She pointed at the hearth where there was evidence of an earlier fire. "Are you cold?"

"No! I am warmed by this conversation," then returned to the thread of the dialogue. "I knew of the nickname but had not heard he was killed by Herod. I have heard nothing about John since the Council of Jerusalem."

"Then you know John was thrown into prison with my father and later went with him to visit the newly converted in Samaria. When Herod Agrippa began persecuting Christians, John scattered with the others into the provinces of Rome." She reached up and pulled her scarf back slightly from around her face. "My father went to Rome and John to Asia Minor, around Ephesus. That is all I know, and it was passed to me through others."

"You know more than I," he said. "I did not know your father or John had been in prison. I have been in Tyre for the past twenty years and only recently returned."

"But your home is Jerusalem. My father went there often. He spoke kindly of your mother, of her care for him and others and especially of the food she prepared."

"Your father was always generous with his words. This is true. He came with Jesus and the other disciples and continued his visitations even after Jesus' crucifixion. I saw him last at the big council in Jerusalem and then not again."

"Did you have family in Tyre?" she asked, her eyes averted, shifting her posture nervously.

"No. My mother is my only family," he said. "My brother was killed and my sister possibly abducted, we do not know. One day she was with us, and the next she disappeared. We thought she was visiting someone in Bethany or Bethphage and would return, but we never saw her again."

"This is very sad. I am very sorry," she said. In the shadows, he could not see her full reaction. The scarf she had pushed back had shifted forward, placing her face again in shadows. But her voice was filled with sincere emotion. "Trouble seems to fall more on Christians than others in these times. At least you were safe in Tyre."

"After traveling with my cousin Barnabas and a man named Saul—

"Oh, yes," she said, animated for the first time. "My father spoke of him. He was also at the Jerusalem conference. He was persecuting Christians, then claimed he saw Christ on the road to Damascus, converted to the faith and changed his name to Paul."

"All of that is true," John Mark confirmed. "But there were conflicts. I parted ways and needed a place to write. Tyre was that place."

"To write?"

He pointed at his satchel at his feet. "The scrolls I carry are the products of my time in Tyre. When your father came to our home, he said someone must write the story of the gospel lest it be lost forever. Others were writing. The man Paul was writing letters to churches, but an apostle, one who was with Jesus, needed to tell the story. In all respects, your father was a wise man but not a man of letters, so he told the story and I wrote."

"Not at one time," she said, doubtfully.

"No, over several years. I copied what he told on papyrus leaves I collected. Over time I arranged them, weaved the stories and message, Jesus' parables and sayings, into a narrative form. Most of the master scroll came from your father, but I interviewed others. I was present at some events. The scroll is nearly complete."

"It is most appropriate you come to Galilee to finish. She smiled and opened her arms. "I feel honored you stopped at my home, the home of my father."

"Your father needs to speak again through his daughter," he said, pointing at her.

"I do not understand." She shrugged and turned up her palms.

"Of all the times I was with your father, through all of our discussions, not once," he gestured with a raised finger, "did he mention seeing the resurrected Christ. He did leave Jerusalem and returned to Galilee as the women at the empty tomb had said Jesus told the disciples to do. That I remember." He slapped his knee with confidence.

"That is true. He and the others came here. They said they had been told to come."

"What happened?" he asked.

"Nothing. I was only twenty, but I remember. They sat around. My father was different. He was very sad and downcast. He did not believe the women who went to the tomb."

"Yet, he did as they said," he added. "He came here."

"Where else was he to go after the death of a dear friend, the best of his life? This was his home." She was leaning close to him, her eyes flashing with emotion. "This was where they had spent most of their time together. What do you do when you want to feel close to someone who has gone? You return to the places of memory. Then my father said, 'Let's go fishing.'"

There was a commotion outside, men talking and some rattling sounds. She stood up and looked out the back window toward the sea and waved a nonchalant hand. "Some fishermen returning for the day and pulling their boats ashore." The scene caused her to pause, raise a finger to her eye then resume. "The other three fishermen—his brother, Andrew, and James and John—got their nets and followed him to the boats. What else were they to do? Life goes on. I do not know what happened to Levi and to some of the other disciples."

John Mark leaned in closer to her. "Others with whom I have spoken said Jesus appeared to two walking on the road to Emmaus the same day the empty tomb was reported. They did not say they were his disciples, but close followers. The name of one was Cleopas. I had never heard of him. Did your father mention this name?"

"No." She tilted her head back and shook it. "I do not recall that name."

"In the story, as it was told to me, these two followers retuned to Jerusalem to tell your father and the other disciples what they had seen and heard, and suddenly Jesus appeared in the room."

Her mouth dropped and her brows flew up. "He entered the room?"

"No," he said calmly, "He appeared, as a ghost or phantom appears."

"This is unbelievable," she exclaimed, rolling her eyes and bringing both hands down on her knees with a slight slap. "My father never spoke of this to me."

"Nor to me," he said. "Those who related these things told more. They said Jesus led them to Bethany, blessed them, then was taken up into heaven, and the disciples returned to Jerusalem with much joy and stayed continually at the Temple."

Miriam shook her head. "This is incredible. My father said none of this to me, certainly nothing about Jesus rising from the earth into the heavens like Elijah. The disciples could not have stayed at the Temple if they came here."

"Your father said nothing to you about Jesus appearing in a room with his disciples where the doors were locked and how he told Thomas, one of the doubters, to put his finger on his hands and in his side where the nails and spear had pierced?"

"Nothing." She seemed almost angry. "This sounds like a different Jesus than the one my father knew. I recall my father saying often that wonderful things happened. When I asked, he said, "Jesus said not to tell. He had his doubts about the empty tomb, but he eventually believed in the resurrection. However, it was not that kind of resurrection.""

"What kind of resurrection was it?" John Mark asked eagerly.

"I do not know how to say it in words."

He raised a finger. "Just a moment. Do not speak further." He reached down and opened the bag at his feet. He pulled out the smaller scroll and untied it, turned it over on his knees and began unrolling it, scrolling to a certain point and stopped.

"What are you doing?" she said, bemusement in the rising tone of her voice.

"You will see." He pulled a pen and inkhorn from the bag. "Do you have a small bowl?"

"Yes," she said. She rose immediately, crossed the room to a shelf, retrieved a small shallow dish and handed it to him.

He poured a small amount of ink from the inkhorn into the dish. He dipped the pen. "Now," he said looking up at her with anticipation. "What kind of resurrection was it?"

"I told you, I do not know how to say it," she said, her palms upturned again.

"How did your father say it? He came back, but he did not stay. He returned to Jerusalem. Something happened here to turn him and the others around. Something he did not tell me, but he might have told you, or you witnessed it."

She paused. She thought a long while. "When he came here after the women discovered the empty tomb, he was sad. The first day or two, all of them were sad. They went fishing. Then something did happen on the shore after they had been fishing. My father was not descriptive. He did not speak for the others, but he said he was with Jesus. He was 'in his presence' or 'felt his presence,' I do not remember exactly, but those were words he used. I did not ask him what he meant. His mood was different. He was excited. He spoke of returning to Jerusalem, that there was much work to do."

It took him a while to catch up to her then he paused. "Did you question your father further?"

Her face grew serious. "You have been with my father. You know him. He is not one you easily question, a reason perhaps you are now questioning me."

He smiled empathically and nodded.

"My mother and I were happy that he and my brother Andrew were cheerful again. Then they were gone, all of them."

John Mark commenced writing again.

"I only saw my father a few times after that. He was a different man, a new man. That is the resurrection I remember, the one I witnessed, not of the Christ, but my father feeling the presence of the Christ. Something more spiritual than physical, something happened inside of him, not outside. Who is saying these things about appearances?" She rolled her eyes again.

"It does not matter." He finished her last comment and stopped. "I can write only what I know to be true. Perhaps others know a different story. I can write only to be true to the message I heard and saw and was encouraged to pass on. I cannot bear false witness. Let others write of a different resurrection if they choose, but I believe the man and his message stand on their own. Many did not believe even as they witnessed miracles. A resurrection is just one more miracle one can choose to believe or not to believe." He paused, to gather a thought. "The resurrection of Lazarus, the brother of Martha and Mary in Bethany, did not create a new faith. Perhaps your father, if he did see the risen Christ, never spoke of it because he was told to keep silent, as he and all of us were told to do at each miracle, including the resurrection of Jairus' daughter." He extended a hand to her. "You have helped me, Miriam."

She pulled back her head covering and shook her hair. He could see the flecks of gray in the dark strands, a face not yet turned old, its youth still evident. *I was young then; you were older.* She could not have been much younger than he. He shuddered to think what he looked like to her. All he could see was a beauty undiminished by years, one shining with a radiance that recalled his own mother in earlier years. He smiled at her. "But you have not told me the truth about the time I came here years ago."

She smirked. "You jest. Surely, I have."

"You could not have been a young girl when I came here years ago. You were not even born."

She laughed. "You flatter me, John Mark. You must be hungry. May I feed you?"

"What will your husband say?" he said, amazed how the question sprang from his mouth.

She looked startled. "I am a widow."

"I am sorry," he said.

"You need not apologize. It was a long time ago."

"Was he ill?" he asked.

"No. It was horrible. He was fishing alone and fell from his boat into the nets and drowned. Others in the village found him near Bethsaida. I had to go with friends and bring his body back to Capernaum. He is buried in the cemetery up the hill. We had a small house not far from here."

"And your children?"

"We had no children, which, as you know according to Jewish law, was grounds for divorce, but he loved me." She raised a hand and wiped a tear. "My husband's brother had the right to marry me. I was legally engaged and could not marry anyone else until he and all of his brothers refused me."

He wondered how any man could refuse such beauty and decency. "You were trapped," he said.

"Only temporarily. My brother-in-law was not in good means. He did not need another mouth to feed. I did not need another bed to share or children that were not my own. He freed me in the ceremony of *halitza*. Before a court of three in the synagogue, I had to remove his shoe, spit upon the ground, and recite the words of the liturgy."

"Jewish law can be so humiliating," John Mark said. "Thanks to Jesus for freeing us."

"I am afraid Jesus could not help me in this matter," she responded, her eyes downcast. "This is still a Jewish community. If I wanted to remain single, I had to abide by Jewish law. It is still the law of our land."

"What did you do?"

"My husband's parents were dead, so I came to live with my parents. My father was away most of the time on the mission, but my mother was here."

She paused, as if she would add something else about her family, but did not continue and looked at him. "And you?"

She had inquired earlier, subtly, and he had answered partially. Now the question came from a meekness he thought incapable of being blunt. There was only the truth to tell, of which he was not ashamed. "I am unsure of the reason. Perhaps the distraction of Jesus and his ministry, the mission after he was gone, the traveling—"

"But you were in Tyre for a long time," she interrupted, challenged him.

He was aware he was hedging. "I know Jewish men are supposed to marry, but, much to the disapproval of my family, I never did. Jesus told me I could marry or not marry, that the end was near, and it did not matter. Besides, I was too busy for a wedding. I could not spare a week."

She chuckled at the humor. "If you are happy, it is not so bad to not marry. Many are less happy after they marry."

"Are you happy?" he asked.

"Yes, but I could be happier." She arose. "Now, you rest while I prepare some food."

She stoked the fire smoldering in the hearth and added some thorn branches and animal dung. A flame appeared and she placed some small timbers around it. He watched her movements, agile and limber, the figure of her youth evident beneath her tunic. Her face was lit by the fire and looked warm, dark and beautifully aged. She left the room and returned with a mattress of straw and wool, which she laid on a raised platform and motioned to him. "Come and rest." She was gentle but firm in her directness.

He did as she bid, returned his scroll and writing supplies to his bag, arose, and reclined on the soft mattress.

She placed a goat's hair blanket over him and turned it back to his waist. Her hands were tender and gentle. "You may get warm as the fire burns, but the wind turns cool in the late afternoon through the window above you."

He had forgotten the time, not noticed the lengthening of shadows in the room. He had almost forgotten where he was, almost forgotten why he was there. He had almost forgotten existing.

A pleasant aroma awoke him. He did not know how long he had been asleep. The room was darker, oil lamps and moonlight providing the only light. Food was spread on a mat before the hearth: fish, bread, beans, leeks, almonds, pomegranates, grapes, olives, and beside his plate an earthen goblet of wine.

He joined her around the mat, looked at the food, and recalled the widow in the Temple, the poorest of the poor who gave all she had. "This is a feast. Forgive me, but widows are supposed to be poor."

"The times are different, at least for Jewish Christians. Jesus had concern for widows." She leveled her eyes at him. "Surely, you have written of this in your scroll."

He nodded but did not tell her what he'd written, not then. He felt embarrassed to reveal the passage prompting the comment. Or the one preceding it about the Sadducees who did not believe in resurrection and their question to Jesus about a certain widow and her marriages to several brothers-in-law and who her husband would be in heaven. In his response, Jesus did not challenge the law and side with the woman as he had done on other occasions, but told about how there would be no marriage in heaven.

"Jesus urged his followers to collect alms for widows," she pressed. "There are few widows in Capernaum and the deacons of the small Christian fellowship here ensure I am cared for. I also have many friends. I eat very little, so you are helping me with food that would go to waste."

After dinner he helped her clean up and they sat by the fire. Outside, the night was accomplished, a cool breeze blew through the windows, and the inevitable subject came up.

"Where are you going next?" she asked.

He sat observing her, her legs curled beneath her, her hair flowing around her shoulders. Her cheeks glowed bronze and above them the flames of the fire danced in her dark eyes. He did not want to leave but ... "To Caesarea Philippi, then Damascus."

"Caesarea Philippi is two days away, Damascus much farther," she said, astonished. "It is night. You must not leave in the dark."

"Where would I sleep? You are a widower, and I a single man."

"You will stay here," she said adamantly. "Sleep where you rested earlier. I will go to the house of my elderly neighbor, the one who thinks I cannot hear. She, too, is a widow and would welcome my company. Her name is

Rachael. You knew her husband, Andrew, my uncle. She probably knows of you and your mother."

"I feel protective of you, concern for what others might think," he said.

"They will think nothing, or they will think what they will. We are two old friends."

At that moment, he did not want to think *old*. He did not want to think *friends*. What he was thinking, he was not supposed to think. "I accept your kind hospitality. Perhaps I can repay the favor someday."

She reached over and lightly tapped his knee with her finger. Was it a flirting gesture? "Nonsense," she pouted and then grinned playfully like a little girl. "Grace never needs to be returned, only accepted."

In that one sentence, her faith knew no bounds. "That is so very true," he said. "I must practice what I write."

"And this gospel you are writing, why is it you must go to Caesarea Philippi and Damascus? You could stay here and write."

"You sound like my mother," he said, smiling. "I have only one bundle of papyrus. My ink ingredients are almost depleted and I have only two reed pens remaining that must be replenished. The reeds break easily. All of these are available in Caesarea Phillipi. Damascus has a strong community of Christians, a library and places to buy supplies."

"But you said you are almost finished. I understand about needing supplies from Caesarea, but Damascus?" She raised her hands in disbelief.

"I am almost finished with the master draft," he responded. "I must make copies. They must be distributed to other Christian communities, to Antioch, to Alexandria, Jerusalem and Rome. In Damascus, there are scribes who can help me make copies. Time is important. One Roman emperor has already persecuted Christians. I fear we are in a lull, and it will happen again. The gospel must be published and protected."

She looked away from him into the fire. From the side, her face drew downward; her eyes seemed half-closed. From that view, it was as though he could see her thoughts working from her head into her eyes, down the slope of her face into her mouth. When she turned and they came out, he was surprised.

"May I see your scroll?"

"Even though unfinished, I am happy for you to see it. The bag is behind you."

She handed it to him and he withdrew the large scroll, untied the leather string that bound it, and gave it to her. Effortlessly, as though she had had practice, she opened and began unrolling it. She reached the beginning and read aloud, the oil lamp flame flickering over the page and her face, dancing in her eyes, "The beginning of the gospel about Jesus Christ, the Son of God. It is written in Isaiah the prophet I will send my messenger..." The wind would flatten the flame beside her, the page go dark for a moment, and she would continue.

He sat up astonished. He wanted to interrupt, but he had never heard his work read by another, albeit a woman with a voice so clear and smooth it might have come from heaven. After a few minutes she stopped.

"That was beautiful," he said. "Where did you learn to read, and in Greek, the *koine*?"

"My father, as you know, was illiterate. He insisted all of his children learn to read and write. My brothers went to the synagogue school. I was taught at home by my mother and in the homes of other women in the village."

"You have done well," he commended.

"I can also write. When papyrus is available, I enjoy writing poetry."

"May I see some of your poetry?" he asked.

"Unfortunately, there is none to see," she said. "The sheets were used as fuel for the fire. But I write when I have papyrus," she said and she looked down at the bag.

"Of course," he said and quickly removed the smaller scroll. "This was my first attempt but I made numerous errors and started fresh on the one you just read but kept this first one. The reverse side has been useful."

"I know. I always used the verso. The writing is more difficult on that side because the papyrus reeds align differently."

He nodded understanding as he opened the smaller scroll to the last fresh leaf. He took the larger scroll she was still holding and laid it flat on the hearth and gave her the smaller scroll which she placed in her lap. He retrieved an oil lamp, placed it beside her on the hearth, and moved the bowl of ink where he had left it earlier within comfortable reach. He handed her a pen. "Now," he pointed, "write what you just read."

The smaller scroll secure in her lap, she leaned forward, the bloom of the oil lamp on her face, glinting in her hair. Reading by the waver of firelight and lamp, she began carefully and deftly bringing the vacant page to life. Her left hand holding the papyrus flat, her right hand moving steadily, unerringly, letters appearing as if breathed onto the page. He recalled the hands that washed his feet, adjusted the blanket around him, put food before him, poured his wine, and something about them that evoked a caring and security he watched unfold before him.

CHAPTER THIRTEEN

On the road to Damascus, October 30, 2011

Kate leaned forward from the back seat and said something to the driver, and he responded to her.

"What did you say to him?" Chris asked.

"I asked him why he didn't tell us he was the taxi sent to the airport to pick us up."

"What did he say?"

"He said we never asked."

"I speak English," Muhammed said.

"Thank you, Muhammed," Chris said. "Just get us to Maaloula in one piece, and we will praise Allah."

"Yes, I get you there." He flashed two fingers as he gunned the car around a slow moving truck. "In two pieces."

"Maybe we should praise Allah now," Kate whispered.

"I speak English," Muhammed whispered louder. "Also Christian, not Muslim. Praise Jesus."

They barreled through the streets of Beirut, the car sweeping and swerving through frantic and chaotic beeping traffic. Driving with one hand, Muhammed caressed a string of worry beads dangling from his rearview mirror. Stop lights glowed red but Muhammed couldn't seem to find the brake. At each intersection, tragedy threatened. Slow-moving women draped in flowing burkas and veils escaped sudden death.

The route took them through a remodeled part of the city. They passed the old Holiday Inn, used in the war of 2006 as a sniper hangout, the results of the damage still visible. Chris thought how, despite all the war and conflict, the city survived and was still the "Paris of the East." They sped through the quieter outer suburbs. The four-lane thoroughfare began ascending the Lebanon Mountain Range, up and out of seaside Beirut, the road turning in bends and switchbacks. Chris recalled reading somewhere that Beirut was the only place in the world where you could be sunbathing on a beach and snow-skiing within half-an-hour.

The road snaked in a twisting series of chicanes and hairpins. Traffic thinned. Muhammed seemed to settle down and tuned the radio to some Arabic music. They drove past strings of gaudy shops and gas stations flooded in florescent light. Higher up, apartment complexes rose like dimly lit honeycombs. In places, the road was under construction.

"Saudi money," Muhammed said. "Two years they work on this road. Maybe finish soon."

"What's that?" Chris said, pointing to the brown paper package Kate had placed on the seat between them.

She looked startled, as though she'd forgotten about it, raised a finger to her lips and mouthed, "A gun."

"A gun!" he exclaimed, dragging his hands down his face.

"Gun?" Muhammed reacted. "We have gun?"

"Muhammed, everything's okay." She shot Chris a tight-lipped disgusted look.

"We not far from border and you have gun? Not good."

"It's no problem, Muhammed," Chris said, returning a hard glance at Kate. "We can get rid of it."

"We will not get rid of it," Kate snapped curtly. "First of all, it is not mine to get rid of. Secondly, we may need it to keep someone from getting rid of us. And, Muhammed, turn down that ghastly noise so we can hear each other without shouting."

Muhammed turned down the volume on the radio, but the discordant Arabic music continued filling the air.

"What kind of gun is it?" Chris asked.

"I haven't looked, but I requested a Glock Seventeen."

"That's a semi-automatic."

"Yes," she concurred tartly, picking up the package and unwrapping the heavy brown paper. She unholstered the gun, held it in her palm and looked at it with admiration. "A ten millimeter, to be precise, with an effective range of fifty meters, short recoil, locked breech, adjustable sight."

"To be more precise," he said with mock fear. "Point it away from me."

She snapped something back and forth on the gun then brought it to her eyes, sighted out the window, then lowered it. "How did you know it was a semi?" she asked. "I thought you knew only about spears and clubs."

"That's an insult I'll let pass. Is there a clip in it now?"

"I requested one." She turned it up with the barrel head down and looked. "Yes."

"My God. Point the barrel out the window."

"The safety is on," she said.

"I don't care," he reacted. "You'd be amazed how many people are shot with the safety on. How many cartridges in the clip?"

"Seventeen."

"You don't need more?" he questioned sarcastically.

"I hope I don't need these. If I do, it will only be once." She raised her chin defiantly to him. "I do not miss."

"Just what do you propose we do with it?" he asked. "We will be searched and frisked at the border. The Syrians mean business."

Muhammed raised his hand and snapped his fingers. "I have idea."

They groaned.

"Give me gun," he said.

"I thought we would just put it under the seat," Kate said.

"Bad idea," Muhammed said. "They search car, under hood, under wheels, under seat. Bad idea."

"You got a better one?" Chris asked.

"Yes. Give me gun. I show you."

Muhammed reached back. Kate re-holstered the gun, loosely rewrapped it and handed the package to him. He took it, weighed it in his palm, and then placed it above the visor.

"My God, Muhammed," Chris said. "You want to get us all thrown into jail."

"Jail?" I do not know this word.

Kate used a word he understood.

"Ah! No, no." He pointed at the visor. "This last place they look."

Chris slapped a hand to his forehead.

"If they look, it my gun. Every Arab has gun. You see on television. They shoot guns in cars, in trucks, on streets. It is nothing, no problem. My gun," he said and slapped his hands on the wheel in a gesture of finality.

Chris and Kate settled back in their seats.

"The next thing to worry about is my passport and the Israeli stamps," Chris murmured.

Muhammed's ear was cocked. "Gun, no problem. Israel, problem. Lebanon no strict. Syria much strict."

"He doesn't miss a trick," Chris whispered to her.

"Let's wait and see," she said. "Maybe they won't see it. The first one, the entry stamp, is faded. The second overlaps it and is blurred. Whoever stamped that day may have had a hangover."

"Worst-case scenario, they turn me away," he said.

"Worst-case scenario is a delay. There're ways of getting around this," she said with assurance.

"In normal times, but this is not a normal time," Chris cautioned.

Driving stiff-armed, Muhammed was still leaning back listening. "I think no problem."

"Is anything ever a problem with you?" Chris asked then gave him no chance to answer. "There's a revolution going on in Syria. They hate Americans. Why is this not a problem?"

"You have *bakshish*?" Muhammed asked.

"I have some Syrian pounds and American dollars," Chris responded.

"How much dollars you have?"

"Why not pounds?" he asked.

"Syrian pounds bad money, dollars good money," Muhammed replied.

"I've got several hundred dollars," Chris said. He had more, a few thousand in a money belt.

"That is good. Give me one hundred dollars," Muhammed requested.

Chris looked at Kate.

She flipped her palms up, a *Why not?* gesture.

He opened his billfold and pulled out a hundred dollar bill and handed it over the seat to Muhammed. "There's a lot of trust invested here, Muhammed."

"Yes. Trust me. No problem."

Up ahead on the left, they saw lights and a row of shops. Muhammed slowed and turned on his blinker.

"What are you doing, Muhammed?" Kate asked, almost shouting.

"Stopping for you to buy."

"We don't want to stop and buy, keep going," she blared.

"But you get American candy, Coca Cola, nice jewelry."

"Muhammed!" Kate said loudly. "You can get your kickback with your next customer. We no stop." She said it again to him in Arabic.

He shook his head, turned off the blinker and continued.

At the border, Muhammed stopped behind a line of cars and pointed to the building they must enter. "I wait. Inside, you not need me, not this stop."

Because of the late hour, the line inside the building was short. A passport official stamped their passports and motioned them on.

Outside, Muhammed had moved up further in the traffic queue. "Get in," he said. "They search taxi."

A uniformed official circled the car with a flashlight. He got down on the ground on one side and shined the beam under the car, moved to the other side and did the same. Muhammed sat whistling, drumming his fingers on the steering wheel. The official then tapped the hood with his flashlight and motioned Muhammed forward.

"Why didn't they make us get out for the search?" Chris asked.

"Sometimes they do and sometimes no," Muhammed replied. "They concerned about cigarette cartons you hide on you." He fluttered his hands across his chest and crotch. "Maybe they know me. Many times I come here."

They drove through a no man's land. Chris looked and couldn't believe his eyes. There in the middle of the backside of nowhere, on a forlorn mountaintop between two Mid-eastern countries, was a Dunkin' Donuts. "We've come a long way from the wayside stops of the first century," he remarked to Kate.

"I didn't believe it either the first time I saw it," she said.

"The first time?" She had told him she was driven overland from Beirut to Damascus but nothing about traveling this route.

"I told you I was driven from Beirut to Damascus in two thousand five to claim my husband's body. It was a horrible trip. I was by myself with only a U. N. official I'd never met who was driving a U. N. vehicle. It was neutral. I felt the U.N. should have stood for United Neutral. You told me Professor

Stewart told you about about my husband's death but did he tell you he was on a peacekeeping tour of duty, shot in the back of the head in the middle of night on the Golan Heights?"

He nodded. "I don't know what to say. No telling how you felt then."

"I did not feel. I was numb. Like I said, neutral, surreal."

"Okey dokey," Muhammed interrupted. "We here," he said as they pulled up to the Syrian border. He queued behind a line of cars for inspection. An official approached the car, motioned them out, and pointed toward a lit-up concrete building. Clutching the hundred dollar bill, Muhammed followed them. At the mountain pass, the night air was chilled, the sky clear with stars, a cycled moon high within them like the flag of a nearby country.

Kate went first, smiling flirtatiously at the official, a large burly man with iron rusty gray hair, rusty eyebrows and big-knuckled hands. He looked her up and down, quickly stamped her passport, then gave her a green fifteen day visa card and motioned her aside.

Chris stepped up and presented his passport.

The man opened it perfunctorily, flipped through the pages, then laid it down.

Home free, Chris thought. *He didn't see it.*

Then the official picked the passport back up and flipped to the second page. "No!" he said to Chris. "You cannot enter Syria." He held up the open passport and pointed to the Israeli stamps.

"Look at the date," Chris requested. "That was nine years ago. I am a doctor. I was there only two days to give a speech, in and out."

"What kind of doctor you are?"

"Archaeology. I am a professor of Archaeology. I have been here before in your country but over ten years ago."

"Where you come in Syria?"

This was good. The man was asking questions. He had a chance. "To Daraa."

"Daraa?"

"Yes. To study artifacts in the caves there." Kate was standing beside him. He was waiting for her to jump in with her marriage story, but she just stood there smiling at the official who obviously noticed the gesture.

The man continued studying the passport. He looked up at Chris, over at Kate who kept the riveted smile on him, then back at the passport, tapped his finger on the counter.

Chris was about to add something when Muhammed stepped forward and slowly slid his hand holding the one hundred dollar bill into the official's line of vision. The official glanced at the bill. Again, he looked up at Chris, over at Kate, and back at the passport. He gave furtive glances sideways at officials in adjoining booths. His finger stopped tapping. His hand inched forward in a crab crawl across the counter. Muhammed slowly moved his hand forward, released the bill and then withdrew. The drama played out in seconds as the bill lay there, slowly unfolding from its crinkled form like something small returning to life, then gobbled into the official's large fist as he brought the stamp down with the other hand onto the passport, next the green visa card and said, "Welcome to Syria," and they were out of there.

The car passed inspection.

Once inside the car, Chris leaned over and patted Muhammed on the shoulder. "Muhammed, you belong in the movies."

Muhammed laughed. "All of us in movies." He thumbed over his shoulders to the border they were leaving. "Cameras. But they not see money. I very careful. The cop, he very careful."

Kate said, "Muhammed, that may be the best one hundred dollars Chris has ever spent. Thank you very much."

"I kept waiting for your romantic lovey-dovey marriage ploy," Chris said to her.

She rolled her eyes. "The magic worked once. I wasn't going to push our luck. Muhammed's plan seemed better."

Muhammed reached up, retrieved the gun from the visor and handed it over the seat to her, carefully, as if it was something he might spill.

"That plan, too," she said as she took the package and placed it beside her.

"Border officials tired," Muhammed murmured.

"Why's that?" Chris asked.

"They not check luggage," Muhammed said. "Usually take an hour. Tonight not long. Tired border cops, little traffic."

They began the descent into Damascus, into the heart of Arab spring and a revolution.

"John Mark wouldn't have had these problems," Chris stated. "The Roman Empire was an open system, good roads, sixty-three thousand miles of them, easy travel. The only ones who needed passports were prestigious officials privileged to stay overnight in special mansions."

"Unless you were a Jew," Kate said.

"Even if you were a Jew," Chris added, "you could travel within a certain area undeterred."

"You left out the road taxes, the bridge and road money," she mentioned. "The ones who collected them were the publicans in the New Testament. They were at every bridge and city entrance. We have discovered records where they threw bales off carts, opened letters. It was big business. They even formed joint stock companies and sold revenues at a fixed price."

"That was what Matthew did," Chris reminded. "He sat on a busy road, the Via Maris that ran through Carpernaum, and collected taxes. That's where we left John Mark."

"And I said he would have crossed the Jordan north of Scythopolis at Gesher. I've revised that plan. Instead of traveling to Ashtaroth and a direct road north, he may have taken a route along the eastern side of Galilee."

"Today's Golan Heights," he clarified.

She paused and looked away, as though his words hit too hard, and then looked back at him. "Yes. Then on to Caesarea Philippi, which, as you know, today is an archaeological ruin within the Golan."

"I did know that. Regardless of whose theory is right, John Mark did go to Caesarea Philippi. We are on the same page."

"Intriguing. So, you left him in Capernaum. Tell me more. Convince me." She said with a cocky smirk.

Again, Muhammed had his head back, quietly absorbing the dialogue.

"He would have stopped at Peter's house," Chris said. "Some of his family would have still been alive, sons and daughters. He could not travel to the town and not stop, visit, ask questions." He was turned sideways on the seat, facing her. "After all, he is a reporter, reporting the greatest story on earth. His writing style is that of a reporter. His gospel is the shortest. He wastes no words and is more polished than Matthew or Luke."

"So, he stops in Capernaum, makes some visits. That's it?" she summarized.

"Perhaps not. I imagine he was lonely." He leaned forward. "Muhammed, what does a man do when he's lonely."

"He find woman," Muhammed said and laughed.

"You two are impossible," Kate chided.

"May I continue?" Chris prodded. "The writer has a lonely life, and John Mark was a writer trying to complete a story. He had left his mother in Jerusalem. His family was behind him, like Jacob when he left his family. He was near the end of his gospel, wrung out emotionally. We know little of Peter's family but surely he had one, probably several children. Some would have still been living."

"Any daughters would have been married and living elsewhere," she said.

"Or widowed," he added.

"If so, they'd be living with her deceased husband's parents."

"Possibly," he said. "For whatever reason, there was one still there. Play along with me. Our man John Mark lingers."

"He cannot linger," she insists. "He is on a mission."

"Okay, he stays over night. She tends to him."

"That's a bit much," she said. "You're embellishing with reckless abandon."

"It gets more reckless. He stays at Peter's and falls in love." He laughed.

She heaved a sarcastic gasp.

"Good, good," Muhammed shouted and clapped his hands.

"Not good. Men!" she said disgustedly. "They want women to be dependent on them."

"*Au Contraire*," Chris said. "John Mark is the one becoming dependent. He is looking for help and finds it."

"Deliver me," she said, exasperated.

He touched her arm to get her attention. "Recall the copied segment on the verso, our discussion."

"Yes?"

"You said it was a feminine hand. You were adamant."

"I don't like where this is going," she remarked caustically.

"The segment is sandwiched between Bethany and a notation of two reams of papyrus and jar of ink he bought in Caesarea Philippi. Capernaum lies between the two cities. The geography and time frame fit. John Mark finds a copyist."

Her hands and eyebrows shot up. "That's a bit farfetched."

"I challenge you to come up with something better. It is possible but not as logical he met someone in Caesarea Philippi before he bought the papyrus." He was leaning across the seat almost in her face, only the gun between them. "I contend the manuscript was copied by someone in Capernaum, someone with a feminine hand, someone he would have known or known about. Wherever he would have stopped in Capernaum, he would have had connections. The most likely place was at Peter's house."

"I do not challenge that logic," she responded as she scooted back toward the door. "And I like the idea of Peter's daughter serving as a copyist. It just seems a bit over the top. Would she have traveled with him?"

"Yes, yes," shouted Muhammed gleefully from the front. "She go with him."

From Kate, a dubious smile.

"John Mark has a cheerleader," Chris said and chuckled. "If she is going to copy documents for him, he will not leave his master manuscript behind. She would have to travel with him."

They approached signs pointing to the touristy mountain villages of Bloudan and Zabadani. Muhammed slowed.

"We go," he said. "Nice."

"We not go, Muhammed," Kate said resolutely. "I see them in Scotland, and he sees them in America."

Muhammed shrugged and accelerated.

"Muhammed," she addressed him again, louder. "Turn the radio to a Damascus station, one in English with the news."

He nodded, leaned over, spun the dial through a blur of music and voices, and stopped on an Arab voice with a British accent.

"Excellent," she said. "Now you can turn it back up."

Frustrated hands went into the air as Muhammed followed her request.

The announcer said rescue workers were searching for survivors beneath wreckage caused by a 5.2 Richter scale earthquake that hit the city of Van in eastern Turkey on the 29th, the date rescue workers halted search for survivors of the 7.2 magnitude tremors only days before on the 23rd.

"Too close to home," Chris said. "That's the North Anatolian Fault."

"How can it be too close to home?" she questioned. "That's northern Turkey."

"The Dead Sea Rift, part of the Arabian plate which abuts the Anatolian plate," he commented, "intersects the East Anatolian Fault which runs due north of it. The East Anatolian junctures with the North Anatolian Fault, which is probably where this quake occurred." He reached over and touched her arm again, a habit he had when speaking close range with someone. "The Serghaya Fault is a branch of the Dead Sea fault in western Syria and eastern Lebanon. Seismic activity along one fault ripples into others. They are holistically interconnected. That's why it's too close to home."

The announcer continued, "Syrian President Bashar-al-Assad ..."

"Listen!" she said sharply, punching him on his arm as if returning the gesture.

"... has warned of an 'earthquake' if the West intervenes in his country as hundreds of demonstrators in Damascus suburbs went out chanting for freedom and an end to the Assad regime. One demonstration, which began in the neighborhood of Muhajreen behind the Al-Aziz Mosque, chanted for the trial of the president. In Homs, an elderly civilian was sniped dead by security forces while driving his car in the Al-Kahalidiyah neighborhood. The number of martyrs has risen to ten. In Egypt, the Hosni Mubarak trial has been postponed ..."

"Muhammed, how far are we from Damascus?" she asked.

"Not very far. About twenty kilometers. But we not go Damascus. Too dangerous."

"If we are not going to Damascus, how are we going to Maaloula?" she inquired.

"Very soon, at As'Saboura, we turn, go through Qudssaya Suburb then to Ma'arouneh. There take road north to Heleh then Al Tawani, Jabadeen, then you there ... Maaloula."

She probed further. "Is that the quickest route?"

"No. quickest route through Damascus on M One then M Five."

"I don't like the sound of this," Chris injected.

"Do you know Muhajreen, the Al-Aziz Mosque?" she persisted.

"Don't even think it," Chris snapped at her. "And don't start speaking Arabic."

"Yes," Muhammed said.

"Do we go close to it?"

"If we go straight," Muhammed responded.

"How close?" she inquired.

"Don't listen to her, Muhammed," Chris admonished.

"A few kilometers past Qudssaya, at Nazeem Basha Street but it take much time."

"Thank you, Muhammed," Chris said. "Time is important not to mention staying alive."

She was silent. Her mouth was set hard, her look determined, her eyes glowing with defiance.

The As'Saboura turn was approaching.

"What do you think John Mark would have done?" he said glaring at her. "Risk the manuscript of all time. Jeopardize the message that could save the world?"

She looked the other way.

"Which way I go?" Muhammed called out.

"Turn! Muhammed," Chris said decisively and shot Kate a hard look. "No need looking for a revolution that may be looking for us."

CHAPTER FOURTEEN

On the Road to Damascus, 70 A.D.

"I do not know for certain. Based upon my father's description, though, I believe this is the place where he said Jesus was the Christ." Miriam was pointing to a temple in front of a large cave and rock cliff. To the right was a cluster of pagan temples and cult niches with statues in them shaded with verdant oaks, sycamores, citron and orange trees. They stood beside a rushing stream that flowed from the cave down a long slope, the infant River Jordan. Not far from them, to their backs, was the city of Caesarea Philippi, newly built by Herod Agrippa and before them, towering over the scene, snow-capped Mount Hermon.

They had traveled two days from Capernaum, followed the higher terrain around the Huleh Swamp and Lake Semachontis before descending into the Valley Dan and skirting the city to find the place, going only by the directions and description her father had given to her. Caesarea Philippi was not that much out of the way and she wanted to go. John Mark had reasons of his own for readily agreeing.

"My father said Jesus looked at him as though he had said something of great importance to impart and then told them to say nothing about it."

John Mark smiled at her.

"Why are you smiling?"

"Jesus said that often. It is in the scroll." He patted the satchel slung from his shoulder. "I wrote it the same as you spoke it, and neither of us was present. Taking in the sight makes me wish I had written more. I am not speaking of what Jesus said, but where he was when he said it. Just look," he said, sweeping his hand over the scene. "Your father made the statement surrounded by the marbled splendor of Caesar worship, the Temples of the Syrian gods, Greek gods looking down, the beginning of the Jordan. It is as if Jesus deliberately set himself against the background of the world's religions."

"And my father said he was the Christ as though he demanded to be compared with them," she said, her eyes bright and excited in the morning sun. "Afterwards, my father said they went up the mountain, that there was a great light and in the great light was Moses and Elijah, and my father was overcome with emotion and did not want to leave." She stopped to put down her traveling bag and catch her breath. "Some people say this meeting with the prophets happened on Mount Tabor in lower Galilee at the end of the Jezreel Valley, but it surely happened here, after my father said Jesus was the Christ."

"I believe you are correct," he affirmed. "At that time, many people lived on Mount Tabor. There was a Hasmonean fortress at its summit. This is the more fitting and logical place."

"And you cannot see Mount Tabor from far away," she said. "You can see Mount Hermon from all of Israel, even as far as the Asphalt Sea. Mount Tabor is not near the Jordan, the river of our life and religion, and here it flows at our feet."

As she spoke, John Mark listened intently, reflecting on her earlier comments about writing poetry.

She broke her train of thought. "That look you have. You disagree?"

"Absolutely not, Miriam. You are very articulate. I was thinking you should write more than poetry."

She waved a shy hand at him and continued. "My father said he was never the same after those visions of the prophets with Jesus. He spoke of this moment often and would get excited. He told me to never forget that it happened after he said Jesus was the Christ."

"That is interesting," he said.

"What is interesting?"

"Your father said he was never the same after that event. In the gospel, the event is at the midpoint, and it is the high point, the climax."

"I am eager to read it, not just this part but the entire scroll," she said.

"You surely will when you copy it," he said. "I believe you will approve."

"But I must read it first, before I copy. I must know it. I must feel it."

He nodded understanding and observed her, how weary, but confident and strong she looked, her eyes flashing with determination. Two days they had been traveling on the Via Maris. The first night they had stayed in the home of friends of her father in Bethsaida, the second in the home of one of her friends in Seleucia in Gaulanitis near Lake Semechonities and the Huleh Swamp, rising early that morning for the seven mile trek to Caesarea Philippi. During the journey she had not complained, not even when the road had turned up and they had to climb the mountain slopes to avoid the swampland. He had offered to carry her cloth bag that held her essentials but she had refused.

He had not encouraged her to come. She had insisted. Besides copying the stories and message her father told him, she had said she could tend to his other needs. She could cook for him and wash his clothes, keep his life organized so he could finish the gospel and send it out. It did not matter they were not married, not at their age. For safety, women often traveled with men. "Did not women, Mary Magdalene and others, travel with Jesus and the disciples?" she had reminded him. She had felt a useless widow, eking out her own survival. Now she had a mission; she felt needed. His coming to her home was, as she said, "like spring after a long winter," her smile and cheeks radiant as she spoke. "Besides, I have always wanted to go to Caesarea Philippi and see the place, be near the spot, where my father declared Jesus was the Christ."

They lingered, walked around the grounds, but kept their distance from the Temples and local hubbub. A time or two she would stop and say, "It happened here, I think," while standing on an elevated ledge with the stream running below. Then later, "No, perhaps there," pointing to a large pomegranate tree that would have been there at the time.

John Mark was still pondering the general location, the extravagant idolatry juxtaposed with the person, the Messiah, the Son of the living God. He turned to her and said, "We must go. It is a long way to Damascus, almost forty miles, four days at least and no homes of friends along the way, no towns."

For the first time she showed anxiety, as if she had not fully thought through her decision. "Then, where will we stay?"

"As the master would often say, the Lord will provide. The Via Maris is a major trade route. There are people and inns along the way."

Thanks to the Roman road markers every mile, they could measure their journey. The road from Caesarea Philippi to Damascus, cut partly through solid rock, was also called the Via Egnatia. It had been the route Paul and his companions had often traveled between ports on the Great Sea and Damascus. The first leg took them due east following the southern flank of Mount Hermon.

They stayed the night with an old man and his wife who said they were Jewish Christians and followed the rule of hospitality to strangers. They had little to offer to eat so John Mark and Miriam shared the food they had brought with them. They departed early the next morning with embraces and hopes they would see the couple again.

The second day the sky was high and blue and clear, a desert sky. The road leveled off, and they made better time, covering almost twelve miles. In the long lonely stretches when they passed no caravans or travelers, they talked.

"Did my father tell you about the night Jesus walked on water?" she asked.

"Yes."

"And you wrote about it in your scroll?"

"I did," he said. "At first, I was reluctant. I did not want to write about things that did not seem real, that were too much like the Greek gods. But your father was very convincing."

"He could be very convincing," she responded. "I remember when it happened. He and the other fishermen were out all night. A strong wind was blowing. You could hear it whistling through the rocks of the walls of the house. It blew things off the roof. When my father returned, it was early morning."

"He told me the storm had happened around the fourth watch," John Mark said.

"That would be accurate," she agreed. "When I arose to see what was happening, because I could hear him speaking loudly to my mother, the sun was coming up. He said they were in the middle of the lake and a strong wind began blowing from the shore. Their oars could not move the boat against it. Suddenly, my father said they saw something coming toward them from the shore, like a shadow moving across the water." Her face became animated as she spoke, her eyes lively. "They all saw it. As he told how they all thought it an illusion or ghost, his hands waved in the air and his eyes grew large in his face," she gestured with her hands. "They became afraid, my father said, more of this apparition they saw than the storm. As the shadow moved closer, he and the others saw it was Jesus. He had an aura around him. He was walking as though he was on land, moving steadily toward them. They thought he was going to pass them, but he told them to be strong and not fear, that it was he. Then he entered the boat and the storm calmed. It was one of my father's favorite stories. I think he told it so often others thought he walked on the sea, too."

John Mark listened intently to her telling of the story. He enjoyed feeling her excitement, the enthusiasm of her commitment, its contagious influence. Both were so engrossed they did not acknowledge another traveler passing on the other side of the road. "Your last comment is interesting. Did your father ever speak to you of his walking on water with Jesus?"

"I did not hear this from him," she said. "It was told to me only recently, by someone traveling through Capernaum."

"The information was second hand."

"Yes," she nodded.

"Likewise, I had heard this part of the story, when I was in Tyre," he said.

"The person who told me," she said, "was from Jerusalem. They had heard many stories of Jesus. Some I had heard also, one in particular about feeding thousands with only a few loaves and fish."

"Many stories about Jesus are circulating," John Mark said, "but I wrote only about things witnessed by disciples or others who had eyes to see and ears to hear. These two about feeding the multitudes your father related also to me. Jesus performed this deed not once, but twice. The feedings occurred near in time to each other in Galilee but in different locations and the number of people varied. The first time it was five thousand and the second, four thousand. Your father had a tendency to exaggerate, but the crowds were probably very large."

"And you wrote of both?" she asked, surprised. "It would seem one would be enough."

"I wrote of both because, the way they were told to me by your father, Jesus twice performed the deed to emphasize giving food to the hungry."

She nodded in agreement.

"Look!" he exclaimed, pointing ahead of them. "As we discuss feeding the hungry, an inn for our food and lodging appears."

"The Lord truly does provide," she said and smiled.

They continued on. Before they reached the inn, a caravan approached and stopped as it drew beside them.

"Greetings, my friend," John Mark said, hailing the leader of the caravan. "From whence do you travel?"

"We come from Mari in Mesopotamia and travel to Egypt."

"Is that an inn we see in the distance?" John Marked asked.

The man pivoted in his saddle and peered behind him. "It is an inn and a good one." Then he looked down at Miriam and added, "But possibly not for the lady."

John Mark understood about some of the inns, how innkeepers were often not reputable, and where there were no housemistresses, women might not be welcome.

The man said, "But there are others in the town."

"There is a town?" John Mark asked nonplussed.

"Ammoxtem," the caravan leader disclosed.

"I have not heard of this place," John Mark replied.

"You will find food and lodging there," the caravan leader advised. "Now we must go. It is a long way to Egypt." He slapped the camels flank with a short tasseled whip and the caravan moved forward.

John Mark turned to Miriam. "Ammoxtem."

"You said there were no towns." She slapped him gently on the back and smiled.

"I knew not of this place, but am glad."

They found a small but safe family-run inn on the eastern fringe of the town. The owner said three men traveling from Damascus to Caesarea Maritime on the coast were lodging there but he had room for two more. Evening and morning meals cost extra, but John Mark paid a lower lodging rate because they had no animals to shelter. They slept beside the three men on a raised platform adjacent an earthen floor where the camels belonging to the men, plus a few sheep, were kept. John Mark positioned himself between the men and Miriam who lay on the outside next to the animals. He slept with his bag tucked beneath his arms and her bag as a pillow. She offered it saying her head did not need support. She made a veil of her headscarf to dull the odor. It had been many years since she had animals to shelter inside her father's house in Capernaum.

Early next morning, they lay still as the men made a clattering ruckus, saddled their camels, and left, taking the food the mistress of the inn had prepared for them. Suddenly, John Mark realized something was missing. His satchel was gone. He jumped up frantically and headed for the door, as if to run after the men when Miriam shouted, "What is wrong?"

"The scrolls are gone, I fear taken by the men who slept beside us."

She raised up and smiled. "Dear John Mark, please be at ease. The scrolls are here." She reached behind her head and brought the bag forward. "I pulled it from you in the night to use as a pillow. I told you I do not sleep with one but the planks beneath my head were warped. I did not think you would object."

He heaved a sigh of relief. "I cannot think of losing this," he said as he clutched it to his breast, still emotional at the possible loss.

"All the more reason we need to get to Damascus and make copies."

"Yes, but even if we make a hundred copies, this, the original," he said, still clutching it close, "must be preserved. Others will copy the copies. They will make changes."

"I know what you say is true."

"This happened to some of Paul's letters," he continued still excited. "I read two that were circulating among Christians in Ephesus then the same letters two years later in Tyre. They were not written by the same person. An original must be preserved. Paul always carried originals with him in small tablets. The integrity of this gospel must be protected."

"I agree, but talking prolongs our departure." She was still lying on the floor and he was standing over her.

"You and my dear mother; she would say the same," he said and reached down to help her up.

The mistress of the inn came down the steps with bread and dried meat for their journey. She looked decrepit and disheveled, so John Mark handed her an extra coin. The mistress bade them farewell and petitioned they stay again with her should they travel that way, and they agreed they would.

The road was dusty. A slight wind blew from the south. Snow-capped Mount Hermon loomed behind them, and the sun blazed over the eastern Ghuta plateau, the oasis where Damascus was located. Jerusalem was southwest almost two hundred miles, the Great Sea and the cities of Tyre and Sidon sixty miles behind them. A man and a woman far from home traveling together could not have been more alone in that part of the world, yet they seemed oblivious to the isolation. As far as they could see, like a promise of glory and great things to come, was a rich and never-ending blue sky,

"Back at the inn, you understood my concerns about writing and what can happen to one's work," he said, initiating discussion a short way from the town, the episode still fermenting in his mind. "I feel confident you have read the writings of others."

She nodded. "Some. That was one benefit, among others, of living in Capernaum."

"I do not understand. Capernaum has no libraries like Tyre or Sidon."

"But it is on the Via Maris. Merchants, sellers of manuscripts and scrolls, would travel through and stop. A wealthy neighbor would buy a scroll, more than one if she could talk the man lower in his price. When she finished reading the scroll, she would share it with others in the village. I was one of those fortunate."

"What did you read?" his interest piqued.

"I would not bore you with all I have read. Reading was my salvation."

"Surely, you cannot bore me on this desolate road. You are an oasis that moves with me. Regardless, you could never bore me about reading, a passion of mine as well."

"One of the more important ones I recall was Livy's *History of Rome*. Not the entire work, but a few of the books. I enjoyed reading Ovid's *Metamorphoses* and a few of Seneca's *Essays*, one I remember especially, *On Tranquility of Mind*. And, of course, *The Scriptures*. *The Psalms* and *Proverbs* I particularly enjoyed when I had the opportunity."

He stopped and looked at her, his eyes wide in amazement. "So you read Latin?"

"I read some Latin, not fluently. Ovid and Seneca were in Greek."

"You read Greek, classical and the *koine*. You read Latin. You read Hebrew. Is there any language you do not read," he said in comic exasperation.

"I know of no others," she responded, her hand covering a chuckle at his reaction.

A man and his family approached with a cart and several dogs and children. He was Jewish and leaving Damascus he said because of the persecution of his people.

John Mark commented, "That was several years ago. I heard the persecutions had stopped."

"Perhaps they have stopped killing people, but not in their minds. They hate the Jews," the man remarked, as he whipped the donkey pulling the cart and moved on, his hostility lingering in the dusty air.

"This is not good," John Mark commented.

"Perhaps it is not bad," Miriam, the ever hopeful one, said. "We are Jews, but we are Christian Jews."

"Some do not know the difference," he opined.

"The Lord does, and I feel his strong presence. It began when you came to my home. Something special is going to happen, I thought. Then we stayed at that inn."

"The inn?" He raised a brow.

"Yes."

"What was special about the inn?"

"It is a story," she began, "I have heard, about the birth of our Christ to a virgin, that it happened in Bethlehem, in an inn with animals nearby. Three men came from the East bearing gifts to worship the newborn child. We stayed in an inn among animals, with three men from the East. Lying there, my head resting on the gospel, on Christ's words, my thoughts on these occurrences. I felt all was right and we were safe."

"You inspire me, Miriam. I am deeply touched and uplifted by these thoughts."

"Have you not heard the story?" She looked at him quizzically. "Is it in the gospel you write?"

A long pause covered their footsteps on the paved Roman road. He stared straight ahead at the rising sun, conjuring a response.

"John Mark?" She nudged him.

"I heard you. Yes, I had heard the story, actually two versions of it. No, I did not include it in the gospel I have written. I—"

"It is not there?" she said dismayed, pointing at the bag slung over his shoulder.

"Please allow me to continue," he said, an edge in his voice at her persistence. "I had a different message, one of a suffering Christ and his humanity. A virgin birth did not fit. It sounded too Greek, like Athena springing from the head of Zeus. Our Christ is different from all other gods."

"But His divinity also makes him different," she insisted.

"Divinity is part of the problem. What makes Jesus truly different from all other divinities is that his divinity became incarnate; it took on human flesh. This is the core of the gospel message. It sets Christ apart from all other religions, including our own Judaism."

She responded with emphasis. "I do not see this problem. I believe the story."

"Please do not misunderstand me," he pleaded. "I am not denying the concept or possibility of a virgin birth and respect the opinions of others who believe this. Everyone sees Christ differently. He is for all people, all times, not just a select few who might perceive him in a certain light. In discussions with the Apostle Paul, with whom I and my cousin Barnabas traveled, a virgin birth was never mentioned. It is absent in his letters I have read."

"As you said, that does not mean it is not important to others."

"This is true," he insisted. "Perhaps others will tell the story."

For several mile markers they did not speak. The wind had calmed, and the sun was high overhead, the stones warm beneath their sandaled feet. They began peeling back their layered clothing.

Past a marker showing they were six miles from Damascus, Miriam, as though she had been carrying the thought a long way and needed to lift the load, spoke suddenly. "If you have problems with a virgin birth, then you have problems with a resurrection."

The remark stopped him. "This is not true. With God all things are possible. We discussed this back in your home. Your description of your father's reaction to a spiritually risen Lord was compelling. I have problems with resurrections that turn Jesus into a ghost or phantom, something unreal."

"I meant only that you have problems with a physical resurrection," she persisted.

"No. There is one in this gospel," he countered. "You will read about it, a small girl who had died, but only for a short while, maybe minutes, and was brought back to life by Jesus. You may have known her. She was Jairus' daughter."

"Yes, I know these people. She and her father are still alive," she responded. "Perhaps, then, I have been unfair. The emphasis in the gospel is not on what people see, hear, or touch, but on faith. Faith does not see, hear, or touch. It merely and simply … believes."

He stood looking at her as though an aura surrounded her. "I must write that. Do not let me forget."

They began walking again and he stopped again. "But we will speak further of resurrection," he said and they started again, the plateau of Ghuta rising out of the plain, appearing like a bluish blur across the horizon.

CHAPTER FIFTEEN

On the Road to Maaloula, October 30, 2011

Chris could feel the heat of her anger across the leather seat. She sat partially turned from him, her face patterned by the passing streetlights of the Qudssaya suburb. To the right and below them, in the amber-pebbled dark, Damascus appeared as tranquil as any city at night. But the news blaring from the radio continued to speak of anti-government demonstrations, bloodshed and calls for the ouster of Assad.

"The violence has now entered Damascus," Chris said, hoping to engage conversation with her. "I wonder what we can expect in Maaloula."

Kate did not respond.

"No violence in Maaloula," Muhammed picked up. "Maaloula quiet place. Only quiet people and priests. Not many tourists now."

Without turning, she finally spoke. "The fact sheet we have says the population is only two thousand."

"This true," Muhammed said. "Now, two thousand. In summer, six thousand."

"It's also ninety percent Christian," Chris said. "which may be another reason it's quiet. Assad has protected them."

Muhammed nodded in agreement.

"How far from Maaloula are we, Muhammed?" she asked, shifting her posture so she was looking straight ahead.

"About forty kilometers, madam, maybe an hour," he answered.

"Shouldn't we make it in less than an hour?" Chris asked.

"We not on A Five, on small road. Go through small towns."

Chris glanced at his watch. A few minutes past eight. They'd departed Beirut around seven and, thanks to Muhammed's magic at the border, made better time than he'd expected. Barring any unforeseen circumstances, they'd arrive in Maaloula around nine o'clock. Monastery prayer times varied, but the monks and nuns at Mar Thecla might be in prayers or compline, the final service of the day, before bedtime. He had no idea where Muhammed was staying and was afraid to ask.

After several miles they passed through the village of At-tal, a few miles later, Minin, and then the desert dark. She sat crouched in the corner, enwrapped in her arms as though deep in thought, her mind, Chris guessed, six years away. Only now did he fully understand why she wanted to go to Damascus. The revolution might have been part of it. But that was where she picked up her husband's body. For her, this was a pilgrimage, and he was now sorry he'd been so adamant. He wanted to talk but would not interrupt her retreat into another time, another place.

Several miles they rode in silence. She shifted posture and began looking out the window again. He found himself observing her profile. She was stunning in her concentration, whatever the focus of her mind. He thought of a subject that might hook her and arouse her from her isolation. "In Edinburgh, we spoke only briefly about the mysterious absence of Mark's final page. The professor argued for a missing leaf, one that had become frayed and perhaps detached from the scroll. You had a different perspective."

She spun around, arms folded. Her chin was raised, her face set. He was a target, he felt, pinned by her glare.

"Precisely," she clipped. "Mystery is a good word. In Mark's gospel, consistently, Jesus implores his disciples to remain silent about his miracles and his identity. 'Tell no one,' he says to them. It is in Mark's gospel, when the Pharisees asked for a sign from heaven, he replied, 'Why does this generation ask for a miraculous sign? I tell you the truth no sign will be given to it.'"

He extended a hand. "Please continue."

Her smile was ice cold. "The theme surfaces in other places. I believe, therefore, the conclusion, as it stands today, is consistent with Mark's theme of messianic secrecy. The emphasis is on faith, one that transcends miracles, becomes their foundation, not the contrary."

He had hooked her. Her concentration was a coiled spring wound up and ready to be tripped. She spoke in her lecture voice, that authoritative tone he was learning she'd shift into when she was digging in her heels. At least, she was engaging him. He forwarded the discussion. "So, Jesus leaves the world with an empty tomb and three trembling and bewildered women who say nothing to anyone because they are afraid."

She opened her mouth as if she had something to add, and then closed it, satisfied she'd made her point.

"If I might play the devil's advocate once more," he risked.

"Please do. You do make a splendid devil's advocate," she said smiling smugly.

Hearing *devil's advocate*, Muhammed straightened his arms on the steering wheel and tilted back his head.

"There are two primary reasons the gospel would not end dangling in that fashion," Chris ventured, aware he may have launched another squabble. "First, and foremost, there is a pattern in the gospel of Mark."

"Exactly!" she pounced. "Messianic secret, mystery, faith."

"I understand," he said reasonably. "You made your case, now allow me. Each of Jesus' predictions throughout Mark is actually fulfilled in narrative form. Thus, since Jesus announced that he would see his disciples in Galilee, the narrative should have depicted an actual appearance of the risen Christ to his disciples in Galilee."

"Jesus was not that predictable," she countered. "At times, he was unpredictable. But go on. Your second point?"

"It seems improbable, and a bit incredible, that Mark, who so often in the gospel quotes Jesus as telling others to 'be not afraid,' would end his gospel on a note of fear. I reference the storm scene where he walks on water and tells the disciples to 'Take courage ... don't be afraid.' In the fourth chapter, another storm scene, Jesus says to his disciples, 'Why are you so afraid? Do you still have no faith?' There are others I could quote, ones you know as well." He caught himself reaching to touch her again for emphasis. "Of particular interest is what happens at the raising of Jairus' daughter, a resurrection story. He tells the ruler of the synagogue, who fell at his feet trembling with fear, not to be afraid, but believe. My point is this. Why would this writer go to such great lengths to emphasize faith overcoming fear, yet leave the last words of his opus hanging on fear?"

For a while, she said nothing, sat there arms wrapped around herself, glaring at him, the green dials of the dash pulsing, like something alien, in her hazel eyes. Then: "You have certainly given this theme much thought."

"I wore out my hotel Gideon's last night," he snapped back.

"Or it wore you out."

"Your response," he persisted.

She came right back. "In a way, you have given it."

"I don't get it."

"Your emphasis on faith," she said.

"My emphasis was on fear, that a writer who stresses courage and 'fear not' would not end his gospel on fear. There should be more, the page that is missing, lost."

"But that precisely is the point."

She was about to get on his nerves again. She loved that word, "Precisely." With her Scottish-English accent, it sliced the air like a razor. "All right. Clarify the point," he said dryly.

She lowered her brows. Her eyes centered on him slowly, as though he was a piece in a game to be moved. "There is no final page because Mark intended to leave the end dangling, a titillation to the spiritual mind, an existential something to think on. Have you ever read Kierkegaard's *Fear and Trembling*?"

"A long time ago."

"Perhaps you recall the author took the pseudonym John the Silent and the title from a line in Philippians chapter two, verse twelve—'continue to work out your salvation with fear and trembling.'"

"I do remember," he said.

"Faith is not a done deal. It is a challenge, a struggle." She sat erect, unfolded her arms. "There are no givens. I think of Alfred Lord Tennyson's lines in the Prologue of *In Memoriam*, 'We have but faith, we cannot know for knowledge is of things we see, and yet we trust it comes from thee, a beam in darkness, let it grow.'"

Muhammed's ears were cocked trying to understand.

She was on the edge of the seat leaning toward Chris, speaking with emotion as though preaching, "You see, fear and doubt are not the opposite of faith but the same side of the coin. Cynicism and apathy are the opposite of faith."

He waited a moment before responding. "That was beautiful. And I do not disagree with your assessment of faith and doubt. I can quote your beloved Tennyson myself. In that same work he said, 'There lives more faith in honest doubt, believe me, than in half the creeds.' But that is not the issue. I believe Mark intended to say more about the resurrection. Think about it." He shifted closer to her, his face near hers. "Peter is John Mark's source. The last we hear of Peter in this gospel, he disowns Jesus and breaks down crying. From then on, and this part you'll like, women hold center stage. Peter does not reappear. Do you really think John Mark would leave his mentor weeping? Would we not find him in Galilee waiting for his risen master, not crying in the flickering shadows of a Roman soldier's fire?"

She stiffened her back but remained silent.

"No comment?" he beckoned.

Her face hardened. She shook her head no.

He had her on the ropes. *Go for the knockout punch.* "May I proceed?"

"If you prefer," she said glumly.

"The old tradition has little description of the actual resurrection appearances, but it does record there was a physical resurrection."

She quickly countered. "Early Christians thought it sufficient to proclaim the Lord's resurrection and were little concerned with the details, another piece of logic that fits my theory and why another page was unnecessary. Mark does not stress the physical or material nature of Jesus' risen body. In fact, he presents no account of any resurrection appearance by Jesus."

He responded. "The gospels of Matthew and Luke were based mostly on Mark. In Matthew, the resurrected Jesus meets the disciples in Galilee."

She countered. "In Luke, Jesus meets them and appears among them in Jerusalem. The accounts conflict. Mark eliminates the conflict. He leaves the conclusion, the leap of faith, up to the reader."

Chris was ready. "John Mark traveled with Paul. Paul stressed the resurrection. It was a major theme in his writings."

Immediately, she came back. "Paul was equally emphatic about faith and what it could accomplish."

Trying to follow the dialogue, Muhammed was distracted, at times weaving in the road.

Incredible. She doesn't miss a thing Chris thought. "I must say I'm impressed. No offense, but one wouldn't think a former special forces agent would know their New Testament so well."

"No offense taken. Thanks for the compliment. Surely, you don't think I get it by osmosis, analyzing ancient texts day in and day out. But how did you know about the special forces?"

"The Professor."

"What else did he tell you?" She asked, annoyed.

"That you were a language specialist in the British army, an ancient manuscript expert, and 'on loan,' his words, to him from the British Museum."

She looked startled. "Why, that old codger."

"He spoke very highly of you, said you were the best, that no one could touch you."

She forced a smile. "Well, he's a nice old codger," the edge to her voice gone. "If he were younger, I could fall in love with him."

"I believe in the resurrection of the body," said Muhammed loudly from the front. "That is our creed."

"Muhammed?" she asked.

"Yes, madam."

"What if news came over the radio just now that Jesus' body had been discovered in a tomb in Jerusalem." She looked at Chris. "Would you suddenly toss the Christian faith, dump its morals, values, and teachings? Would they suddenly become useless, unimportant, valueless simply because there was no physical resurrection?"

Muhammed was silent. Then, "That is most difficult. I might become Muslim again."

Chris smothered a laugh.

Lights appeared in the distance, and soon they were driving through a town named Seidnayya.

"Next, Jabadeen, then Maaloula," Muhammed said. "Much to see in Maaloula."

They looked at each other. They couldn't tell him they don't have time, that they are not really tourists.

Past Seidnayya, the desert darkness engulfed them once more, and again they found entertainment in their subject.

"Though I am not a gambler, I will make you a wager," he offered.

"I am a gambler," she said flatly. "I gamble every day I wake up. What is your wager?"

"If we find the autograph and the last page is no longer lost and the one we have now, I will, at my own expense, fly you to Arizona and personally show you the Grand Canyon."

She let out a slight whoop. "Oh my! Confident one, aren't you? Here is my wager. If there is a final page with express reference to the physical resurrection of the risen Christ, I will cook for you a seven course meal in my Scottish manor and give you a personal tour of Dunbar and the castle where Queen Mary was whisked away, to use your term, plus a personal guided jaunt through the Lowlands."

He couldn't remember the last time a woman had cooked for him. Did he detect a slight flirtation? She was not the same woman after they skirted Damascus. "You say that with much pleasure, as through there is no sacrifice, no loss."

"I am a realist, Dr. Jordan. I do not know how much more time you have in Scotland. It is a wager I could meet. After all, a bet is a bet. Pain, or pleasure, are not necessarily part and parcel of the wager."

He leaned over, offered her his hand and she shook it. That was that, but it wasn't. She wouldn't let the issue die, or live, depending on one's perspective.

"Win, lose or draw, a religion built solely on resurrection is thin," she said.

"Here we go again," he murmured.

"It hangs tenuously from one peg. Jesus knew well enough the world at that time was populated with resurrection stories. Why do you think he told the disciples and those around him to say nothing of Jairus' daughter's raising? That's why he emphasized faith over the miraculous. What if the great mystery was revealed? What if it was proven fact? What would happen to a belief we accept by faith? Besides, making resurrection the centerpiece of one's religion means waiting for salvation on the periphery of life, not experiencing it at its core, in the present."

"What is pifery?" Muhammed asked.

They looked at each other and grinned.

She responded. "It means death, Muhammed, when we die."

Chris leaned up and spoke into Muhammed's ear. "It means dying in this taxi unless you get us to Maaloula in two pieces, three counting you."

"Oh!" he said, smiling at them in the rearview. "No problem, no problem. We not pifery," he said as he swerved around a big semi straddling the center line. Suddenly, they saw blue lights ahead and traffic backed up.

Muhammed turned and looked at Kate, his face serious, a frozen look of concern in his eyes. "Give me gun again."

"Is there a problem?" she asked, handing him the brown package.

"It is possible," he said and then tucked the gun again over the visor. "Road blocked."

Uniformed officials were walking down the line of cars, flashing lights in windows, under carriages, and around wheels. They came to their car. Muhammed slid the window down. There was a conversation, and then the official moved to the next car.

"Why the road block?" Chris asked.

"Security forces," Muhammed said. "They look for rebels, liberation people."

Chris looked at Kate. "So much for resurrection."

"We're not dead yet," she quipped.

"Maybe pifery," Muhammed said, not laughing this time.

Quickly, Chris removed his passport from his front shirt pocket, and then the green tourist card he was given at the border. He opened the passport and placed the green card in the second page so it covered the Israeli stamps.

"Smart," Kate said, observing the move.

One of the officials shined his flashlight in Muhammed's face, muttered something, and made him get out.

Muhammed looked back as he was exiting. "He say all get out."

The car emptied, the doors remained open.

Speaking in rapid Arabic, Muhammed began explaining something to the official. By the motion of his hands he was describing where they had been and were going. Chris detected the word "tourist."

Kate leaned over and whispered to him, "He's told him we are tourists going to Maaloula."

The official turned to them.

"He want to see your passport and green card," Muhammed advised.

Chris removed his passport and handed it to the official. Kate followed.

It seemed the official was more interested in the green card. He removed them from the passports, shined the light on them separately and then returned them.

Muhammed pointed to the trunk. The official shook his head and motioned them back into the car. They had to wait. There was a problem with the car in front of them, and they could not proceed until it was cleared.

"Why are they inspecting the luggage of the car in front of us and not ours?" Chris asked.

He pointed at the license plate. "They from Homs. Much fighting in Homs. Much revolution."

The official motioned the car in front of them to pull over, and they were able to proceed.

"That was close," Kate sighed.

"They look for guns going to Homs," Muhammed said. "Not tourists. Tourists bring money, not guns. Syria need money."

They entered Jabadeen, a small town they passed through quickly. Muhammed noted it was one of three that still spoke the ancient Aramaic. Minutes later, he pointed ahead at a bulge of light in the night sky, a lurid glare beneath the stars, and shouted, "Maaloula!"

CHAPTER SIXTEEN

Damascus, 70 A.D.

Before they even saw the city, Damascus had loomed in their minds. It was one of the oldest and largest cities in the world. Abraham had chased invading kings north of Damascus to recover Lot. Abraham's servant Eliezer had come from Damascus. From then on, it had been referenced often in the Scriptures. Many Jews had lived there, perhaps a legacy from the commercial community set up by King Ahab, famous ruler of the northern kingdom of Israel. From this early settlement, a community of Christian disciples had grown. It was the city where Paul had been converted and had re-visited on his return from Arabia. It was the city where he had preached perhaps more than in any other, the city where the teachings of Christ had been planted and spread throughout the region. Damascus was the city second only to Antioch of importance to the followers of Jesus.

As John Mark and Miriam approached the city, the setting sun behind them cast a golden glow on its walls, and they were awed at its size. John Mark's eyes grew tired scanning it from north to south. He had been told it was twice as long east to west.

"It is larger than I had ever imagined," remarked Miriam.

They could not enter the western gate immediately, but had to stand aside and allow a long caravan to pass. Once inside, they were overwhelmed with the noise and energy of the people. Jerusalem, in comparison, was a quiet city. In Jerusalem, John Mark could hear four languages—Hebrew, Greek, Aramaic, and Latin—occasionally one he did not recognize. They were in Damascus only a short time and multiple languages mingled in the congested air. He heard more than he could count on his fingers.

They stood at the end of a wide double-colonnaded street aligned with houses and shops. Pedestrians used the side passages, carts and horsemen moved noisily in different directions down the middle thoroughfare. Both sides were lined with covered patios flanked by shops. Before them was the imposing Temple of Jupiter. The sun's leveling rays struck its massive entablature and pediment as they spread the wall's long shadow down the crowded street and across the city. Nearby was a large theater they would learn later was built by Herod the Great.

They moved further into the city to escape the bottleneck of heavy traffic around the busy gate—venders hawking their wares, beggars crying out in nasal voices, tax agents checking caravans, farmers pulling carts loaded with produce and animals. They had already discussed their plan, to find the street called Straight and hope Judas or Ananias was still alive. If not, they hoped they could find other Christians in the area who would offer them food and shelter. John Mark still had money, but they would be there a long time, and he was not yet established as a scribe. He was confident, however, that in short time, others would hear of his ability and services, as they had in Tyre, and he could generate income, perhaps enough to lease or purchase their own quarters. First, they had to find the street called Straight. The popular name for it was the *Decumanus,* the main thoroughfare crossing the city from west to east.

Ask a shopkeeper, John Mark thought. They were housed in *insulae* or street-front shops or workshops and lived above and behind the working areas. Behind the colonnades, as far as he could see in the waning dusk light, shops lined both sides of the wide street. He saw a tin smith, bakery and laundry. One sold pots, another idols. There were fruit and vegetable stalls and spices, their aroma filling the passageway. Further down the street were some taverns and a brothel. Most of the shops he saw were probably family-owned. They would have been there thirty-five years ago when Paul was in Damascus. He guided Miriam toward a shop he reasoned might have an affiliation with Paul, a tanner. Across the entrance, leather hides hung from elevated horizontal poles. He spoke first to the shopkeeper in Greek and drew a blank face in response. Miriam spoke to him in Aramaic and his eyes lit up.

"This is the Straight street, the Decumanus," he said, a finger pointing toward the ground. He was a bearded diminutive man with discolored hands from the years of his trade.

"Are you Jewish?" she asked.

"Yes, yes," he said eagerly, as though anticipating something special in the next question.

"Do you know a man named Ananias?" she inquired further.

The shopkeeper put his hand on his head and thought a moment.

"There are many with that name, you must tell me more," he requested and lowered his hand.

John Mark decided on another approach. "Do you know a man named Judas? He would be old. He lived on this street."

The shopkeeper thought again and again put his hand on his head as if the gesture generated memory. "This name, many people have this name in Damascus."

"The name Paul," John Mark probed again. "Or Saul, his former name. Have you heard of this man? He taught about Jesus—"

"About the Christ!" the shopkeeper interrupted, his eyes ballooning, his face animated, his hand bouncing on his head. "Yes, yes. He taught in the synagogue."

"Your synagogue?" John Mark asked.

"Yes, yes, mine," he said, patting the same hand on his chest and pointing down the street. "It is not far from here. A man Judas helped him when he was blind. He is in my ecclesia. Paul stayed in his house. It is on this street, maybe three hundred meters."

"And the man Judas, the same who helped Paul, he is still alive?" John Mark inquired.

"Yes. He lives there. Like you said, he is very old. I know, too, now, this Ananias."

"Is he still alive?" Miriam asked.

"No, he died."

"When?" Miriam asked again..

"A few years ago. But Judas, he is alive. I can take you there if you wish."

"That would be most generous of you," John Mark said gratefully.

"What about your shop?" Miriam questioned with concern.

The shopkeeper looked up at the sky, down at the long shadows filling the street. "Time to close."

John Mark and Miriam waited for him to take down his selections of leather hides and goods and clear the tables. He moved methodically, a routine he followed daily. He secured and locked everything in a room at the back of his display area. He stepped into the street and motioned them to follow him.

They were a few steps from the shop, and John Mark felt bumped from behind. When he reached around, his satchel was gone. The man who took it was running toward the west gate. "Thief!" John Mark shouted running after him, followed by the shopkeeper. The man's clothing flew like flags in the air behind him and a sandal fell off.

"Stop!" joined in the shopkeeper, "Thief!"

Suddenly, the satchel fell from the man's arms, and he fell face down on the stone pavement. The shopkeeper began beating the man but John Mark restrained him.

"He is injured," Miriam said arriving quickly on the scene. "He needs help."

"But he just stole from him," the shopkeeper cried.

"He stole because he is poor," John Mark said. "We must tend to him."

Miriam stooped down and inquired if the man could rise. He said he could, and she helped him up. He was an older man, emaciated, with only a few yellowed teeth. His right hand was bleeding and his forehead scraped. John Mark went back and retrieved his sandal. A thong had broken. When he returned, Miriam was wiping the man's hand with the edge of her outer garment. The shopkeeper stood looking on in disbelief.

"The leather thong on his sandal ripped apart," John Mark observed, showing the damage to the shopkeeper. "Can you repair it? I will pay you."

The tanner stared at him, a confused look on his face. "Yes. It will not take long. But he tried to steal from you."

"I know," John Mark concurred. "That is all the more reason I must show kindness. He will be gratified for your kindness as well."

The shopkeeper took the sandal and returned to his shop. Miriam continued tending to the man, his face as confused as the shopkeeper's. John Mark walked back to the gate where he had seen some food venders. He bought a portion of fish with vegetables and cheese and a small flask of wine. Thinking the food possible poisoned, at first the injured man was reluctant to accept it.

Sensing his concern, Miriam pinched a bit of the cheese and put it into her mouth. "It is good, please eat."

With trembling hands, the man began picking at the food. Keeping his eyes on his benefactors, he plunged both hands into the small dish wrapped in thin dry bread and he ate rapidly.

"Here, drink this," John Mark said kindly, handing him the wine.

In seconds, it vanished.

The tanner returned with the repaired sandal.

"How much do I owe you?" John Mark asked him.

"Nothing. You and your wife are true followers of the Christ."

John Mark thought to correct him about the status of his relationship with Miriam but decided against it. The comment would only be confusing. He looked over at her. She was smiling.

The man finished the meal. They bade him good wishes but before they departed the shopkeeper invited him to a fellowship meeting of Christians, his ecclesia. The man inquired the place.

Eliezar pointed. "It is there above my tanning shop. Tomorrow night, after sundown."

"I will come," the man replied, smiled weakly and waddled off.

"Another convert," John Mark said, clapping the tanner on the shoulders. "Well done."

"If anyone was converted, it was not I who was responsible, but you and your wife."

John Mark glanced over at Miriam and she smiled again.

Headed down the street called Straight, the tanner said, "The bag, it is made of good leather. How did you come by it?"

"I bought it in Tyre."

"It is waxed to protect from moister," the tanner said. "Does it contain anything of value? You ran hard after the thief."

"Yes," John Mark replied. "Something of great value."

"May I enquire the contents?"

"You may and happily I will tell you. It contains a scroll, the gospel, the good news of Jesus Christ."

The tanner halted and they stopped with him. "I have heard of nothing like this," the tanner said, "nothing that is written. You must bring it to our fellowship, our *agape* meal tomorrow night, and read from it."

"It is agreed," John Mark said.

"You do not meet in the synagogue?" Miriam questioned.

"Years ago, we did," the tanner said. "When Paul returned from Arabia and began preaching in the synagogues that Jesus was the long awaited 'Anointed One,' the Jews, even some of the Jewish followers of Jesus, became angry. Some sought to kill him. His preaching also angered King Aretas of Nabatea, the governor of Syria. To escape his soldiers, Paul was lowered in a basket through the window in a city wall and escaped an attempt to capture him."

"That was when he came to Jerusalem," John Mark said, all too familiar with the problems caused there among the Jewish followers of Jesus. "Even Greek Jews sought to kill him."

"It was then that he attempted to meet with my father and James, the brother of Jesus," Miriam said.

"Your father?" the tanner said.

"Her father was Peter the Apostle," John Mark said, knowing Miriam's shyness in making the reference herself.

The tanner stopped walking again. He turned and looked at her. "Your father was Peter the Apostle?"

She nodded.

He dropped to his knees. "My Lord and my God, I am in the presence of the daughter of Peter." He reached out a trembling hand.

She clasped and held it, felt the tremors as though they belonged to her own hand.

He bowed his head and began weeping. "I am not worthy to hold the hand of the daughter of an apostle. I was beating the thief, and you were trying to save him. Have mercy upon me."

"Please rise," she urged.

He stood.

She continued holding his hand. "Tell us your name, for we do not fully know you."

"I am Eliezar the Tanner, which is how I am known in Damascus. My name in Hebrew means 'God has helped.' Now you know me."

She released his hand. "Have you always been a tanner?"

"Yes. That is how I met Paul. He was a tanner. That is how he partly financed his travels and ministry."

"I know," said John Mark. "For a time, I traveled with him, to Antioch and places in the Great Sea—Cyprus, Salamis, Paphos."

"You traveled with Paul?" the tanner's emotions rising again, near hysteria. He raised his hands into the air. "Blessed is this day. I meet the daughter of Peter and now a companion of Paul."

"The world of the followers of Jesus is small," John Mark said. "We feel blessed the Lord has brought us to you."

Miriam nodded in agreement.

John Mark continued. "Please tell us more of your relationship with Paul."

"When he came to Damascus, I helped him. He had a small shop here on the Decumanus, not far from mine. When he departed for Jerusalem, he closed his shop and gave me much of his leather. The leather used to repair the man's sandal, it belonged once to Paul."

John Mark laid a hand on his shoulder. "Eliezar, you are true to your name. God has helped you, and you have helped Paul. Now you help us. Take us to the house of Judas."

They continued down the street called Straight. The sun was fully set, its glow lingering in the western sky, the shadow of the walls in the street now gone, taken over by the dark. From columns lining the thoroughfare, torches burned, the smell of their oil pungent in the night air.

They had walked a long way, almost to the other end of the city it seemed when Eliezar stopped and pointed. "This is the place."

The house was two-storied and flat-roofed with a small front balcony and an arched doorway with openings for windows either side. A dim light flickered inside. Eliezar stepped forward and knocked on the wooden door. They stood waiting, but the door did not open.

CHAPTER SEVENTEEN

Maaloula, October 31, 2011

As they neared the city, the view developed into spotlighted golden cliffs, steeples and minarets. Bright splashes of halogen lighted domes and crosses. Other varied lights scattered up the sides and across the dark mountains.

"The place is lit up like a Christmas tree," Chris exclaimed. "Is this a holiday, Muhammed?"

"No, always like this. Holy place. Every day holiday. The lights up high," he said excitedly, pointing straight ahead at a row of bright halogen lights atop a mountain, "Mar Sarkis!"

"But we're not going to the monastery of Saint Sergius," Kate clarified.

"Correct. We go to Mar Thecla, in the town below Mar Sarkis."

They turned left off the main highway and followed a curving road. A sign with blue graphics on white had an unusual block script at the top, Arabic below that , and then MAALOULA in English at the bottom.

"Three languages," Kate said. "The one on top is Aramaic. Most of the people here speak it."

Just beyond, a smaller sign read WELCOME TO MAALOULA, also in the three languages.

They entered a long smoothly paved street. On the left, behind continuous decorative wrought-iron railing, flat-roofed houses with satellite dishes swept by; on the right, cedar trees candlelabraed the road. They passed occasional shops, cars pulled up on the curb in front of them. In the faint street light against the yellow limestone cliffs, the buildings all seemed painted the same color. A few were butter-yellow but most were of a pale blue wash.

"Muhammed," Chris said, "most of the houses are painted blue."

"The color a gesture of respect for mother of Jesus."

"Look!" Kate shouted.

They were still on the outskirts but suddenly ahead of them were tiers of houses climbing the sides of the mountain..

"This is like Positano," she said animated. She looked at Chris. "Have you ever been to Positano?"

"No. I take it you have."

"Yes. Fabulous place. The houses are like these, stacked up the sides of the mountain, one atop the other. You must go some time. It's on the Amalfi Drive, the best of Italy."

Although he was listening to her, Chris was captivated with the houses, how they seemed to hang onto the edge of the mountain, as though suspended in mid-air. He had only heard of Maaloula, never seen pictures. Then he saw, poised over the city like the figure on the prow of a ship, a spot-lit statue. "Muhammed, who's the statue straight ahead, the one on top the mountain?"

"The Virgin Mary. Here, no statue of Muhammed," he said and laughed.

At a roundabout which appeared to be the city center, they veered right down another long straight street that gradually ascended. At the end of the tunnel of buildings they saw a cubed lighted cross atop a dome.

Muhammed turned a corner and pulled into a large parking lot. In front of a closed garage door he stopped. "Mar Taklas," he said.

A brightly lit sign a couple of stories above them confirmed: CONVENT OF SAINT TAKLAS.

Muhammed got out, opened the trunk and handed them their luggage. "We go here." He pointed to a decorative wrought-iron double-gate. To the right of the gate were signs forbidding the use of cameras or cell phones.

Muhammed tried the gate. It was locked. Except for the bright sign and lighted crosses atop the buildings and chapel, the steps behind the gate were dark.

Chris looked at his watch. Nine o'clock.

Muhammed pushed a button beside the gate. Kate and Chris stood holding their luggage. Muhammed pushed the button again. Soon, footsteps hurriedly descended the steps. A young nun dressed in Greek Orthodox habit, head and body in a sheath of black, only her face showing, approached the gate. She said something in a language that was not Arabic.

Muhammed said something back to her.

"What's going on?" Chris asked Kate.

"She spoke to him in Aramaic, and he didn't understand, could she please speak Arabic and ... she's responding now, listen."

The young nun nervously told them the convent was closed for the day. Muhammed introduced Kate and Chris, explained who they were and why there were there. The nun smiled. She unlocked the gate and motioned them through. Apologetically, she acknowledged Chris and Kate. In fluent English, she said that the convent had been expecting them but sooner in the day and that everyone would be relieved they arrived safely.

Muhammed was bouncing on his feet and seemed antsy. "You okay now, I go," he said.

"You go? Where do you go?" Kate asked.

"To Beirut."

"How will we get back?" Chris asked.

"Use cell phone. Call Dr. Krekorian. He send me."

He shook hands with them and like a genie was off as quickly as he'd materialized in their lives.

The young nun led them up the steps, through a second entrance and foyer, and then up another flight of stairs to a spacious courtyard surrounded by buildings. Chris noted they were of recent origin. Looking around, he saw no evidence of surviving Byzantine work. At the end of the courtyard, a V of diagonal stairs led up a wall of icons and crosses to the next level that appeared to be two or three stories of apartments with flower boxes. The windows were all decoratively barred in white wrought-iron. A final set of stairs led to an enclosed area on the side of the mountain. He was getting a better idea of how the buildings climbed the mountain.

They crossed the mosaic marble courtyard. The nun asked them to stop at a baptistery of black marble with small sphinx-like statuettes at the corners. She walked to a door off the courtyard and entered. In a few minutes she returned, following an older woman in similar habit, a brilliant silver cross hanging from her neck. Her eyes were dark and deep set, her hands large and fleshy as she shook theirs and greeted them in a heavy, dull voice with remarkable English.

"Please allow me. I am Malasia Sayaf, the Mother Superior of the convent. Anina," she gestured to the young nun at her side, "I presume you have met."

Kate responded accordingly. "I am Dr. Kate Ferguson. With me is Dr. Christopher Jordan. Dr. Andrew Stewart of Edinburgh sends you his kind regards and thanks for your hospitality."

The Mother Superior bowed slightly in acknowledgment. "We enjoyed his visit here and only wish he could have stayed longer. We are glad, however, he sends his friends. Your accommodations are ready. Anina will show you to your rooms. If you need any assistance, my office is just there off the courtyard." She was speaking politely with her hands folded, at times bowing slightly. "Breakfast is served in our cafeteria at eight o'clock. If you prefer to have other meals with us, please inform me and arrangements will be made. In the morning, I will be honored to give you a tour of our convent, and Anina will give you a walking tour of our ancient and sacred city, the city where Jesus came as a young man and where St. Paul himself founded a church and where Saint Takla is buried, there," she said as she pointed to the encased area on the mountain at the top of the final stairway. "We trust your stay will be lengthy. Please sleep well tonight. I leave you with Anina's care," and she departed.

Kate and Chris swapped nervous glances but said nothing. All the professor had told the Mother Superior was that they were coming to Maaloula to conduct linguistic research and explore graphics and symbols on the interior walls of the caves.

Anina motioned them to follow her again, this time up one of the diagonal stairs at the end of the courtyard, and to another level and another courtyard then up yet another set of stairs. Their rooms, side by side on the third floor, opened onto a balcony overlooking the main courtyard and a panorama of the bespangled city. Above, a waxing crescent moon hung in a clear sky glittered with stars.

Anina pulled keys from a pocket, looked at the tags on them, and handed one to each. "The water in your room you can drink. If you need something, my room is down," she pointed below, "by Mother Superior."

They thanked her, and she left, floating, not walking, it seemed in her flowing dark habit.

Kate opened her door and said, "Sleep well," before entering her room.

He stood there a moment pondering. That was what Allyson always told him. He really wasn't ready to turn in for the night. He rarely went to bed before ten, and jet lag twice in two days, not to mention the carnival lights surrounding him, had thrown him off schedule. He opened the door and flipped on the light. The room was small but clean and neat with the basics: bed, nightstand and lamp, chest of drawers, closet, a cushioned straight-back chair and micro bathroom. The accommodations had something else very basic: security. From what Chris could tell, unless someone scaled the concrete walls, the only entrance was through the front gate that was iron-grilled and bolted. He put his small luggage on the bed and heard a tap at the door. *Anina probably back with something she forgot.* "Come in," he said.

"What if I just stand in the door?" Kate said, pushing it open with the toe of her boot. "No need to get on their black list the first night."

"I see. Well, I'll come out there." He walked onto the balcony with her. She'd let her ponytail down so her hair flowed around her shoulders and put on a heavier jacket for the cooler weather. The temperature he guessed was around forty. Weather forecast for the evening was just below freezing, but the dry air made it feel warmer.

"You up for a drink or cup of tea?" she asked. "It's midnight Edinburgh time. I'm wide awake."

"You and me both," he added. "I'm as wired as these lights. Tea wouldn't help sleep, but a drink might. I doubt there's a drop of Glenfiddich in the country much less this village."

"They have something better," Kate said smiling mischievously. "Arak."

"I'd forgotten. That's the traditional beverage of the Mid-east. Powerful stuff."

"It's from the anise family and more powerful than Glenfiddich," she said. "One hundred proof."

"So much for Muslim abstinence. I saw a small restaurant near the entrance of the monastery. Let me get my key." He locked his door and noted she'd already locked hers. With or without him, she was going out.

Down the first flight of stairs and crossing the courtyard, Chris stopped.

"What is it?" she questioned.

"We can't get out. The front gate is locked."

Kate knocked on Anina's door. Of course, she would be happy to assist them and readily escorted them down the entrance steps to the gate.

"Ring the bell when you return but before midnight, please," Anina said, raising an authoritative finger.

They agreed and thanked her.

The café was around the corner next to a kiosk that displayed everything from pomegranates to Kit Kat candy bars. There were tables and chairs outside, but they chose inside where it was warmer. The owner was shooing away a vagrant when they arrived. They sat near the window away from two other customers seated toward the back. The place felt more subdued than the energy of the town. The waiter, a small mustached male, brought them a menu. One side was in Arabic, the other in Aramaic.

"You select something for me," Chris requested.

"You're living dangerously," she said, casting that roguish smile again.

"I was living dangerously when I told the professor I'd come to Edinburgh within twenty-four hours. Right now, I'm famished and need something to eat to live, dangerously or not."

She pointed at the Arabic side of the menu and said something to the waiter in that language. He said something back, the expression on his face suggesting he was correcting her order. Then he pulled up his sleeve and showed something tattooed on his forearm. He gathered the menus, and she said something else, the gesture with her forefinger and thumb indicating a small amount.

"What did you order?" Chris asked.

"You'll see. You'll like it."

"And this." He mimicked the gesture with his finger and thumb.

"You'll like it even better."

"What did he say back to you after you ordered, the deal about the tattoo?"

She chuckled. "He was correcting my Arabic, said I should learn Aramaic, then he displayed his name tattooed in Aramaic on his arm. These people are very passionate about their language."

"The professor said you knew many languages," Chris said. "I take it Aramaic is not among them."

"It is not. But I plan to learn some while I'm here."

The waiter brought a tray with a decorative blue bottle, a bronze cup with a spout and a wooden handle, and two small bell-shaped glass cups filled with ice. The bottle had a silver cap with silver lettering. Chris didn't recognize the brand, El Massaya, but the word "Arak" was in smaller print toward the bottom.

"This is a ritual," she said. "You must watch," as if that was not what he was already doing, a bit spell-bound by the procedure.

The waiter mixed one-third Arak with two-thirds water in the long-handled bronze cup.

"That is called an ibrik," she said, pointing to the cup. "It is a Levantine water vessel."

Next, the waiter poured the mixture into the ice-filled cups. The dilution caused the clear liquor to turn a translucent milky-white color.

She added another touch of her inexhaustible knowledge. "It turns this color because the oil of anise is soluble in alcohol, but not in water."

"You don't miss a beat, do you?" he teased.

"I'm sorry," she said. "Too much information. I tend to do that."

"No. I'm impressed." He raised his glass to hers. "To John Mark and the autograph."

They touched glasses.

He watched her first, how she let the first taste coast over her tongue as though it was an anesthetic, no change of expression on her face, this woman who drank Glenfiddich and ate haggis. The acrid odor of the drink carried across the table.

He took a timid sip, felt the vapor-rising, chemical-generated heat, the dull thump as the ball of fire hit his stomach and spread warmly through his body drawing tears to his eyes. One more sip would replace every party or celebration in his life he'd ever had, past or future, every high and reckless moment and every disconnect with reality and good judgment. "What's in this stuff?"

"Distilled alcohol with sugar, grapes, dates or plums. It all depends where it came from. This bottle came from Lebanon, so probably grapes. You have to develop a taste for it."

"If I have a one left. Tell the waiter I want a beer, a Syrian beer."

She spoke again to the waiter. He smiled and quickly brought a bottle and set it on the table beside the glass of arak. "Al-Sharq," the waiter said, "Syrian."

"Shukran," Chris said and downed half of it with the waiter standing there. He tapped the top of the bottle with a finger and held it up. "One more."

"You just complimented him," she said. "The Syrians believe their area of the world invented beer thousands of years ago."

The waiter brought him another beer along with their food, a simple dish of warmed hummus, fruity olive oil and baked flat bread.

They ate quietly for a while before he said: "I apologize for being so insistent about going around Damascus. I realize now it was more an emotional thing for you, a pilgrimage."

She put her fork down and looked at him oddly. "Emotional? Pilgrimage?"

"Your husband."

"No, that was not the reason, though I did reflect on it. I was wrapped up in our quest. I wanted to go where he went, John Mark, follow in his footsteps. Maaloula may not have even existed then, but Damascus did. I wanted to go to the Old City and see again the Via Recta, the street called Straight and experience the ambience."

He'd badly missed the mark and recalled something the professor had said about her feel for history, ability to grasp the mindset of a culture within any given time frame. She could do it because she'd been to all the places, studied them, and injected herself beneath the skin of their separate histories. "That's where Paul went, to the house of Judas" he said. "It's recorded in Acts."

"Yes. That's where Ananias found him blinded from the vision, laid his hands on him according to the Lord's instructions and 'the scales fell from his eyes and he regained his sight.' Don't know why I'm telling you all this. You're the New Testament scholar."

"Unsure about the scholar bit," he ceded. "Paul was baptized on the spot, ate some food and gained his strength and spent several days with other disciples in Damascus before going to Arabia."

"The new Jewish reform movement was small at that time," Kate added. "John Mark would have known of the strong Jewish Christian community in Damascus, probably one of the reasons he went there. Paul's letters were circulating." She took a sip of arak. "He would have heard about them or read some of them. Whether he knew the names Ananias or Judas is speculative, but it would not have taken him long to locate Christians who would give him food and shelter."

"And a place for him and his lady friend to settle down to the business of making copies of the gospel," he said.

"The part about the girl friend is speculative," she said doubtfully, "but your point is well taken. How do you like your food?"

"Wonderful. Good decision, except for the arak. Speaking of decisions, we need to put together a plan. The convent already has one for us. They want to show us around. I'm not sure the professor's bit about being linguistic research scholars and graphic spelunkers sank in. They think we're going to be here a while."

"Tell them up front we have an agenda," she said. "Accept their offer to show us the convent in the morning. I'm sure the walking tour of the town by Anina would be helpful and informative but we'd prefer to see Maaloula on our own. The professor gave me the name of the shop where he bought the scroll. Then it's off to find the beggar," raising the last bite of food to her mouth as she finished the sentence.

The waiter brought the bill. Chris paid it and thanked him again, "Shukran."

"Tavdi," the small waiter said and wagged a scolding finger back and forth before his eyes. "No Shukran,"

"He's giving us a lesson," she advised. "We've learned our first word in Aramaic."

Chris left a tip but the waiter waved a hand over it, the gesture meaning it was included.

They walked back to the convent. The air was turning cooler it seemed and the stars above burning brighter as though in competition with the city lights. They rang the bell. It was eleven o'clock. Anina hurried down the stairs and let them in and said she would see them in the morning at breakfast, eight o'clock.

On the balcony, he pointed at the flood-lit cliffs towering over them. "You see how many caves there are? And those are just the ones we can see at night. Our return flight is in four days. No way we'll see them all in four days."

"That is not the idea, dear Chris." She reached over and touched his wrist, an intentional gesture. "We are looking for only one beggar, one cave."

CHAPTER EIGHTEEN

Damascus, 70 A.D.

Eliezar turned and looked at them. "He is old," he said and knocked again and this time called out, "Judas! Judas!"

Finally, the door creaked. A small wizened face peered through a slight opening. A weak, hoarse voice said, "Who is there?"

"I am Eliezar the Tanner, a member of the ecclesia and—"

"Yes, I know you. What do you want?" the voice on the other side of the door said impatiently as if he could not stand much longer and hold the door.

"Followers of Christ have arrived from a long journey and wish to see you," Eliezar said loudly. "One traveled with Paul the Apostle and the lady," he pointed behind him at Miriam "is the daughter of Peter the Apostle."

The door flew wide open. Beyond its threshold stood a stooped, white-haired man of ancient days, his glaucous eyes wide and blinking. He managed to shuffle closer until he stood in the doorway, an arm leaning on its jamb, the hand hanging limply motioning. "Come closer … come closer."

"Stay, sir!" John Mark entreated. "We will come to you."

John Mark and Miriam stepped forward and stood in front of the old man, almost touching him. He placed a hand on his boney shoulder, and Miriam held the hand at his side. His entire body trembled.

Judas looked up at John Mark. "You … you are the apostle?"

"I am an apostle, dear sir. I am John Mark. At times I was with Jesus and his twelve disciples. I traveled with Paul the Apostle."

He looked down at Miriam. "You are Paul's daughter. I did not know he had a daughter."

"No, sir. I am Miriam the daughter of Peter, the disciple of Jesus."

He breathed deeply. "Oh, my God. Oh, my God," was all he could say between gasps of breath. Before they could catch him, he collapsed onto the threshold. He was still trying to speak. "The daughter of Peter ... Peter ... here ... in my house." He began wiping her feet with the hem of his tunic.

John Mark and Miriam reached down, placed their hands beneath his arms, and lifted him.

"Paul the Apostle lived in your house," Miriam said. "I am but a visitor."

The old man looked back and forth at them in seeming confusion then said, "Who's the man behind you?"

"I am Eliezar."

"Oh, yes. Eliezar, of course. Please come in," he motioned limply with his hand.

They followed his slow shuffling gait into a large room. As they entered, immediately to the right steps led to an upper room and the roof. There was a long cushioned bench across the far wall, a couple of wooden armed chairs and stool and before them a small square table which held an odd collection of painted pottery and earthenware, and another taller table in a far corner with a bowl of fruit. Cushions were thrown up against a vacant corner hearth, one probably used only to provide warmth in the colder months. Beside the hearth was a clay oven that appeared unused and next to it a large decorated urn, similar to those in Israel used to transport water. A few rugs were scattered around the stone floor. One oil lamp burned on a thin mantel above the hearth and another on the shelf of a small back window that was open, occasional breezes stirring the flame. Also on the mantel was a candelabra and hanging above it from a silver chain was a large silver medallion. A doorway at the back by the bench probably opened onto an unroofed courtyard or atrium. A quick scan of the place would suggest its owner was well-to-do and had, at one time, prospered.

"Please sit," he said, as he lowered himself, with Miriam's assistance, into one of the cushioned chairs.

She sat in the chair beside him. John Mark sat on the hearth near them. Eliezar remained standing.

Judas looked at Miriam, his eyes, his face, still filled with disbelief. "You are the daughter of Peter, the Apostle."

She nodded.

The old man raised his eyes slowly to the ceiling and folded his hands. He mumbled something in a low unintelligible voice then looked at her again. "Where is your father?"

"He is dead. He was crucified in Rome."

Slowly, he swung his eyes on John Mark in front of the hearth. "And Paul, you traveled with him. Where is he?"

"He is dead, too, sir," John Mark responded. "He died in Rome, in prison."

Judas lowered his head. "Rome ... Rome," he whispered. "Everyone goes to Rome. Why not Damascus?"

As if no one had an answer, silence filled the room. The oil flame fluttered in the window and street noise filtered through two small windows beside the closed front door.

Miriam placed a hand on Judas' arm, looked at him and smiled. "We have come to Damascus, sir."

Faint but distinct, the first smile creased his wrinkled face. "You have, indeed. But for what purpose?"

"To spread the life and word of Jesus Christ," John Mark said. He did not want to mention another reason, to escape the revolt in his country. As his mother had reminded him, it was in Damascus that only a few years earlier gentiles had murdered Jews.

The old man thought a moment. "His word has come here. It was here before Paul," he said, his thoughts and memory connecting better on things of old rather than recent. "Paul came." He pointed a finger at Eliezar who nodded. "He spread Christ's teachings further."

They all nodded. No one disagreed.

"So ..." his head bobbed as if waiting for the words to fall into place, "Christ's word is preached in Damascus. Does the city need more preachers?" His head quit bobbing and he looked at his listeners for a response, first at John Mark, then Miriam who looked at John Mark.

John Mark spoke. "With all respects, sir, the spoken words are a testament to your great city and its champion of our faith."

From the elderly one, another smile.

"But as our faith at one time had to be preserved in writing in *The Scriptures*," John Mark continued, "the time has come for the new faith to be committed to writing."

"Show him your scroll," Miriam said, her impatient tone suggesting action rather than words.

Since the theft incident, he had switched the strap to his back so the bag hung across his chest. He opened it, retrieved the large scroll and laid it on the table beside the pottery, carefully moving pieces aside to make room. "This is the gospel of Jesus Christ," he said and patted it for emphasis.

The old man leaned over for a closer look, touched the scroll, ran a marbled hand up and down its length then looked at Miriam. "Read to me."

She untied the scroll, rewound it to the beginning, and began reading. Eliezar moved closer and sat on the stool. The old man's head was down, as if in prayer, but he was listening, his finger tapping on the arm of the chair to the cadence of her voice. A trapezoid of light had drifted up from the floor, framing her as she read. She read a long time, and the light moved on, leaving her in shadow. Except for the first few phrases, words she herself had not previously seen or read, the tone of her voice was reflective of that wonder and discovery. She had finished the story of Jesus healing a man with leprosy and began the section that read, "See that you do not tell this to anyone, but go and show yourself to the priest," down to, "Yet the people came to him from everywhere."

Judas raised his hand.

"Yes?" she asked.

He took a deep breath as if preparing to say something of great length, then lifted his eyes, and said, "Hallelujah!" His eyes grew misty. "Amen ... amen," and he wiped away a tear.

John Mark looked over at Eliezar, at the tears falling from his eyes and pooling on the floor, and great emotion filled him. He had experienced a power when writing, felt an emotion, heavier at times than others, but this was the first time he had observed someone hearing the words he had written. More than ever, he felt an urgency to complete the work and begin its publishing process. But there were necessary steps. The first was finding a place to stay.

"Should I continue?" Miriam petitioned.

"Yes, but later," Judas said, his voice weak. "The evening is growing, and I am tiring. Tomorrow, please, tomorrow where you stopped."

She had nothing to mark the place and the scroll needed to be rolled up. Sensing her dilemma, Eliezar pulled a knife from his apron pouch, sliced a strip of cloth from the sleeve of his mantel, and handed it to her. She laid the thin strip of cloth on the papyrus leaf and began rolling the scroll.

Eliezar also sensed something else. "You have just arrived. Where will you stay in Damascus?"

"We have no place," John Mark replied.

The old man's mind seemed in another world, perhaps still savoring all he had heard, but his head snapped upward at John Mark's comment. "My home is your home. You must stay here."

"But you have space for one person," Miriam said scanning the room.

"Do you so easily forget," Judas said, the tone gently admonishing, "that Paul stayed here. If you can climb those," he pointed to the stairs they passed when they entered, "there are two rooms upstairs." He gestured toward the back door, "and an atrium in the rear of the house with a guesthouse. I can no longer climb the stairs, and I use the guesthouse when the weather is warmer. When it turns cool, I light a fire with one of the lamps and sleep in this room on the bench."

"We would not want to be in your way," said Miriam.

"You would be a welcome addition," he assured them. "As you can see, I am old and growing older. Some of the women in our ecclesia tend to me, bring me food, and once a month clean the house. I am not asking you to do these things, but there would be ways of paying for your stay."

"I fear that would not be enough," said John Mark.

Judas waved a flippant hand. "Nonsense. It is more than enough. Paul, if he were here, would have something to say about grace and charity and possibly even scold you." He smiled again.

"Very well," John Mark agreed. "Miriam and I accept your kind hospitality."

"Your name is Miriam," Judas said, looking directly at her.

"Yes. I was named for the sister of Moses and Aaron, but I am not obstinate or rebellious as the meaning suggests."

"I believe you," the elderly Judas said then grinned, "but one would think the daughter of Peter might possess some obstinacy."

Everyone in the room laughed.

"Now that my new friends have a place to stay," inserted Eliezar, "I must leave. I fear my wife is concerned about me. She would delight in having two guests for dinner."

"Many thanks, Eliezar," John Mark expressed. "We are indebted to you. We saw places to eat nearby."

"Eliezar, John Mark means we accept your gracious gestures," Miriam clarified, "but we would not impose on your wife at this hour. We will dine with you another time."

"I will come tomorrow," Eliezar said. He gave Judas a farewell bow and departed.

Judas pushed himself up from the chair, lifted the oil lamp from the mantel, and motioned his two new guests to follow him. He showed them the courtyard and guest house. Beyond the back wall, they heard carts clattering over a cobblestone street and voices.

"Another street," their new host said. "Damascus has many streets. Only one called Straight." He directed them back to the stairs, handed them the lamp, and instructed them to view their rooms.

· · ·

"Are they adequate?" Judas asked, after John Mark and Miriam descended the stairs.

"They are more than adequate, kind sir," Miriam stated. "There is a table in one and light through the windows, both adequate for writing."

"Writing?" Judas asked.

"Yes, sir," John Mark answered. "The words Miriam read to you from the master scroll must be copied. Other scrolls must be created and sent to other ecclesias, to Antioch, Ephesus, Jerusalem, Alexander, and eventually to Rome." He paused to interpret Miriam's look. "But, of course, the first will go to your church here in Damascus."

"You were moved with the words I read to you," Miriam reminded him, "yet you seem unsure, questioning."

"What you read *was* moving," Judas emphasized. "Perhaps I wonder why you write when the end is near."

"But no one knows this," said John Mark. "Jesus himself was absolute on this issue. Tomorrow or the next day, when Miriam reads, you will hear his words: 'No one knows about that day or hour, not even the angels in heaven, not the Son, but only the Father.'"

"He said this?" Judas questioned, his tone skeptical. He placed a hand to prop himself against the stairs where they still stood.

"Yes," John Mark responded.

"Paul spoke different words," Judas said. "He said it was soon. Did you hear this on your own or did someone else tell you?"

John Mark looked at Miriam. "Her father, Peter. He could not write, but his mind was keen, his ability to recall words near perfect."

"My father also had the benefit of repetition," she added. "Jesus spoke certain words not once, but often, and to different audiences but almost always in the presence of his disciples."

"It is unfortunate I never met your father," the elderly one said. "And Paul had not met him when he was here. That meeting came later. I do not doubt what you tell me and look forward to hearing more." He pushed himself away from the stairway. "But I must, must recline. I have nothing at the moment for you to eat, just some pomegranates in a bowl on the table. But, as you observed, there are venders still in the street outside."

"Before you go, sir, there is one thing we must tell you," Miriam said, looking sheepishly at John Mark.

"Yes? Is it important?"

"Indeed," John Mark agreed. "Miriam and I are not married. We are good friends on a mission."

"You are kind and trusting to tell me, but it was unnecessary. When you reach my age, these things do not matter," he said and smiled.

"Sir, we are but a few years behind you," Miriam said and returned the smile.

CHAPTER NINETEEN

Maaloula, October 31, 2011

Chris couldn't sleep. He'd always had trouble the first two nights after traveling long distances. He put on his robe and walked onto the balcony. Kate's light was on, so she must be experiencing the same. The village had a pleasant, fresh early morning smell. The dry cool air and clear sky made him feel like he was back in Arizona. Backlit by the first blush of dawn, the eastern foothills of the Anti-Lebanon Mountains resembled something cut and pasted on the horizon. In the bright cold dawn, the entire scene looked like a picture book; the town below tucked between the hovering spot-lighted cliffs, the glowing crosses and domes, the Virgin Mary perched high above. He glanced at his watch: five-thirty. A few cars moved along the clean streets below.

From his vantage point Chris had a panoramic view of the entire village, population two-thousand, spreading out from the mountain and outcrop of rocks, an innocent town that would soon be sucked into revolution and counter-revolution. He thought of small towns in Arizona. Everyone knew everyone, including the beggars and street people who, by their dress and oddities of behavior, stood out. They shouldn't have trouble locating one beggar in this small place, if he was still there. He couldn't have gone far. There were two small villages near Maaloula. He could have walked there or collected enough money for bus fare to Damascus. He thought it ironic. A beggar might help them find the Gospel of Mark and one purpose of the book was to lead people to help beggars.

The sun came blasting over the eastern rim of hills, its bright orange rays striking gold into the limestone cliffs, revealing dark pock marks, the caves, hundreds of them. If they couldn't locate the beggar, they had to go into the caves, one by one. Chris caught himself rushing to judgment and slapped the side of his head just as Kate emerged from her room.

"Mosquito?" she asked. She was wearing a pink gown and no makeup, her hair clamped back so it fell loosely around her shoulders. He'd known very few women who looked good without makeup. She looked better. The sunlight striking her face added a natural color to her cheeks and lips.

"Just trying to knock out some stinking thinking."

"The way you smacked it, you succeeded," she grinned.

"I started thinking, out there somewhere is Mark's autograph. I might even be looking at the spot, yet it seems so far away if we can't find the beggar."

She touched his arm again, as she had the evening before, "You're not alone. I couldn't sleep thinking about it."

"And we have to waste the morning with tours."

"It may not be wasted," she said. "Part of the Saint Takla tour goes through the canyon behind the convent. We'll get a close up of some of the caves."

• • •

Along with other nuns and priests, they met for breakfast in a large dining room. Kate was wearing a black burka which looked odd on her, and dressed very simply in dark slacks with minimal makeup and no jewelry. Chris noted she wore flats, no heels. Anina introduced them to the group and then said a blessing. After a vegetable omelet with fruits and pomegranate juice, their tour of the convent began, conducted by Anina instead of the Mother Superior who was not feeling well.

"Here we are in the Chapel of Saint Takla," Anina began her lecture as they entered a large spacious room adorned by icons and an ornate altar. "Saint Takla was the daughter of a Seleucid prince and disciple of Saint Paul. She was pursued by soldiers sent by her father to kill her because of her Christian faith." Anina was articulate and poised, making appropriate gestures as she spoke. "Trapped against these sheer cliffs, she prayed to God for help, and God answered her prayer. A narrow cleft opened in the rock face allowing her to escape to a small cave high above in the cliffs." She turned and pointed at the shrine higher up against the rock. "Locally, she is recognized as the first Christian martyr though others say she lived to old age in the cave where she died. The cleft is how Maaloula gets its name. In Aramaic, it means, 'entrance.'"

After visiting the small shrine on the face of the cliff, they descended to the parking lot where, to the left of the convent, a path led up through a narrow defile, the rock on either side pressing in, almost tunneling in places. Along the length of the siq, numerous shrines and caves had been dug into the rock. The defile brought them out at the top of the cliffs and to a restaurant with a pleasant garden terrace set among poplar trees where they sat and rested.

"Anina, do people live in these caves?" Kate asked.

"Yes, in some they do. But there are many where no people live."

"Why is that?" Chris followed up.

"Getting to them is difficult. The only people who go to them are people who hide from something or someone. They, how do you say in English, break laws."

"Criminals," Kate said.

"Yes, criminals," Anina responded. "Some people say many treasures are hidden in the caves."

"Have any been found?" Chris probed.

"I do not know," Anina said. "There are Christian symbols on the walls of some caves. Early Christians came here to hide from persecution. They came from Damascus, some as far away as Caesarea Philippi. Perhaps they brought their valuables with them and left them or died with them. Only God knows. By now, I think they would be gone. Many people explore the caves."

Chris thought of the eras, the generations—Romans, Persians, Arabs, Crusaders—picking their way through these caves like scavengers do a shipwreck. It was a miracle anything was left.

"Beggars from Maaloula live there," Kate commented.

"Some do," Anina agreed.

"Do you have many?" Chris asked.

"In Damascus, they are not allowed," Anina said. "The police stop them. But tourists come to Maaloula, so we have a few. You see them in front of the tourist sites, the mosques and churches. You must be careful. Some have been known to attack tourists, especially Americans," she said as she looked at Chris.

"Now it is time for me to show you the city," she said arising.

Kate glanced at Chris, their eyes telegraphing the same message.

"Anina, you have been most helpful," Kate said, laying a hand on their guide's shoulder. "But we would like to explore the city on our own."

"Oh?"

"Yes," said Chris. "It has to do with getting to know your city firsthand. Then, if we have questions, we can return to you for help."

Anina politely assented and bowed. They followed her down the steps, back through the canyon to the parking lot where they thanked her again and she bowed again.

"Anything in particular you look for?" Anina asked.

"Our friend, who was here earlier this year, Doctor Stewart ..." Kate began.

"Yes. I remember him. Very nice man."

"He mentioned an antique shop in Maaloula," Kate finished. "I am fond of antiques."

"Maaloula has several shops of antiques," Anina replied. "There is one down this street and others nearby. You should have no trouble. Remember, dinner is served at six o'clock."

"We may not return in time," Kate said.

"For only two people, that is no problem," and she departed toward the convent gate.

CHAPTER TWENTY

Damascus, 70 A.D.

The next morning John Mark and Miriam arose early as the sun was breaking and ate some pomegranates and additional fruits they had purchased in the street the night before. Their host had not yet appeared, still asleep they presumed in the guest house. They would not awaken him and left quietly. There was much to accomplish.

Eliezar was to show them "his" city, but the shops were not yet open so they explored it on their own. They continued on Straight Street toward the rising sun, John Mark looking for a shop that might sell writing materials but saw none. He had purchased two packages of papyrus and a jar of ink at Caesarea Philippi, but he needed more. At the *Cardus Maximus*, the major thoroughfare perpendicular to Straight Street, they turned north. The street, like the Decumanus, appeared to be joined at right angles by streets that probably led to various gates. In silence, they walked a long way, taking in the width and breadth of the city, its many faces and voices, as people began to stream from their homes into the street. They eventually came to the north gate and Abana River bounding the northern side of the city and beyond the river, the bare hills of the desert where everything shifted, nothing was permanent, nothing was celebrated but water, nothing was revered but God.

They took a different route back to Straight Street and Eliezar's shop. The streets were not wide and straight and bathed in sunlight but narrow and tortuous and filled with deep shadows. The houses looked like those in Jerusalem and Capernaum, flat roofs and clustered around courtyards. Most were nice, indicating success of the families inhabiting them. Damascus was obviously a prosperous city.

"To know a city, one must lose himself in it," John Mark said.

"I do not desire to be lost, I have just been found." She looked up at him and smiled. "My life has meaning. I am doing something worthwhile with it."

"I understand, but you chose to go with me. You risked in order to find yourself. That is faith."

"And you risked coming to Damascus to flee the revolt," she declared.

"And we are risking now," he said, laughing softly.

"We are risking more than one thing."

He returned her smile. "I do not feel I have recently met you. I do not feel I am learning to know you. I feel I have known you all of my life."

She reached and held his hand. "And I feel the same. This is a good thing. We do not have to lose ourselves in each other."

Blood rushed to his face, and he suddenly felt hot all over.

She squeezed gently on his hand. "We are found."

He looked at her. "Therefore, if you would have me, I would like to marry you."

"We are already married, privately, in the eyes of God."

"Yes, but I want to be married to you as Christ is married to his church."

"Then, in its time, it will happen," she said.

"May I put my arm around you?"

"If you wish, but I have your hand. That is enough." The words came from her on a sound that was not of this world, and her voice carried their truth, one where pity, compassion and truth were blended. Goodness and truth shone from her as from a true saint of the faith. He did not know how to respond so he gently returned her squeeze, and they continued on.

Eliezar's shop was open, and he was glad to see them. Yes, he said, writing supplies were sold in several places but the nearest *chartarii* was on the Decumanus, about five hundred meters beyond the Cordus Maximus. "It is on the left, on this side. The man's name is Ezra. I know him. He is a friend and a Jewish follower of Christ. We worship together."

"His name is most fitting," commented Miriam.

"You mean Ezra, the Scribe of *The Scriptures*?" asked Eliezar.

"There is no other," she said.

"Tell him Eliezar sent you."

"We must speak more of scribes," John Mark said. "I am a scribe. In Tyre, that was my trade. I would be very indebted to you," he looked at Miriam, "I mean, I would be most grateful if you could make others aware of my craft and skills. My hand is sure and steady, my work solid, without error. I have samples."

"There are a number of scribes in the city, but none I think on the Decumanus," Eliezar assessed. "I will happily tell others of you, that they can find you at the house of Judas. Everyone knows Judas. His house is well located, mid-way on the Straight Street."

They turned to leave and Eliezar called them back. "Do not forget, tomorrow night, my house," he reminded them and pointed upward again.

They had no trouble finding the papyrus vendor in the market who also sold inks and pens. He was lean and middle-aged with thinning hair and a thin scraggly beard where food from his morning meal was lodged. The vendor immediately tried to interest John Mark in a codex, a stack of papyrus pages sewn together on one edge, but he told the vendor he was an old-fashioned Jew and preferred the scroll.

Miriam pulled at his sleeve. "But this codex is more practical and economical," she argued. "You can write on both sides and flip back and forth quickly rather than tediously unrolling and rolling," she said, demonstrating with her hands.

The vendor was grinning, his head pumping up and down, some of the food scraps flying from his beard.

"But the codex costs more," said John Mark. He stayed with the scroll and bought two *chartes*, forty sheets of papyrus, about twenty-four feet which he told the vender he estimated he would need for one book.

"But we are writing more than one manuscript," Miriam stressed. "You bought two *chartes* in Caesarea Philippi. This makes enough for two scrolls. I will copy one, you will use my one to copy another and so on."

John Mark made a frustrated nod and flashed two fingers to the vendor. "We will return for more, I am sure. We have much to write."

"You have much to write, you need many pens and much ink," the vendor beamed, rocking back cockily on his heels. "Here is some fine red ink of ochre, gelatin, gum and bee wax."

"No red ink," John Mark stated. "Black only."

"Very well," the man said. He reached across his setup table and lifted a small vial. "This is from Egypt, made with iron-salts, nutgalls and gums."

"You have none made with lamp black and gum Arabic?" John Mark inquired.

"Yes, but it is not protected from water or moisture."

"I prefer the lamp black and gum Arabic to erase mistakes more easily," he said. "Give me two vials for now and ten reed pens," and he pointed at the bamboo stem types.

"You are writing much," the vendor said, obviously impressed. He gathered the purchases, bundled the scrolls of papyrus with a string and wrapped the ink and pens in cloth. With the ink and cloth, he included two smoothened oak sticks for rolling the papyrus and a small container of glue for attaching one roll to another. He handed John Mark the package and said, "Eight dinars."

John Mark did not have eight dinars, mostly drachma. He offered him ten drachma, near the exchange rate, and the vendor was happy.

They returned to Judas' house and found him up and dressed and seated on a bench in the courtyard.

The elderly man pushed himself up when they walked through the domicile's backdoor. "I was hopeful you had not departed, at least not without a farewell," he said smiling.

"We went to buy writing materials," John Mark informed him, showing him the bundle.

"You have a large package," Judas observed. "You will be writing more than one scroll."

"Yes," John Mark said. "Many. We may be here a long time."

"That is good news," Judas said and sat down. "You can bury me."

"That is not good news," Miriam said and frowned. "I returned to read more to you. It is bright and pleasant in the courtyard. I will return shortly."

"I have work to do," John Mark said apologetically. "Do you have another table, like the one in the bedroom upstairs?"

"There is one in the large room," and Judas pointed inside.

"The shorter one is actually better," John Mark said. "I can write as I sit. Often, I write seated with the scroll balanced in my lap."

Miriam returned with the scroll and seated herself on the bench beside Judas, beneath an acacia tree which grew behind them. She unrolled it to the place marked by the strand of cloth and began reading. While she read, John Mark climbed the stairs and began arranging and storing their writing tools, placing the table before the window for good morning light. A small corner cabinet was perfect for storing the papyrus, pens and other items.

• • •

That evening, all three attended the fellowship, the *agape* meal held at Eliezar's.

The meeting took place in a large second story room over Eliezar's shop and adjacent small living quarters. They were introduced to Eliezar's wife, a short, plump woman of excessive apologies that there was not enough room for everyone to sit. She quickly found a chair for Judas. She was constantly moving back and forth from the room to another in the living quarters, presumably the kitchen. A U-shaped table was set with inexpensive plates, goblets and utensils. Several men, elders, were in charge of the service. Eliezar was one of them and he presided at the service. He introduced his guests. Everyone knew Judas and welcomed him back after an absence. Food was brought to the table by Eliezar's wife and her helpers. A prayer was said by Eliezar and everyone sat except those standing who had plates brought to them by servants.

The atmosphere surrounding the meal was convivial and joyous. Christ and his presence were mentioned often. John Mark found it interesting that the emphasis was on the joy of Christ's resurrection and his presence, not the elements, the bread and wine, which were brought later by Eliezar's wife and placed before her husband. In his initial prayer, Eliezar had said, "Lord, come eat with us." The theme was that of joyful communion with Christ's presence, not his death. John Mark had read one of Paul's letters to the church in Corinth where the emphasis was upon the death of Jesus, not his resurrection.

The ritual following the meal, after the initiates had been dismissed, was simple. Only the baptized were allowed to stay, which included John Mark and Miriam, something they had not experienced in other agape meals. A text from "The Prophets" of *The Scriptures* was read followed by a short homily. Everyone stood for a solemn prayer that concluded with a kiss of peace to each other. Eliezar gave thanks over the bread that was presented, broke it and each person partook. Wine was poured by the deacons in each cup. No words were spoken. Following the service, members of the fellowship took the left over pieces of bread to those who were sick and in prison. John Mark and Miriam were deeply touched by the service and the distribution of food afterward.

On the way back to the house of Judas, John Mark recalled, "This was unlike other communion services I have attended. Most follow a procedure set up by Paul in one of his letters, to the church in Corinth, I believe. There were words of institution, 'This is my body,' and 'This is my blood.' The emphasis was upon the crucifixion."

"This was about his resurrection, his living presence," Miriam mentioned. "It reminded me of my father's belief."

They were supporting Judas who ambled between them. He was quiet, as if he had not heard them, but after a while spoke: "I am familiar with both. Both have meaning. But the earliest agape meal, and believe me," he looked at one then the other, "the early ones celebrated Christ's resurrection and his appearances with disciples when they were supping."

No more was said as they continued back to their domicile on the street called Straight.

CHAPTER TWENTY-ONE

Maaloula, October 31, 2011

"According to these directions the professor provided," Kate said, pointing at the sheet of paper, "the shop is actually just where Anina said, near the convent about three blocks down."

They walked the short distance, their eyes vigilant for beggars.

They entered the shop, which by its clutter of old and dusty items was definitely an antique store. The owner was busy with a customer so they pretended to look around. To the right of the entrance were shelves of old books. On the floor, at the far end of the shelving, sat a jar, possibly *the* jar. Chris nudged Kate and pointed it out to her. They kept looking.

The shopkeeper was eyeing them over the top of his glasses while assisting his customer and spoke to them in English. "You look for anything special?"

"Just looking," Chris said. "We heard you had old books."

"Yes, they are there," and he pointed at the shelving of books they had seen and returned his attention to his customer. The customer paid him and left, and the shopkeeper directed his full attention to his two new customers. He was tall and stubbly jowled with keen sunken eyes and a thin mouth. On his head, anchored with a single black rope band, he wore a *khafia*, the traditional Arabic headdress with its distinctive red and white check pattern.

"So, you are American?"

"I am," Chris replied. "She is British."

"Scottish!" she frowned, lowered her eyes and corrected him.

The shopkeeper smiled. "Regardless, both of you are interested in old books. Please take your time and look."

"What about the jar on the floor," Kate said. "Is it for sale?"

"Yes, of course. Everything is for sale."

"Is it old?" Chris asked. "Does it have a history?"

"Yes, it is very old," the shopkeeper said and launched into the story they had heard from the professor about the drunk and the manuscript inside and how he sold it to someone, "actually, he was Scottish, an old man."

"We are interested in the jar," Kate said keenly. "We collect old jars."

"And this one, because of its design, is of particular interest," said Chris. "This person who brought the jar to you with the manuscript, does he have other jars similar to this one?"

The shopkeeper perused the jar, walked over, and moved his fingers around the lip. "I do not know the answer to this question. I have not seen him again in my shop."

"In your shop," Kate said, "but perhaps somewhere else. If he is a beggar, as you described him, maybe you see him other places in the city. Maaloula is small."

"Yes. He is a local beggar who lives in one of the caves. Often he is on the streets, more in summer months when the tourists are here."

"Do you know his name?" Chris asked.

"No." He stroked his chin then raised a finger. "But I tell you, I will try and find this beggar and, if he has more jars, I will get them for you."

"Do you know the location of his cave?" Chris pried further.

"There are hundreds," he said making a wide sweep of his hand as if they were merchandize in his shop.

"We appreciate your effort," Kate said gratefully. "You are most generous ... your name?"

"Walid, madam. Walid."

"Thank you, Walid," she said. "If you find this beggar, we would be most interested in buying his jars ... all of them."

"And we will pay you a fair price," Chris added. "Can you provide a description of this beggar? Perhaps we might see him and inquire ourselves of his jars."

The shopkeeper seemed reluctant, tapping a finger on his lower lip. "I can tell you this. He is small and stooped. He wears a tattered robe, gray in color. His right hand is crooked. He begs *bakshish* with his left hand. He has a high voice, like a small child."

"We are most grateful," Kate said, bowing slightly

"When I close my shop today, I look ... for you and for me," he said without conviction and grinned broadly.

"Thank you, Walid," Chris said. "We'll come back tomorrow and check on the jars."

After they had left the shop and walked further down the street Chris turned to Kate. "That's one way to skin a cat."

"We may be the cat," she said ironically. "We told him too much. I shouldn't have said 'all of them' and you shouldn't have said 'fair price.' Now he thinks they're valuable, and we're cash cows."

"That could be good. Greed is a motivator."

"Yes, but it would behoove us to find the beggar before he does," she said, making quick strides down the pavement. "He was not going to look for him until he closed his shop. So, we have the afternoon. We should be able to find one beggar among two thousand people."

"One with a crooked right hand," he remarked, "probably one that was broken and never set."

"And a ragged gray robe, which doesn't tell us much. Most I've seen on men were gray and ragged."

They had developed a sense of the town. There were two main streets that converged in the center at a roundabout where there was a church then split in oblique directions toward the cliffs. Streets veering from them ran irregular circuitous routes. Statues of Christ and the Virgin on the mountain served as reference points in the small jungle of houses and shops that erratically climbed the cliffs.

They came to the roundabout and stood in front of the church that faced the way they had entered the city.

"Which way should we go?" she questioned.

"We could split up. You take one side of the city, I'll take the other."

"If our cell phones had service at this elevation, that's a splendid idea," she said. "But mine shows service only higher up the cliffs at the convent."

"Then perhaps we stay together, explore the old city behind us. It's not the high tourist season but there are tourists. Where there are tourists, there are beggars. As we work our way higher, and the phones work, we can split."

"That's a plan," she agreed.

They began walking up a street that veered to the right off the roundabout. Passing nothing of significance, two blocks away they came to a small café. The sign high above the door said Chieser Bakery. Out front were a red plastic table and chairs. The place was unimpressive but one of the few cafes they'd seen. It was a clear bright day. Sunlight bouncing off the cliffs had warmed the air, so they sat outside. The waiter was a large burly man with a servile demeanor. Kate ordered a chocolate croissant and he a small pizza covered with cheese and thyme. Both ordered a Syrian beer.

The mid-day weather was perfect. He'd taken off his sweater and looped it loosely around his neck. The small café, the weather, the beer—they could've been in Paris or Florence or Barcelona, he thought. But they were in one of the most remote places on the planet, and his mind was on a paradox. She appeared prettier in a simple unadorned burka, little makeup, no jewelry, this offspring of Scottish royalty. Trying not to look beautiful, she was more beautiful. The awareness of his thoughts made him slightly nervous. He wondered if she sensed his intense observation of her, that she was growing on him. "I'm having to adjust to your burka," he said.

"I have been in Arab countries before. They are attracted to Western women. This was one trip I did not need to receive attention."

He was about to tell her it didn't matter how she looked, what she wore or didn't wear. In any culture, on any street, at any café, her height and classic look was going to attract attention. Her calmness and poise magnified her beauty, a charisma, he surmised, that realigned a room of people when she entered. The waiter brought their beer and two glasses and Chris turned the conversation in a different direction. "I still wonder how Mark's rough draft, and possibly the autograph, ended up in this place."

"It's a touch of irony," Kate said, pouring the beer into her glass. "We are in Syria in a time of revolution, yet there is no revolution here in this out of the way place." She lifted the glass and eyed him seriously over the top. "We are looking for a hidden document. If we were being persecuted in the first century and had something of great value, I would want to be here. I'll let you connect the dots from there."

"That would have been Domitian, about eighty-five C. E., possibly later. If John Mark was a youth or in his early twenties when Christ was crucified, he would have been in his seventies, possibly eighties. Or dead."

"And his female companion?" she questioned.

"If she was alive in that period, she was younger so she would have been in her late sixties, early seventies," he computed.

"It doesn't matter," she said flipping a hand. "If not dead, they were both very old. They could not have made it here. There has to be another reason this scroll or scrolls made it to this outpost."

"They were old, but old people got around better in those days than today," he said, and took a swallow of beer. "They were tougher. However, it is more likely John Mark entrusted the manuscripts to someone, perhaps one of the leaders in the early church in Damascus."

"Legend has it he's buried in Venice," she said, "his bones beneath the altar of Saint Mark's Cathedral."

"I don't think he ever left Syria," Chris considered, turning his glass in his hand. "Maybe Damascus, possibly as far as Antioch, but no farther. Like Paul, he used runners. There was a strong Christian church in Damascus." He uncrossed his legs and took a sip of beer. "At the time, allegedly, there were more Christians in Damascus than any other major city in the Empire, including Rome. In our twenty-first century arrogance, we forget that the first century literary world in which Christianity emerged was sophisticated and productive. Networking thrived."

She acquiesced with a single nod. Her primary concern was elsewhere. "What if we don't find the beggar?"

"We follow the antique dealer," he enjoined. "He's got a stake in this."

The waiter brought their order.

They were eating quietly, and Chris thought the timing appropriate for the question. "Do you believe in the resurrection?"

She narrowed her eyes and pointed her fork at him. "You don't let up, do you?" she said with long smooth vowels. "You do realize this has nothing to do with our wager."

"I wasn't referring to the bet," he said. "I'd like to know, with all your philosophizing on fear and doubt, what you *really* believe."

"The answer is yes."

"And?"

"Yes!"

"Foul!" he exclaimed.

"I answered your question," she said nonchalantly, spearing a bite of croissant with her fork.

"You know what I mean. Do you believe that Jesus physically rose from the dead or was it some type of spiritual resurrection?"

"I thought I'd already commented on that," she stated flatly.

"You commented on what others had said, but you never said what you actually believe and you're dancing around it now."

"I've always wanted to see the Grand Canyon."

"You told me that; it's in the wager," he said. "What does that have to do with the question? Now you're not dancing; you're dodging."

"I read a story once about a wee lad whose dream was to see the Grand Canyon. So, his mommy made arrangements and took him, flew him from Glasgow to New York, then to Phoenix. They rented a car and drove. When they arrived, the wee lad couldn't wait. He ran on ahead of his mommy. She was running after him. He stopped at the edge, looked back at her, and said, "Mommy, something big happened here."

He sat looking at her waiting for the rest. "So?"

"That's it. I believe the resurrection was something big that my faith accepts. To answer your question again, YES! THE END!"

"Finished?" the waiter said emerging from inside.

"Yes!" she replied. "We are finished."

Chris paid the bill and they continued up the street, passing shops with merchandise arranged outside and homes with clothes drying along porches. All the signs they saw were in two languages.

"We're not going to know Mark's take on the resurrection until we find the autograph," he said.

"We may not even know then," she added.

"What if we're both wrong?"

She grinned. "That's called a compromise."

He motioned her to stop at a street vendor selling fresh pomegranate juice. He bought a cup and handed it to her. "Peace."

"Peace," she responded and smiled, accepting the token gesture.

Their eyes met. There was something different in the way she looked at him, an expression he'd not seen before, a softness about her. Something was missing, gone, something he'd clearly detected before. The wall. Her next move reconfirmed. Or did it? Perhaps it was a gesture of habit, one from another time, another person. Perhaps she did it when she felt comfortable with someone, male or female, as she casually looped her hand through his arm. Perhaps it was genuine and she was farther along in their relationship than he. He'd begun to feel some attraction to her but thought it situational, two people in a foreign and hostile country, only each other to look to. Time, distance and circumstance can make strange bedfellows. He remembered once running into an old adversary in a hotel bar in Quito, Ecuador. You'd have thought they were best friends when they saw each other, hail fellow, well met and all that. Unsure the reason of her gesture, he was glad to feel her closer.

Her hand through the crook of his arm, they continued working their way up the street. They reached the top at the Monastery of St. Sergius and had not been approached by or seen a beggar. They walked in front of the hotel next door, the Maaloula Safir Hotel. If one were going to stay in a hotel in Maaloula, this would be the place. Near the very front, two beggars accosted them but neither resembled their man. They continued higher, checked out a few caves. All were inhabited. Most of the people were friendly. One lady offered to make them tea. One man was hostile. They saw no one, male or female, with a crooked right hand or heard anyone who spoke in a high voice.

"At least we got our feet wet," he discerned as they made their way back down the mountain.

Late afternoon shadows moved across the city, stretched across the shops and houses to the green irrigated plots they had seen when they first entered. They came to the small café by the kiosk where they had eaten the previous evening. Standing by the door was the same server. Waving his arm for them to enter, he welcomed them with exaggerated fanfare.

"I think I'd rather sit out," she said.

Chris agreed.

The waiter acknowledged and pulled the flimsy plastic chairs out for them.

"Tavdi," Chris said.

The waiter smiled and gave him a thumbs up.

"You're a quick study," she complimented.

"On some things," he replied.

They ordered Coca Colas the waiter quickly brought and began reviewing the small, plastic menu.

The suspiring sound came from behind them. At first inaudible, it came again, like a smothered whisper, "Bakshish!" They turned and saw the graveled teeth and pitiful face of a beggar. Their eyes moved down to the outstretched hand, the dirty curled fingers, and the right hand crooked and tucked against his side.

CHAPTER TWENTY-TWO

Damascus, Spring, 90 A.D.

It was an early spring morning, a slight chill in the air. John Mark sat on the bench beneath the acacia tree. Beside the bench bloomed clusters of yellow and blue flowers. A splinter of moon hung low in the eastern sky, and birds were chirping around him. Miriam was inside stirring around. The door was open, and he could hear her clattering about in the kitchen, cleaning up after breakfast. When she finished, she would join him for their morning devotion. In his lap was a new book he had acquired. His vision had gone, but hers was still sharp as an eagle's, and she would read to him. Then they would have to pack their belongings, place them in a cart, along with an ass he had purchased, and leave the only home they had known their twenty years in Damascus on the street called Straight. He thought of all that had happened in that time.

Thanks to the grace of God, they were still alive, in advanced years, and enduring. Thanks also to Judas, they had a home. Nights, moonlight slid across the ceiling lulling them to sleep, and days, sunlight did the same awakening them. Early on, they had set up places to write and fallen into a comfortable routine. Arising at daybreak, they had copied; he upstairs in one of the rooms facing east and she downstairs beneath him near the back window, outside in the courtyard on warm days where the sun would dry the ink faster. Both had kept a rag with a string tied to their waist to erase mistakes. The ends of their fingers had become discolored from spitting on them to aid in making the erasures. They had written until their hands cramped and had spent time rubbing each other's so feeling would return to them. After a day of writing and their evening meal, she had sat in the patio looking up at the stars and he on the balcony looking down at her. Then they would find each other, she usually the one who found him. At night, he would check on her sleeping body, her mind probably miles away in Capernaum on the shore, a landscape painted by the moon.

He had decided on the ending for the gospel. If his count was accurate, they had copied and distributed thirty scrolls. He personally had delivered books to congregations in Caesarea Philippi, Antioch and Jerusalem, meeting the scribes in each place who would, in turn, make copies and pass them on. He had learned that some were no longer using the scroll but had switched to the codex he had earlier rejected. Paul had made that format more popular with his letters. Many had wanted to change because the scroll was so identified with Judaism. They desired a new literary form for their new faith. Nonetheless, they had been happy to get his scrolls and the gospel of Christ.

Jerusalem had been his last visit on his wide swing back through Tyre where he had visited old friends and had met new Christians. Rhoda had met him at the gate and, with great emotion, delivered the sad news. His mother had died. She had harbored hopes he would return and take over the house but instead she had given it to Rhoda. He had held Rhoda and they wept. He had spent the night and told all that had happened and Rhoda had encapsulated the movement of the church there, that despite squabbles, it was strong and gaining members. Cleopas, a brother of the Lord, had become the second leader after the one before him, Jacob, another brother of Jesus, died, crushed by a whiffletree. The gospel John Mark had brought would be welcome. All they had were *The Scriptures* and some letters from the Apostle Paul. There were other writings from some called Gnostics, but they were not considered reliable and did not present Christ as human.

Over the twenty years, the church at Damascus had also grown. There were more Christians in Damascus than anywhere in the Empire, many of them women. He and Miriam had watched it grow from an organization similar to the ecclesia in Jerusalem, governed by a council of presbyters, to one led by a single presbyter or *episcope* with presbyters and deacons beneath him. John Mark had seen this structure in Antioch, perhaps the first Christian community to implement it. There, Paul had ordained presbyters and episcopes to exercise general oversight of the congregation but one was in charge. Paul had done the same in Damascus, authorizing Ananias to ordain presbyters and episcopes. The current episcope had adopted the title "patriarch." John Mark had heard from others on his last journey to distribute the gospel, that Rome had followed suit. As the church grew, breaking into more congregations, the episcope or patriarch had appointed a presbyter to pastor the flock in each congregation. The organization of the ecclesia based upon the Jewish synagogue had all but faded. Nowhere was this more evident than in their own lives. Not long after they had arrived, he and Miriam had wed, not by a rabbi, but by a presbyter within the new faith of followers of Christ.

The success of the new Christian faith was the reason they were having to join a small caravan of Christians and leave the city at midnight. Domitian, the emperor, son of Vespasian, the same who destroyed Jerusalem, had set himself up as a reformer of morals and religion and deified himself, assuming the title of "Lord and God." In Judea, Domitian had stepped up the policy introduced by his father of persecuting Jews claiming descent from their ancient king David, and the oppression had spread to Damascus. The persecution had also involved the destruction of their libraries, their books and scrolls. People loyal to the Empire had reported to the authorities the identities of Jews and Christians who were disloyal to the Emperor and had refused to worship him. Only days before, John Mark had received reliable word that his and Miriam's names had been reported.

The small group had been sworn to secrecy regarding their destination. Many, however, had known of it, word passing down that it was where a woman named Thecla, one of Paul's disciples, had been chased by Roman soldiers and a miracle had happened. The mountain she was trapped against had opened for her and had allowed her to escape. The passage, they had been told, was very narrow, with caves all around, a perfect place to hide from oppression. Others had gone on before and sent word that there were many caves, enough for everyone. John Mark had wondered if the secret was not too big, that others, including Roman officials, would learn of the location.

Miriam was tarrying. He was eager for her to come and read. The document, in codex form, was written by Clement of Rome to the church in Corinth. It had been copied there and arrived, via the church in Caesarea Philippi, in Damascus only two weeks before their departure. The letter had been read to the entire congregation and then Miriam had been allowed to read it to him privately. Time was of essence. They were to depart at midnight, and they must leave it for others to read before it was copied and distributed.

The manuscript had probably been through several editions. John Mark surmised the author had been concerned about the errors, alterations and redactions that inevitably occur. It was not unusual for an editor to change the wording to fit a particular theological viewpoint. All the more reason his manuscripts should be protected so the world, at some unknown point in time, could see the original gospel, the autograph itself.

In the twenty years John Mark and Miriam had been in Damascus, the copies of two other gospel accounts had made their way to their ecclesia. Similar to other documents that had arrived, including some of Paul's missives, both had been read to the congregation, and later, John Mark had been allowed a private reading. Like the copies he distributed, no names had been attached. The message, not the author, was important. Jesus would not approve of anyone, apostle or not, seeking personal gain or fame from his life and teachings. At Miriam's insistence, however, he had signed his name to his original. At some point in time, the world must know, she argued, the authenticity of the gospel's source. The others, for the same reason, probably signed their originals, she added.

Both gospels had similarities. They began with genealogies, something John Mark had considered unimportant. He had understood their purpose, but the immediacy of the message was important, not lengthy histories preceding it. There was another similarity between the two works. They had independent sources, but it was evident they had copied him, in places their words verbatim. In one, the calling of the first disciples was similar and in both the calling of Levi was almost word-for-word. Jesus' statement, "Pick up your cross and follow me," was placed differently but the words, including "Whoever wants to save his life will lose it but whoever loses his life for me will save it," were the same. John Mark could go on and on. Miriam, as always, was a healthy corrective to his concerns. He was not the only apostle, the only eyewitness, to these events and teachings.

"Dear one, they are writing for the same reason, the same cause, the same Christ," Miriam had reminded him.

As usual, she had been right. There was only one gospel and different accounts of it, different perspectives. His anger had settled, and he had been pleased they had used his work as a base. In places, such as the Temptation of Jesus, they had actually improved his account. Where he had allowed only one paragraph, which they had copied verbatim, they had embellished, creating a stronger message.

His biggest concern was that these authors had given too much away, leaving little room for faith. Jesus' messianic secret was no longer a secret. Sometimes, the whole story needed not be told. He had seen this nowhere more clearly than in their accounts of Jesus' resurrection. The author, whose genealogy extended back to David and Abraham, had given a brief account of the eleven disciples meeting Jesus in Galilee where some had worshipped him, but others had doubted. John Mark had shown that sentence to Miriam and they both smiled.

The other gospel writer, who had proposed to give an eyewitness account to one named Theophilus, had given an extensive account of Jesus' resurrection including appearances to companions on the Emmaus Road who reported back to the disciples in Jerusalem that it was true: Jesus had risen. Later, in this writer's gospel, Jesus had appeared to the disciples, challenging their doubts, showing them the punctures on his hands and feet from the nails on the cross, yet, they still had not believed. He had eaten with them, told them of predictions of *The Scriptures*, had led them out of Jerusalem to the vicinity of Bethany, had lifted up his hands, blessed them, and ascended into heaven. It was as though they had to see him ascending into heaven in order to have belief, proof that contradicted the mystery of faith.

Both of these writers had spoken of the disciples, of their doubt upon having seen Jesus after his crucifixion, and in so doing, had added reality to the struggle of faith. The first writer had done this more than the other, who had seemed to portray Jesus as an Elijah disappearing into the heavens. Neither, in John Mark's opinion, had captured the true essence of Jesus' resurrection. Was it possible their works had already been edited and expanded? Had they really seen or heard of these things? He, John Mark, had not heard of an ascension similar to Elijah's. The answers to these questions, he would probably never know. All he knew was that he could protect his writing, his account, so that someday the truth, as close as he could get to the truth, would be known.

Miriam finally came and sat on the bench across from him. She took the tablet from him, opened the cover, and began reading the letter from Clement of Rome;

> *The church of God which sojourns at Rome, to the church of God sojourning at Corinth, to those who are called and sanctified by the will of God, through our Lord Jesus Christ: grace to you, and peace, from Almighty God through Jesus Christ, be multiplied ...*

The letter had the right tone, John Mark thought, the right words. It was from Clement but sounded like Paul. The message forthcoming would be spiritually up-lifting. Then the tone, the words, changed. Miriam's sighs and facial expression reflected the same disappointment. There was trouble again in Corinth. "Owing, dear brethren, to the sudden and successive calamitous events which have happened to ourselves ..." She read on about the conflicts within the church, how some presbyters had been deposed and John Mark thought again of another problem accompanying the faith's success: quarrels. They had been inevitable. As the small churches had grown, they had taken on more ideas and beliefs that would surely clash. The same conflicts had happened in the history of his old faith, Judaism. The writer, this Clement, was reasserting the authority of the presbyters appointed by the apostles as rulers of the church. This statement was the right and correct thing for him to do, but sad for the reason.

Miriam continued reading, her words faltering on the accounts of the martyrdoms of her father and Paul in Rome, recovering her emotions as Clement told of the results of envy, the importance of repentance and pointed to Christ as an example of humility, His Second-Coming, and then the words,

> *Let us consider, beloved, how the Lord continually proves to us there shall be a future resurrection, of which he has rendered the Lord Jesus Christ the first-fruits by raising Him from the dead. Let us contemplate, beloved, the resurrection ...*

John Mark raised a hand. "Halt!"

"Why must I stop?" she questioned. "We must finish."

"The resurrection," he said, his eyes, thoughtful, looking up. "The resurrection," he whispered then looked down at her. "Did he say 'continually proves?'"

She looked back at the page. "Yes. 'continually proves.'"

"And the rest?"

"'... to us there shall be a future resurrection.'"

"Hmmmm," he murmured. "'Proves.'"

"You are thinking," she said.

He nodded.

"Is the thought worth sharing?" she asked.

"There is something I must add to the gospel, to the last page."

"Dear husband, you can add nothing now. The scrolls are sealed."

She was right. The scrolls, both of them, had been entrusted to Eliezar who had wrapped them in his best leather and waxed for moisture protection. For additional safeguarding, the trusted tanner had enlisted the services of a scribenarii who preserved documents and special papers for wealthy families. The scribenarii obtained clay jars specially crafted for such purposes. The scrolls were placed in jars which had sat in the sun for as long as possible, allowing them and the jar's interior to dry, before they had been sealed with a special wax substance to lock in the dry air and protect from outside moisture. "They will last forever," Eliezar had told John Mark.

"Shall I continue, dear one?" Miriam inquired.

"Not yet. Allow me a moment." Neither of them would live much longer. Where they were going, a strange place on the edge of the world, they would die. Then, only then, he would know about resurrection. He thought of something Paul had written to the same church, how we see a poor reflection as in a mirror, then face to face; how we know in part then someday fully. That someday was not far away.

"Now?" she said, bouncing her legs on her toes as she would do when impatient. "There is much more."

"I think not. The resurrection. That is a good place to stop."

She smiled at him and closed the codex.

"Besides," he reminded, "we have much to gather and pack before we depart."

They ate later than usual that evening, a hearty meal of lamb, vegetables, fruits and a stout wine to sustain them for the first leg of their long journey. Miriam had washed the pot and wooden spoons and dried them before packing them. The last items added to their cart were blankets and rugs, a few cushions, which would serve as a pallet when they needed to rest from walking and a cradle for the two jars Eliezar had sealed. The jar containing the master copy was much larger than the one holding the draft. John Mark wanted both preserved so others at some point in time, might understand the process and difficulties involved. No one knew when that time might be. The last day, the eschaton, had not occurred, as some, including Paul, had predicted. Jesus had said no one, not even he, knew the time, only the Father. John Mark had made sure to include that admonition in the gospel.

At midnight, they led the donkey and cart from the courtyard into the street. Miriam, as instructed by the caravan leaders, had wrapped cloth around the wheels of the cart and the donkey's hooves to muffle their sound on the pavement. Beneath a full moon, they exited through the Eastern Gate, near the place Paul had escaped, and met their small group at a designated spot away from the city. According to what they had been told, their destination lay just over thirty miles away. The journey would take four to five days, depending on how fast or slow they traveled. He and Miriam were the oldest. Despite their good health, John Mark's failing vision an exception; they knew the arduous trek would be difficult. They also knew they might not make it. In case they died in route, John Mark had made provisions for another within the caravan, a trusted friend, to care for and store the jars in a safe and secure place. Everyone knew the contents and their importance. At least, John Mark and Miriam had the cart and could ride when they tired, which they knew would be often. Across the plain it was dark. The sky was hard and prickly with stars. In the light of the full moon they could see the mountains they would skirt to arrive at their destination.

CHAPTER TWENTY-THREE

Maaloula, October 31, 2011

He had been there all along, right under their noses, the vagrant they'd seen the previous night chased away by the waiter. He was lank and boney, hatchet-faced with a sharp-nose, large intense cunning eyes, sunken cheeks, and a pointed chin shaped like a worn boot. He wore a headdress of no significance, possibly one retrieved from a garbage bin. Black hair curled across his forehead. Chris rummaged in his pocket and pulled out a pound note and gave it to the beggar whose broad smile revealed pulpy yellow gums barely, it seemed, holding his rotted teeth. "Shukran," the beggar said, his breath metallic, of garlic and red wine.

"This is good," Kate exclaimed. "He speaks Arabic."

The waiter rushed out to run him off again. Simultaneously, Chris and Kate held up their hands and in Arabic, Kate told him it was all right, no problem. In a huff, the waiter turned and walked back inside.

"Go slow with the beggar," Chris cautioned.

She nodded and asked him to sit in the vacant chair between them. He seemed nervous and unsure, suspicious, looking left to right with only his eyes. But he sat, placing his left hand still gripping the pound note on the table. The right hand remained tucked against his waist. His deep set eyes with tiny pupils assessed them nervously, cautiously.

She asked if he wanted something to drink, perhaps a beer, and he smiled and nodded. She turned and got the waiter's attention, motioned him over to her. He came promptly and she ordered a beer for the beggar.

Speaking again in Arabic, she spoke to the beggar then turned to Chris. "I asked him his name. 'Abdas,' he responded and added something else. He says it means 'servant of God.'"

"If he only knew," Chris mumbled under his breath.

"We'll find out," she sighed.

The waiter brought the beer and set it loudly on the table before the beggar. The beggar eyed it nervously, as though it had some quality about it that could harm him and then, with his left hand, turned it up and drained it. Kate ordered him another.

Chris said, "Ask him about his arm, but go slow."

She inquired. The beggar blinked rapidly and his good hand went into gyrations as he responded. He had a sinister smile, his eyebrows moved wildly and he ran his tongue over his yellow teeth when he spoke. Arabs don't give short simple answers, Chris had learned, so he sat back and awaited the translation. Based upon the hieroglyphics the beggar's hand was carving in the air, it had something to do with falling. When the beggar finished, he leaned back and looked alternately at the two of them, his pupils still nervous beads of jelly. The waiter came and set the second beer before him.

"You were right," she said, then translated. "He says he fell going into his cave and broke his wrist. Apparently there are big rocks at the entrance and he has to climb over them to get in. He is also a philosopher."

"How's that?"

"He is glad the rocks are there because they keep out others. He said you cannot have life both ways. He would rather have the rocks with the broken wrist than no rocks and harassment."

"I wonder what he was before he was a beggar," Chris surmised.

She looked at their vagrant guest and posed the question.

There was another lengthy response, longer than the last. Chris wondered how Arabs ever got anything accomplished. Then she said something back to the beggar which meant another drawn out response. Chris had almost finished his Coke and was ready for another, but the waiter seemed to have disappeared, probably upset at them for their invitation to his daily nuisance. The beggar was not finished, still jabbering away when Kate turned ashen, a look of shock on her face. She reached an unsteady hand for her Coke, lifted it then put it down, the bottle rattling as she returned it to the table, the beggar still talking, his face animated.

"Excuse me!" she said and abruptly rose and left.

The beggar looked up startled, an unfinished look on his face.

Chris thought she was weeping as she left. Her head was down, fingers pinching her eyes. He observed this unusual behavior with concern. She said something to the server just inside the door then disappeared into the small cantina. She was gone for a long time, longer than the time to use the toilet. She'd left him sitting there with the beggar who appeared as uncomfortable as he. In the nervous silence, Chris ordered another Coke. The beggar was downing the last swallow of his beer when Kate returned. She seemed more composed but Chris could tell she'd been affected by something.

"Are you okay?" he asked.

"It's a bit much to digest," she responded, calmer but still shaky.

"We haven't eaten yet," Chris said.

"Not that, what our beggar just told me."

"Too much for you to tell?" he asked calmly.

"Almost. Too much for me to know." She looked at him. "The world just shrunk."

Her face was still pale. Tremors passed across her lips. What could the beggar have said to cause this woman of iron to melt into a nervous state and bolt? "Now, you've really aroused my interest. I may have to learn Arabic." He smiled.

She didn't return the smile. "It's incredible," she said. She motioned to the waiter and ordered beers, one for her and her companion."

"It's that bad?" he questioned.

"Unbelievable." Her voice quavered. "Of all the infinite possibilities."

The waiter brought their beers, the beggar observing all the sudden movement and reaction with interest.

"Our friend over here wonders what the hell is going on and you're driving my curiosity insane," he said exasperated and leaned closer to her.

She reached for her beer, downed a long swallow and held the bottle. "He is a beggar because he was court-martialed from the army." She drank again and planted the bottle on the table, her hand still unsteady.

"What did he do to get court-martialed?"

"He killed a soldier."

"That's acceptable if the soldier's on the other side."

"He was not," she said.

"Which side?"

"Neither."

Chris then knew and understood. He'd let it drop. She did not need to be re-traumatized more. He picked up the beer and drank.

As though she needed to talk about it, she continued. "His unit was not far from a U. N. outpost on the Golan Heights. He was attempting to break and enter, burglarize, one of the buildings. The man he shot was a night sentry. I said incredible that I, of all people, should run into him. Yet the more I think about it, the more it seems less improbable. This small corner of the world is in a smaller corner of this world. Syrian ex-military turned beggars flock where there are tourists. Most of Syria is in upheaval. This area is not." She stopped. cast a nervous glance at the beggar and drank again from her beer.

"I don't know what to say," is all he knew to say and paused. "Ask him when it happened?"

"I did. It was in two thousand five."

"I'm sorry. We can leave."

"No!" Both hands came down on the table and startled the beggar again. He rose, and it seemed he was going to bolt. She spoke something calming to him in Arabic, and he sat back down. "No," she said again, softer. "We have a job to do."

His iron woman was back. He didn't know how she could regain her composure so quickly knowing the beggar across from her was probably the man who shot and killed her husband.

She finished her beer, put the empty bottle down and looked at Chris, steely greenish-brown eyes regarding him seriously. "Someone once said coincidence is God's way of maintaining his anonymity."

"Yes?" he replied, unsure of the context.

"There is something strangely redeeming about this, and the architect is not anonymous."

"The Lord does work his will in strange and mysterious ways," Chris added.

The waiter finally emerged from his snit and asked if they were ready to order. He ignored the beggar.

The beggar licked his lips and dragged the back of his hand across his mouth, a contrived gesture that seemed designed to suggest hunger.

Kate looked at Chris. "If it suits you, I'll order for all three of us." She turned to the beggar and said something to him. He flashed a dark yellow smile and pumped his head gleefully. The waiter's face turned sour, no doubt because his guests were positively reinforcing the unwanted vagrant's behavior. He might give up his cave and pitch a small tent across the street next to the convent walls.

She read from the menu, the waiter wrote.

"Ask him for another Coke," Chris said. "I'm tired of the beer. One, too, for our friend. We don't want to get him drunk."

Kate translated to the waiter. He scribbled again and left.

"I guess now we can go to the next leg of our mission," Chris said.

Speaking in Arabic again, and addressing him by his name, Abdas, she told the beggar about their interest in antique jars and that one Walid, owner of an antique shop, had purchased one from him. At the name Walid, the beggar perked up and nodded up and down.

She relayed to Chris what she'd told him.

"Don't go too fast with him. He detects eagerness like a hawk."

She shot him a don't-tell-me-how-to-do-it look and proceeded to ask Abdas if he had more jars. He responded that he did and raised a finger indicating only one.

"Why didn't he bring that one to Walid?" Chris asked.

She translated.

As expected, the answer was lengthy. The beggar pointed at his right arm then toward the gorge then in the direction of the shop.

"Because it is much bigger than the other jar," she converted, "and he cannot manage it with his arm down the mountain from his cave to the shop."

"Tell him, just a suggestion you understand, that we will buy it from him, go with him to his cave to get it, and that we will pay him much more than Walid."

She interpreted again to the beggar.

For the first time, a short response: "Na'am."

"He says, 'Yes!'"

"We know Walid paid him two hundred and fifty Syrian pounds," Chris stated. "What does he want for it?"

"Do you think we should ask him or make a fair offer?" she questioned.

"Ask him." Chris advised. "He might go lower."

A translation pause.

She had a surprised look on her face. "He wants three hundred Syrian pounds. He wants it in American money."

"Can do. That's a little over five dollars. I have some ten-dollar bills I can't break here. Tell him we'll give him that."

"You were the one who said go slow on this," she reminded him.

"Just tell him I can't get change," Chris said impatiently.

She relayed the message. A lopsided grin creased Abdas' face. He reached his left hand across the table, shook hands with her first then Chris. Their observant and protective waiter brought some hand wipes with the meal.

The beggar observed his food with the same caution he did the first beer, with disbelief, and then touched the food with his hand to confirm it was real. His eyes darted nervously between them and he began eating.

Chris ate in silence, mainly because he couldn't speak Arabic but also because most of the time was absorbed with Kate's translations of small talk with their guest whose high whiney voice was beginning to get on his nerves. She was obviously dancing around any topic relating to the military or the revolution. All Chris wanted to do was get through the meal before dark took over. He had a small flashlight, but it would not provide enough light navigating up and down a tricky mountain slope and through a narrow canyon. He looked at his watch. It was after five. About two hours of sunlight remained. He looked at her and pointed at the sun with his fork.

The waiter came with the check. Chris paid him in Syrian pounds. The waiter's face showed disappointment. He must have overheard the discussion about American dollars going to the vagrant. Nonetheless, he seemed satisfied as they departed with the beggar.

CHAPTER TWENTY-FOUR

Maaloula, Early Spring, 90 A.D.

The small caravan almost made the journey in four days, arriving early morning on the fifth. Sunlight striking the distant cliffs turned them gold, revealing the shadowed cleft in the mountain, as though a hand of God, like a Titan's ax, had come down and split it open. Also in shadows were the numerous caves darkly pitting the sides of the mountain.

Others living there had seen them approaching and came forward to greet them. It was a time of jubilee and celebration. Old friends from the Damascus church hugged and kissed. There were new friends with them, some from as far away as Caesarea Philippi and a few from Seleucia, northeast of Galilee.

For John Mark and Miriam, it was indeed a time of celebration but for a different reason. Both had sores on their feet from walking and over their body from the constant jostling of the cart the times they lay in it. They were hungry and thirsty. They had slept very little and were tired beyond words, yet they were still breathing. They were alive. Holding to each other, they could walk. Their hero was the untiring black donkey who, like the love and mercy of the Lord God, remained steadfast and unwavering.

Members of the welcoming group guided them up the slope to the opening and through a narrow cleft that truly looked like the work of the Almighty. The hand that carved it sliced the mountain with an artistic curve and provided a small stream running through the middle. Rose-colored rocks rose over thirty meters above a footpath that seemed well-trod since Thecla's footprints. In places, the gorge was wide and in other places narrowed to a tunnel. Thankfully, their cart made it through, but a small army could not. Little wonder people sought the place as a safe refuge. Someone commented that Thecla was wise to run to a place like this and fortunate to have God on her side. Members in the welcoming party pointed to a spot on the mountain, a cave that held her bones. People had already begun worshipping her there.

Once they were through the gorge, a younger couple from Caesarea Philippi led them up the mountain, pointing out several of the caves they knew were uninhabited. John Mark and Miriam stood, looked for a moment, and scanned the side of the mountain.

"Are there any where we would not have to climb very high?" he asked. "We are old and have come a long way."

"There are some," the man said. His name was Zacharias and his wife was named Sarah. "But they would be easily found by the Romans. The best caves, for our purposes, are difficult to reach."

"So it is with most things in life," John Mark said, the words *easily found* and *difficult* resonating with him. What he had brought with him was more valuable than their lives, and the caves were the reason he came. Looking at Miriam, John Mark said, "Show us the ones more difficult to access," and she nodded approval.

They continued climbing. They were on the back side of the cliffs they had seen approaching the site, the gorge having taken them through the mountain. There was one aperture hidden in the shadows of a small cleft in the rock facing. It appeared to be a cave, but John Mark was uncertain. The location was on a slope. Access to it was difficult but did not seem insurmountable. The donkey could climb the terrain as well, probably better than they, but not with a full cart. They would surely have to watch their step and not venture out in the dark.

John Mark pointed to the cave, or what he thought was a cave.

Zacharias and Sara went ahead, reaching back with their hands to assist them in the climb. They had to step carefully around the stones, lest they twist an ankle.

As they neared the place, it was clearly a cave and seemed perfect for their purpose. The opening was hidden in the shadows of shelves of rock on both sides with an overhanging ledge. The overhang would provide protection in bad weather. A small ledge before the opening provided an entranceway.

"The Lord does provide," Miriam said.

"Amen!" John Mark agreed.

They entered the cave and a dank, sour odor hit them. Then they saw the crude hearth in a corner and shards and pots, bones beneath the pots.

"My God," Miriam said, a hand flying to her mouth.

"They are just animal bones," Zacharias said. "Put under the pots to hide from foraging animals."

"Someone has used it before," John Mark noted, pointing to the hollows dug into the wall as shelves.

"Long ago," Sarah noted. "The bones you see are old."

"It is no problem," Miriam said. "We can clean the place."

"You have brought belongings," said Zacharias. "Allow Sarah and me to help you bring them up the mountain."

They readily accepted the offer.

By the time John Mark and Miriam were back down the mountain and through the gorge, it was nearing mid-day. Though it was spring, the sun off the mountains made it feel more like summer. They would be exhausted when they finished but they would be safe. John Mark was confident their two new friends would assist them in getting a fire started. He had brought olive oil and clay lamps so they would have light. They had thought ahead and brought rugs for the cave's cold floor and a chair for each of them. Their writing was over, their mission accomplished. All they had to do now was enjoy each other's company in old age and await their deaths. Then John Mark remembered. There was one more very important thing to do: find a home for the scrolls.

Hauling their possessions up the mountain was not as arduous as they had anticipated. The donkey carried the heavy items and Zacharias and Sarah were helpful. They inquired of the two jars, which John Mark said must be handled with great care. When told of their contents, the couple's faces lit up. They had heard the gospel read at their ecclesia in Caesarea Philippi. John Mark told them it was one he had personally delivered. He told them of their past labors, the copies he and Miriam had made and had distributed. Zacharias and Sarah were excited and wanted to read the gospel again. John Mark welcomed them to come to their cave. He and Miriam could tell them the memorized gospel but the original scroll, sealed in one of the jars, was to be soon buried to be read again in God's chosen time.

John Mark and Miriam spent the rest of the day cleaning the cave, preparing for their first night away from home and its comforts, frequently reminding themselves why they were there. One item they brought was a broom Miriam had slipped through the slats of the cart. Once the debris was cleared, the odor would improve. The cave opening afforded a panoramic view of the land below, mostly flat desert from the mountain base to the horizon. The overhang would provide shade as well as protection from the elements. Anyone approaching in daylight could be seen from miles away. Late in the afternoon, a slice of sunlight hit one wall of the cave, and they saw the graphics: several fish and *chi rho* ☧ symbols, an eagle and something they could not see well enough to decipher, a fragment of writing, in Greek, perhaps a scripture. As the light moved across the face of the wall, John Mark was able to translate.

I WILL SEND MY MESSENGER AHEAD OF
YOU WHO WILL PREPARE YOUR WAY
PREPARE THE WAY OF THE LORD
MAKE STRAIGHT PATHS FOR HIM

Astonished, they looked at each other.

"It is from Isaiah," Miriam beamed. "It is the beginning of the gospel."

"Incredible!" he exclaimed. "Whoever was here, they were believers in the new faith."

"And here is another," she said, moving deeper into the cave where the light was beginning to touch. She moved her hand over the chiseled letters, brushing away the accumulated dust and lichen and read aloud.

SURELY THIS IS OUR GOD
WE TRUSTED IN HIM AND
HE SAVED US
THE HAND OF THE
LORD WILL REST ON THIS MOUNTAIN.

"It is also from Isaiah," John Mark observed.

"But they left," she said, confounded.

"That may have been here during Nero's persecution," he guessed. "I heard these caves were used in that time and for the same reason. When the persecutions stopped, they left. They were saved. The scripture is valid."

Just beyond the second script, the wall of the cave dipped inward, forming an enclave.

"This is where I will put them," John Mark said.

"Them?" She looked at him puzzled.

"The scrolls. We can build a wall of rock around this enclave, make it look natural, as though it is part of the cave."

"Then no one will *ever* find them," she said doubtfully.

"They will, some day. Others, after us, will use these caves. Persecutions will continue."

Late in the afternoon, Zacharias came with an oil lamp and helped them start a fire and light their lamps. He offered to bring food, but Miriam said they had brought enough for a few days. Zacharias reminded them about the fresh water in the stream through the gorge and said there was another spring of water up the mountain near the entrance to the defile. When they were out of food, the community had formed a group to ensure a steady supply and then he looked at the donkey. "Your animal may need to be sacrificed."

That would be sad, but they understood. They wanted to do what was right and helpful.

"Hopefully, that will be a while," Miriam said. "He has been our life support. Without him, we would not be here."

Zacharias acknowledged he understood and departed.

That evening, as the sun was setting before them, its glare bright and its rays long, flooding the cave with light, Miriam warmed some dried fish over the fire and cooked a combination of vegetables in the pot they had brought. They ate in the softer light of dusk, listening to the birds and mountain creatures. When they had finished, John Mark read from Psalms and they prayed. Sunlight was leaving the cave, and they reclined in its opening. The oil lamp made shadows on the walls. Beyond the flames of the fire they watched the donkey snatching tufts of grass, his head rising slowly and dropping impatiently.

"How long do you think we will be here?" Miriam asked.

"Only God knows," John Mark responded. His muscles pulled with tiredness, but the ground felt soft. He turned on his side so he could look into her eyes. "But we are not alone. The master went on before us. He is here."

CHAPTER TWENTY-FIVE

Maaloula, October 31, 2011

In deep shadows through the gorge, they followed Abdas. The defile was about a half mile long. They emerged in glaring orange light and had to shield their eyes from the sun's leveling rays. They went a short distance when the beggar stopped and pointed up. The ascent was not steep but tricky. Half-way up, Abdas stopped and pointed again.

Kate asked him what he was pointing to and he said his cave.

She translated to Chris and he said, "I don't see one."

"Neither do I," she concurred.

"You think he's leading us on?"

"I don't think so," she said. "You haven't paid him. He's a cripple, he can't overpower us."

"He's not that crippled," Chris remarked. "We don't know what he has under his tunic."

Abdas stopped and looked back, a curious expression on his face as though he might understand some English after all. Then he turned and plodded upward.

Once they arrived, they understood why they could not see the cave. It was partially hidden in a cleft of the rock facing. Large pieces of rock slab lay in front of the entrance.

"No wonder we couldn't see it," Chris observed. "Even if it was not tucked into the cleft, the entrance is blocked by these huge rocks." He looked up, assessing the geology of the rest of the mountain. "Look, there, over the cave. This was an overhang at one point that snapped and fell, possibly due to an earthquake, another reason the jars were not discovered sooner."

Holding his right hand tightly at his waist, Abdas began climbing over the large rocks. Balancing with his left hand, he motioned them to follow. Chris watched Kate climbing lithely ahead of him. They had to be careful to avoid twisting an ankle or falling and breaking a bone, like their guide, something that could happen to a sober person in this boulder-strewn terrain. Once inside the cave, the sunset was a blessing. Its illumination revealed walls darkened by centuries of oil and candle smoke. As though divinely directed, bolts of light flooded the cavern and simultaneously, they saw the chiseled graphics on the left wall. Abdas was pointing toward the back of the cave, but they were captivated with the passages.

"They are in Greek," Kate remarked immediately.

He walked over to the first passage, brushed his hand over it. Dust and flakes of lichen flew into the air. When the disturbance cleared, he said, "They're both from Isaiah."

She was already translating the first one as he spoke: "I will send my messenger ahead of you who will prepare your way, prepare the way of the Lord, make straight paths for him."

"That's the beginning of Mark's gospel," he said awed. "Did he write this?"

"We've agreed that if he hid the scrolls," she responded, "he would probably have been in his eighties. These are chiseled. He would not have strong hands to do this. Perhaps a younger person followed his direction."

Abdas began jabbering and pointing again.

Kate told him to wait one moment, that the writings were important. She listened as Chris translated the second passage: "Surely this is our God. We trusted in him and he saved us. The hand of the Lord will rest on this mountain." He paused and stepped back. "This is phenomenal."

They turned to Abdas who pointed again to the right of the second graphic, to a portion of wall that had caved in.

"This wall is human made," she assessed.

"Yes, but clearly in a manner that might appear natural," he added.

"It's a fairly shoddy construction, probably designed to last through a time of persecution."

"But which one?" he asked, as he stepped through the jagged aperture, followed by Kate, and they saw immediately the large jar. Beside it on the ground were two ink pots, one clay, the other bronze. The small bronze jar still contained residual dry ink.

Mystified, she asked, "Were they still writing?"

"They were old, but it's possible," he said. "Or they belonged to someone else. These may have been placed here for symbolic and ceremonial reasons."

She pointed at the large jar. "Originally, for no telling how long, it was probably standing. Perhaps the earthquake, the same that toppled the overhang, knocked it over."

"Or our drunk friend," Chris said with sarcasm, "when he fell through the wall."

Abdas was getting anxious. They had the jar, he wanted his money.

"We cannot take this down the mountain," she said. "Syria has laws protecting archaeological finds."

"We can't open it here in front of our new buddy," he advised.

"We have to," she retorted. "It's the only way we'll know its contents."

"I suggest we take it down the mountain, away from Abdas, and open it privately."

"We could do that," she agreed. "It's our jar, we're paying for it. Tell him we want the two small pots."

"We can't take them and the scroll out of the country," he cautioned. "Raises the risk."

"No, but we can give them to the convent. They are valuable relics." She told Abdas they wanted the two pots, and he told her they meant nothing to him. "Go ahead, give him the ten dollars," she instructed Chris.

He turned his back and untucked his shirt. He unzipped the money belt snapped around his waist and pulled out the bill. When he turned around, Abdas's good hand was out. "Now, it's our jar.," Chris said. "We can do as we please with it."

Abdas thought the deal was done. He stood waiting for them to leave.

Chris leaned over and tried to lift the jar. "It's heavier than I thought. Taking it down would be difficult and possibly attract attention."

She reached in to help him. "The scroll, if it's inside, should not be that big. Why is it so heavy?"

"The clay has absorbed moisture," he said, "two thousand years worth. Let's hope it didn't penetrate. That may be why it's so big, for protection of the scroll, if there's one inside. That's the advantage of the desert climate, why so many scrolls have been found intact in Egypt and the Dead Sea valley."

"We're on the edge of the desert here," she pointed out.

"Let's hope it helped. We need to get the jar into the light."

Abdas looked on with curious eyes as each took an end and lifted the jar. Moving slowly, carefully, taking small steps, they worked it through the breach in the fragile wall then a little further, laid it gently beneath the graphics on the wall. Golden beams of late afternoon sunlight poured through the cave's opening. Kate pulled her phone from her pocket and took pictures of the cave, the graphics and the jar then swung the lens on Abdas who raised a hand before his face.

"You're the archaeologist," she said. "How do you open it?"

"Very carefully," he said. He pulled out a Swiss knife and opened a large blade.

"How did you get that through security?" she asked dismayed.

"I put it in the toe of a packed shoe with socks around it and hoped. The scanner may have been asleep. If they confiscated it, I could buy another. They're a dime a dozen on the black market."

He began working the blade around the lip of the jar, chipping off bits and pieces of ancient wax and caked clay. "If there's anything in there, we may have the same luck the professor had. This thing's been sealed for the end of time." He continued working the knife. He'd work a while, stop and try the top. Work longer, try again. "I've never had one this difficult. Usually, they're so primed by time you can hit the tops, and they just pop off. If they've fallen, like this one, they're already off."

"Glad that didn't happen," she said, leaning over observing, listening to him talk to himself.

Abdas stood back. They were so intent they'd forgotten about him.

Then, a loud snap.

"There," Chris said, and drew an audible breath.

"You got it," she commented and patted him on the back.

"Yes." Holding the broad neck of the jar with his left hand, he pulled on the lid, slowly. Millimeter by millimeter, it came out, along with dust and an odor of ancient time. He reached in his top pocket and pulled out the miniature flashlight he always carried, leaned over, and shined a thin beam of light into the wide craw of the large jug. He peered into the dark cavity.

He could see something wrapped in leather, tied at the top around two dark rods. He could not believe what he was seeing. He felt a palpable presence. A shudder passed through him and he bowed his head. He felt her hand on his shoulder.

"Are you all right?" she asked.

"Yes," he managed. "God, yes. I can see the rods. This is sacred. In this place, we are … " His voice wavered … "only years from Christ. This is holy ground."

For several minutes, nothing else was said. An eerie silence filled the cave. A wedge of late afternoon sunlight slid down the wall, a brilliant edge moving over the graphics, across the jar. A soft breeze blew into the cave. Soon, the late afternoon sky would pivot into dusk.

Moving closer for a better look, Kate tripped on his feet. He turned quickly to catch her, but she fell on top of him, pinning him to the ground. Her hands were clutching his shoulders, almost around his neck. There was perspiration on her forehead and around her lips. Their eyes locked, intense; their breathing hard.

"I'm sorry," she said catching her breath.

"Are you all right?" he asked.

"Yes. The scroll," she whispered, "the scroll," and pushed herself up. She brushed herself off.

He turned his attention again to the scroll.

"Why am I afraid to take it out?" he questioned somberly.

"For the same reasons, I'm afraid," she responded. "It may not be what we think. If it is, it will change our lives, possibly forever."

"We won't know for several days. No way we can unscroll it here."

"I agree," she said. "It's getting late."

He glanced up at Abdas who also seemed caught up in the moment, a look of rapture on his face as though he, too, knew something important was happening. Chris looked back down at the jar, shined the light once more then put the light down and ran his hand through the opening. He could touch the leather and the rods. He tried to grip one but they were barely protruding from the leather casing, almost flush with it. "Lift the other end of the jar," he said to her. "It will probably slide out. I can't grip anything through the opening and don't want to cause damage to the scroll. It's probably papyrus like the one the professor found, and fragile."

She nodded, walked around and lifted the bottom of the jar.

Nothing happened, no movement inside.

"Higher," he said. "It may have to slide over the curvature of the neck."

"We would have to be careful, but we could crack it open," she said. "That's how some of the Dead Sea Scrolls were removed."

"I know. If this doesn't work, we will."

She lifted the jar to an angle almost perpendicular with the ground and there was movement. The top of the leather object appeared and protruded from the jar's mouth.

Chris rose, straddled the jar, and put his hands next to hers around the base. "Now, lift," he said.

They raised the large jar upwards and a scroll wrapped in leather slid onto the ground. Its rods were barely visible and it was sealed completely in leather, with leather stitching around the rods at the top and bottom. Immediately, Kate snapped a picture.

They knelt beside it and ran their hands gently, worshipfully, over it.

"Waterproof," she exclaimed.

"What?"

"This leather, it is very fine quality. Only occasionally do we see it. An analysis will tell us where it came from, a time frame, and what was used to treat it. It's done on parchment all the time."

"We are presuming its contents are papyrus," he said.

"We could be fooled. Parchment was replacing papyrus toward the end of the first century. But we must make haste. Just a moment."

She looked up at Abdas and said something to him.

"What did you say to him?" Chris asked.

"I have to tinkle."

"You're kidding," he joked.

"No. We've got to call Dr. Krekorian, get Muhammed here ASAP. If I make a call here, you-know-who is going to get suspicious."

Abdas was listening intently. "Muhammed?"

She said something that seemed to satisfy the beggar, but he was obviously getting antsy about something else.

"What did you tell him?" Chris asked.

"I told him Muhammed was Allah's prophet, and that God was great."

"Do you even have service here?" he asked.

"Yes. I checked when I was taking pictures."

She got up and walked to the cave's entrance and stepped out of view. She was gone a few minutes then returned. "Muhammed is on his way. It should take him an hour."

"Let's hope Muhammed makes it without running over someone or killing himself," Chris said.

"If we needed anyone coming for us in this moment, it's our Muhammed."

"Muhammed? Muhammed?" Abdas exclaimed again, excited.

She repeated to the beggar what she'd said earlier and he said something back to her. She looked at Chris. "Don't ask. He said God is great. We don't need to say Muhammed again. He may think we're religious fanatics who have stumbled onto some valuable Islamic document. That would *not* be good."

Then Abdas pointed at the scroll, said something, opened his hand and said, "Bakshish."

"He wants money for the scroll," she translated. "He says that was not in the deal."

"How much does he want?"

"Give him ten American dollars," she suggested. "That should satisfy him."

Chris turned his back again, went through the same motions with his money belt, and turned around flashing Alexander Hamilton in Abdas' face.

Abdas grinned and snapped up the money with his good hand.

"Tell him he can keep the jar, that we're more than even," Chris said.

She translated and Abdas grinned broader.

"This leather is of good quality but brittle in places," she observed. "We must be careful. We don't want to lose anything, not a flake, if we can help it." She removed her burka and gently wrapped the leather-encased scroll in it. "That should help. The scarf will catch any fragments that falls off."

"That reminds me," he said and began picking up pieces of wax and clay he'd chipped from the lid. He wrapped them in a handkerchief he pulled from his back pocket, placed it in his shirt pocket and buttoned it. He went back through the hole in the makeshift wall and retrieved the two ink pots. "Let's go."

They began to leave but Abdas moved and blocked their passage. "Bakshish!"

"Tell him to step aside," Chris said, adamantly, his voice raised, "that we've paid him all we have."

She translated and Abdas responded, stayed put, his eyes glaring.

She translated. "He says we owe him for the two ink pots."

"So, he's changed his mind," Chris said. He was reflecting on the irony that this was the "servant of God" who probably shot and killed Kate's husband, that she was being exceedingly patient with him when she reached into her blouse, pulled out the gun and pointed at the beggar's head. Abdas dropped the money he was holding and went berserk. His nostrils were dilating and quivering. She said something lengthy to him, and he grew quiet.

"What did you say to him?"

"I told him he was probably the man who killed my husband, gave him the details of time and place so he got the picture, that I was thoroughly pissed off and was going to blow his head off if he didn't stand aside and let us pass without trouble, that if he followed us I would shoot him on the spot. Now let's go."

Abdas stood aside and let them pass out of the cave and down the mountain, Kate clutching the scroll in her burka as though it were a small child rescued from danger. "We need to get to the convent quickly," she said, her voice urgent.

"To hell with our stuff," Chris said. "Let's meet Muhammed at the highway."

"Trust me, Chris. We need to go to the convent."

They were down the mountain and entering the gorge when they heard the loud shrill, like a banshee, coming behind them. The noise echoed crazily through the hollowed siq.

"It's Abdas," she exclaimed. "He knows I won't shoot him here."

They began running, enough dusk light piercing the shadows of the towering dark cliffs to show the way. They reached the entrance, the convent just ahead. The beggar's screams were louder, echoing off the canyon walls.

"What's he hollering?" Chris asked.

"Thief!" she answered.

They reached the front gate just as Abdas was exiting the gorge, only a hundred feet behind them. Luckily, the gate was open. They slammed it shut behind them, slid the bolt and climbed the steps, glanced back at Abdas holding the wrought-iron bars and screaming.

"Quickly, to my room," she said as they ran across the courtyard and up the next tier of steps. Inside her room, she hurried to her carry-on, popped it open and removed a partition.

"What in the world?" he uttered.

"It's a false bottom."

He realized then that's why it was specially made, that she had probably used it before to get manuscripts safely from hostile places, all for the good of culture and history and humankind. He was standing and observing her quick movements. There was a knock on the door. He moved to answer it.

"Just a second," she called out, ensuring her burka was snuggly around the scroll, then laid it in the baggage.

"Here, put this with it," he said opening his shirt pocket and handing her the wadded handkerchief with the wax and clay chips."

"That was smart," she remarked then clamped the partition into place and hastily repacked her clothes. She looked at the door. "Who is it?"

"Anina."

Chris opened the door.

"Are you all right?" Anina's face was animated, her eyes wide and alarmed. "There is a beggar screaming at the gate. He says you are thieves."

"What did he say we stole?" Chris asked.

"He did not know," Anina said excitedly. "It was hidden in a jar."

"We have these two ancient ink pots," Chris said, "but he gave them to us. He said they were worthless. We brought them to you for the convent."

Her face lit up. She took the pots from him and held them up to the light. "They are priceless," she glowed.

"They are yours," Kate said. "Our gift to the convent. Anina, we took nothing from the beggar. We gave him some money, and he wanted more. Now he is very upset."

"He is also a little loco," Chris said, twirling his finger at his temple.

"Loco?"

"Crazy," Kate said.

Anina heaved a sigh of relief. "That is good. I was worried. We do not want the police. Police create many problems here."

Chris didn't want to hear about those problems. They needed to find a way out without attracting more attention. Suddenly, the noise at the gate grew louder. There was more than one voice.

Anina stepped onto the balcony and looked below. "There is another man."

They joined her to see.

"The shopkeeper," Kate said.

"He is shouting 'thief,' too," Anina said. "Please, what is this?"

"Quickly, Anina, we must tell you something," and they stepped back into the room.

"You are Christian," Kate said to her.

"Of course," Anina replied, almost indignant.

"Then you will understand," Kate continued. Without revealing their real reason for being in Maaloula, she recapitulated the events of the day, said they had purchased a jar from the beggar, went to his cave and found what could be the most valuable document in all of Christianity. "If others learn of it, they could bring harm to it or destroy it."

Chris had never seen Kate this animated. She was in the woman's face, the words pouring out of her like the situation was a matter of life or death. With the clamor growing at the gate, it might be. Other voices had joined the two and he heard shouts of "American, American." The worse they had feared seemed to be unfolding.

"Have you heard of the Dead Sea Scrolls?" Chris asked.

"Yes, yes," Anina exclaimed. "We have looked at them on the Internet. They are in Israel. We cannot go to Jerusalem."

"We understand," Kate said. "What we have may be more important."

Anina's eyes widened further. She was clutching the ink pots.

"We've got to get out of here," Chris said. "If your Mother Superior goes to the gate, she will not know any of this."

"We have someone coming from Beirut to get us," Kate said. "He is on his way. Can you help us?"

"What can I do?"

"Get us out of here another way," Chris said. "Do you have a backdoor?"

Anina put the two pots under the bed and said, "Follow me!"

Chris grabbed his things from his room and threw them into his luggage while Kate was completing her packing. The moments moved surreally fast, happening, it seemed, before they were happening.

The only way out of the apartments was down the stairs into the courtyard. Others in the compound were gathered, wondering about the riotous din at the gate, but no one had gone to see. Kate and Chris followed Anina across the courtyard and around the back of the building, down some unlit steps to a small gate. Anina threw the bolt and motioned them through, closed it behind her and rushed ahead of them. They were in a small graveled passageway between a building and the cliff wall then quickly crossed a street into a small alley. The route was circuitous, so they had to stay close to Anina who was weaving left and right, through one passage that dog-legged to another.

"We do not want to get you into trouble," Kate whispered to her as they ran.

"No trouble," she whispered back. "Trouble if I do not help."

They kept running. Chris thought the narrow tilted passages were like the wynds in Edinburgh, wide enough only for one or two people, but no vehicles. Anina was smart. She was keeping them off the streets. Then they heard sirens.

"The police," Anina said. "Someone has called the police."

"Just get us to the highway, the main road into the city," Chris said.

"That is a long way," Anina said.

They were still running.

"You don't have to take us there, Anina," Kate said. "Just point the way."

They ran on, turning sharp corners, up steps, down steps, arousing dogs from their slumber and lethargic denizens who rushed to open windows and doors. Chris almost ran over a donkey that started braying, competing with the police sirens. They moved along the back side of the village, against the floodlit cliffs and entered a narrow street that descended sharply, hit a dead end, took a right into another narrow street that seemed parallel to the main street that brought them into the town.

"Anina, we cannot get on the main street," Chris said, breathing hard as he ran.

"I know ... just up here ... we cross to the oasis."

"We'll be ... in trees?" Kate asked.

"Yes," Anina responded.

Through an alley they came to the main street and stopped. Anina held them back with a hand, looked both ways, then motioned they cross.

They had seen the trees entering the town, giving no thought they would be their salvation out of the place.

"Now, quickly, you go," and she pointed. "The main road there, the trees here. The trees go to the highway."

"Got it," Chris said.

"Thank you, Anina," Kate added. "You will be rewarded for this."

They hugged just as police sirens were nearing. The shopkeeper and his accomplice must have told them a story of great travail. The whole city seemed to be alive with sirens. They watched Anina as she crossed the street, her robes billowing behind her, and into the alley. She would concoct some story explaining her brief absence and the disappearance of their guests. The Mother Superior would understand. They valued relics of the faith. When the true story was revealed, all would be forgiven. That, to Chris, seemed the logical outcome but these were strange illogical times.

They moved deeper into the oasis, away from the street where spotlights could reach them. Rather than use the rollers that would sound like mild thunder moving over the pavement, they had been carrying their luggage, an added physical burden. They reached a point they thought was safe and stopped.

"What time is it?" Kate asked.

He looked at his watch. "About six-thirty their time."

Both of them were speaking in whispers, murmurs.

"I called Dr. Krekorian about six," she recalled.

The sirens were still blaring, and they could see swiveling blue lights along the two major thoroughfares that bracketed the oasis.

"You'd think the 'most wanted' had escaped from prison," he murmured.

"They don't have a high crime rate," Kate remarked. "Bored police. They pull out all the stops."

"We need to think this through," he said. "How is Muhammed going to know to find us here in this jungle?"

"He's not. He only knows to come to the Takla Convent, where he dropped us off. We'll have to intercept him."

"So, we stand out on the highway with our thumbs out and the Maaloula police swarming all over the place," he said ironically.

She offered a suggestion. "We know what his car looks like. We move further up the oasis, get closer to the main intersection where we saw the large 'Welcome' sign, jump out and flag him down."

"Surely, we can come up with something better," he said .

"If you know it, speak it," she said tersely. "If we miss him, Anina is resourceful."

"If push comes to shove, we can bury the scroll, return later, and get it."

"It's shove time. Get down!" she exclaimed and pulled him to the ground with her hand.

A spotlight from a patrol car began sweeping through the trees. They lay flat as the weak beam moved over them. They waited. The light shut down. The patrol car moved on.

They got up and ran hard, straight ahead, paralleling the main street from the highway. The trees thinned and stopped.

"This is it," she said. "The highway." She pointed. "Muhammed will be coming from that direction."

He was standing behind her. "Yes, and we're on the wrong side of the intersection. What's on the other side of the main street at the intersection? Can you see?"

"There is a domed building with what looks like a minaret," she said. "But it couldn't be a mosque, not this far out."

"It might be. The city's mostly Christian."

"Running south of it, towards the intersection are some bushes. Come here and look," she motioned to him. "Nothing's coming."

He stepped up beside her. "Perfect. The right-of-way slopes off from the bushes. There's a short retaining wall. It'll cover us."

Behind them was the city in colorful lights and ahead the desert under the bright crescent moon embedded in a sequined sky.

"We can cross," she urged. "The police have turned back. They will not come this far. We must move quickly."

They scampered out of the low brush, crossed the road and clammered over the low wall. It seemed to have no purpose except to channel water from the road in heavy downfalls. For minutes, no cars passed, coming or going.

"This is still early evening," he said. "We should see something. Maybe they have a roadblock in town. If they do, we definitely need to stop Muhammed. I remember the car is white."

"It's a white Mercedes," she agreed, "late '90's model. It has a yellow taxi light on top. He kept it on bringing us here to identify him at the border crossings. Apparently that helps. He'll have it on. That's our cue, the yellow light."

"Taxis are the norm here for long distance travel," he said. "He's not the only show in town."

"Let's hope he's the only show with a white Mercedes and a yellow taxi light."

They crouched and waited.

A few cars passed. None with a taxi light.

Chris looked at his watch again. "It's still too early."

"What time?"

"Quarter to seven."

"I called him around six," she said again. "It takes a good hour, but that helps narrow our focus. White Mercedes with yellow taxi light coming down that road in fifteen minutes."

Blue lights began strobing again, car motors loud, revving, speeding from town.

He turned to look at her, a flash of uncertainty in her eyes.

"Lay flat" she said, and pulled out her gun.

"Surely, you're not going to use that," he exclaimed, stretching prone on the ground beside her.

"Only if I have to, and only as a bluff … and only if we are threatened. We don't have to wait for Muhammed. We can go cross-country. In the dark, they'd have a hard time finding us."

"We might have a hard time finding us," he added.

"Shush!"

They listened as two cars passed, blue light flashing on the bushes and the minaret and mosque. Then they heard them stop at the intersection.

"They've stopped. This isn't good," he whispered.

She said nothing.

The only people talking were the police among themselves at the intersection. Were they setting up a roadblock? Chris wondered. The beggar would not have known about the phone call. She told him she went to pee and the only word he understood in their conversation was "Muhammed." The only person who knew about the call was Anina. Surely, that was knowledge she wouldn't reveal. She was sympathetic to their cause. She was educated. She knew about the Dead Sea Scrolls. Whatever he and Kate had found might find its way back to her convent, a trophy.

They continued lying low. The police continued talking, their motors still running, lights flashing.

"At least they haven't shut their motors," she said.

They waited. Lights appeared coming from the west.

"Should I look?" he asked.

"Don't risk it."

The lights from the car swung toward them.

"It's turning," he whispered. "No roadblock."

"That's good."

The police cars followed suit.

"That's even better," he said.

"Unless that was Muhammed, and they're on his tail," she murmured.

"It's still not seven. A few minutes to go."

Seven o'clock came and went. Kate was beginning to fidget. Chris was trying to not show his anxiety. Several cars passed. One was a taxi, but it was black. Muhammed would not have swapped cars. At seven thirty, they were about to give up and work their way back to town, see if he was waiting on them there, when lights appeared on the western horizon. As the lights neared, a small yellow light rode on top of them. As Chris and Kate rose to signal to the oncoming car, the flashing blue lights appeared again, coming from the town.

Kate re-holstered her gun. "Come on! Let's make a run for it."

Racing toward the approaching car lights, they began waving their arms. It was Muhammed in the white Mercedes. He stopped and through the open window began making excuses.

Chris jumped into the front seat and shouted, "Drive!"

Muhammed was still jabbering about being late.

"Shut up, Muhammed!" Kate commanded, opening the back door on the passenger side and throwing in her luggage, "and step on it. The police are after us."

Muhammed glanced north at the blue lights headed toward them, spun the car around in the direction he had come and laid down a stretch of rubber.

Chris and Kate fastened their seat belts. Chris recalled something Dr. Krekorian had said about Muhammed having no knowledge of bats out of hell. He was about to get acquainted.

Chris noted the blue lights were further back when Muhammed turned the car around, but the view through the side mirror suggested they were gaining. He looked at the speedometer. The needle quivered on a hundred and forty kilometers, over eighty miles an hour. At that speed, he wondered if the car could last.

Muhammed was muttering something under his breath, an eye on the road and the other on the rearview mirror.

"It's just one car," Kate observed. She was twisted around on the back seat looking through the rear window. "The other one may have dropped away."

Muhammed raised a fist and smiled as though he was winning a race. The lights of Jabadeen came into view. Muhammed did not slow. The strobing blue light was still behind them, the distance steady, about a half mile, Chris estimated. Past the sign that said JABADEEN, Muhammed slowed.

"They will catch up," Kate said loudly from the back.

Muhammed shook his head. In the center of town, he took a sharp right.

"What are you doing?" they both said simultaneously.

"Different way," he said, then gunned the motor through part of the business district and into a residential area, went over a slight rise, slowed and cut the lights. "I think I lose them."

They turned around and watched. For a moment nothing, just the lights of the town and the few cars moving through its dimly lit streets. They waited longer.

"Yes, I lose them," Muhammed said confidently just as the pulsing blue light appeared below the rise, almost from nowhere it seemed. The road rose sharply, and he accelerated into the foothills of the Ante-Lebanon Mountains.

"They are out of their jurisdiction," Chris said. "In America, they could not arrest us."

"In Syria, they arrest you. In Maaloula, Hama, Homs, Damascus—they arrest you," he said. "In Lebanon, they not arrest you."

The car ascended the mountain slopes, the lights of the desert plain falling away behind them. The police car continued chase, its blue throbbing light bouncing off the slopes and hills.

"Where does this take us, Muhammed?" Kate asked.

"Baalbek."

"That's northeast of Beirut," Chris asserted. "Way out of our way."

"Yes, but the police after you. If they follow to the border, much problem. If I lose them, not much problem. Also," he raised a finger, "less traffic this border." He continued up the mountain, a vigilant eye on his rearview."

Chris recalled Dr. Krekorian had made a similar comment.

In less than five miles, the road t-boned with another. "Here, I lose them," he said, and took a quick left then another sharp right, and disappeared into the folds of mountains. "They think I go other way."

"Where are we now?" she asked.

"Not far from Talat Musa and the border."

"How far?" Chris asked.

"Five, six miles. The lights gone," he said, thumbing over his shoulder.

"I'll be," breathed Chris.

"We're not out of the woods yet," Kate cautioned. "They may figure out what happened and double back to the dog-leg."

"That'll take them a few miles," Chris estimated. "By then, we should be across the border."

Muhammed pumped his head in agreement and reached his hand over the seat back. "The gun."

They'd forgotten the gun. Kate handed it to him, holster and all minus the brown wrapping, then took it back.

"The gun," he said again, bouncing his open hand.

"I've got a better place, Muhammed. You drive." She opened her carry-on, removed her clothes and accessories, unsnapped the hidden compartment partition, slid the holstered gun in beside the scroll and reversed the process. "There. Why didn't I think of that in the first place?"

"You did the same thing I did," he said.

"What?"

"Left all of your toiletries and makeup. I'm impressed."

"We didn't have time. I can replace makeup. We can't replace Mark's autograph, if that's what it is."

Minutes away, the border lights glared into the night. The same procedure was followed. Everyone had to get out of the car. Muhammed explained they had been to Maaloula and going next to Baalbek. Yes, they had had a hotel room. Muhammed gave the name of one.

Then another border guard approached. He had been on the phone in the glass booth. He spoke broken English. "Moment," he said. "Have you artifacts that belong to government of Syria?"

"No," Muhammed replied. "Nothing."

The official stepped in front of Chris. "Artifacts?"

"No!" Chris said. "We are tourists."

He turned to Kate, "You, any artifacts?"

"Nothing!" she answered.

"You passport, please."

They pulled out their passports with the green card inside and handed them to him. Chris was thinking, here we go again with the Israeli stamp saga, then wondered who had tipped them off. Maybe the police or the shopkeeper. From the cool airy top, he looked back down the mountain. No blue flashes. Not yet. They could have turned them off. But no reflected headlights were coming up the pass behind them.

The official looked only at the first page of their passports and pointed at the car. "We look."

"*Mafi Mushkili*," Muhammed said.

Chris whispered to Kate, "What did he say?"

"No problem," she whispered back.

They stood aside trying to appear nonchalant while two officials, the one who spoke English and another who joined him, inspected the car. They shined flashlights beneath its carriage, under the seats, and in the trunk, which was empty. They opened Chris' bag first, rummaged madly through it, closed it and opened hers. The official who spoke English removed all of her clothes, ran his hand around the interior, then looked back at her, said something in Arabic, and made a motion of combing his hair and putting on makeup. The others standing around laughed.

"I forgot it," she managed.

"Where you forget?"

She pretended to have a problem with the name.

"She leave it at Hotel Safir," Muhammed said. "I get them there."

The official began running his hand across the bottom. Chris' eyes were on Kate. He was swallowing air. She was holding her breath. The official put her things back in and re-zipped the carry-on.

He turned to them. "Shukran."

Blue flashes appeared down the pass.

"Shukran," Muhammed said and motioned them in the car.

The official motioned with his hand, waving them through the checkpoint.

No cars were lined up either at the Lebanon border. Muhammed and Dr. Krekorian were right, not a very popular crossing, at least at night. Chris and Kate glanced back at the Syrian border. The police car, blue light flashing, had arrived. They'd made it in the nick of time.

"We in Lebanon. You safe now," Muhammed said with a toothy smile.

"For now," affirmed Chris. "We have later to deal with."

"What's later?" she asked. "We're through the roughest part."

"It's something called customs. Then there's airport security, X-rays and scanners, just a few minor details," finishing his comment sarcastically.

"I've not had problems before," she said. "I can explain later."

He glanced at her from the front seat. "Yes, but before you didn't have someone back in Maaloula who … " he glanced at Mohammed at the same time she clamped a finger over her lips. "Nevermind!" he broke off.

"They have no inkling what *it* is," she said. "In fact, neither do we."

"We have an inkling," he said. "That doesn't matter. I just hope your you-know-what holds up."

"Speaking of airports," she threw in, "we need to call Dr. Krekorian and check on airlines out of Beirut tonight."

"We probably cannot get out tonight," he advised. "It's past eight now."

"Probably no service now," Mohammed said.

She pulled out her cell phone and checked. *No Service available.* "Mohammed's right. I'll have to wait until I get closer to Beirut."

"That's not long," Chris calculated.

"Thirty minute, phone okay," said Muhammed.

For a while they rode in silence, the car making its way down the Ante-Lebanon foothills into the Bekaa Valley. In the distance, lights, spotlights casting an orange glow on pillars rising out of the dark.

"Baalbek," Muhammed pointed.

"Heliopolis," Chris whispered.

"No, Baalbek," Muhammed insisted.

"They're the same," Chris said. "Heliopolis is its classical Roman name, 'city of sun.' It is counted as one of the wonders of the ancient world. The Romans transformed the Canaanite god Baal into the Roman god Jupiter."

She leaned forward and placed a hand on Chris' shoulder. "That's where our wedding was going to take place, darling. Remember?"

He turned around and smiled. "Well ... it's not too late."

"No time for wedding," Muhammed said. "No stop."

As they neared, the six rose granite columns of Jupiter, crowned by elaborate capitals, rose majestically from the light like ancient rockets launching into the dark

"On the return trip, I asked the U. N. driver to go out of his way so I could see them," she said solemnly. "Did you know the granite columns were shipped from five hundred miles deep in Egypt, at Aswan, up the eastern Mediterranean coast, over the Lebanon Mountains, then across the Bekaa Valley?"

"I had heard that," he said then turned and looked at her. "Even more impressive is that fragile papyrus from Egypt, if kept dry, can last as long."

She patted his shoulder, one of agreement. Her hand and eyes lingered before she removed the hand, but not the eyes that continued gazing languidly into his. He turned around. She did not sit back. He could feel her arms across the seat back on his shoulders, her breath on his neck. He did not figure her as a touchy feely person and reflected on her fall at the cave, the look in her eyes, the expression on her face. It was not one of pain or embarrassment or concern.

"Try the call again," Chris suggested, hopeful they could fly out tonight. Security might be more lax.

She checked and had cell service, dialed the number. Chris heard a female voice answer, a pause, then a male voice he recognized as Dr. Krekorian's. The conversation that ensued made Kate smile. "Fine. If you have the rooms," she said. "If there is availability, the six o'clock flight in the morning is perfect. It's on Air France so ticket transfers should be no problem."

More talk on the other end.

"Thank you, Dr. Krekorian, for handling that for us. Your kindness exceeds our expectations."

Muhammed took them safely to the hospital but not before they were startled by a flashing blue light. A police car behind them had stopped another vehicle.

All three breathed a sigh of relief.

CHAPTER TWENTY-SIX

Maaloula, Mid-Spring, 90 A.D.

John Mark and Miriam had been there several weeks, their time absorbed mostly in making their new home in the cave more livable. To obliterate the old odors, they had burned some fragrant herbs she had found growing wild nearby. The donkey had been content to forage among the rocks and crevices for his nutrition and had never strayed far from them, returning each evening to his water bowl. To conserve precious olive oil, they had lighted lamps only at night. A fire at the mouth of the cave had been kept alive during the day for cooking. With large flat sandstone and shale slabs, Miriam had designed a hearth with a back and sides to protect the flame from wind and allow for banking the coals in the evenings. She had cooked the provisions they had brought with them which lasted a week, except for the large sack of grain, which should serve them at least a month. A tenth of the grain they had contributed to a communal storage bin. When men in the group had killed wild game, meat was apportioned throughout the community. A steady influx of refugees fleeing persecutions had maintained the food storage. Some of the men, diverting water from the stream, had devised an irrigation system and had begun sowing seeds for small crops. All were hopeful for a fall harvest that would grow as irrigated and cultivated acreage extended outward from the cliffs. All of this activity had made them more vulnerable to detection but they hoped and prayed they were beyond the long arm of persecution. Others before them had succeeded.

Miriam had brought scrolls of *The Scriptures* with them, their only reading material, and they had morning and evening devotions. John Mark's vision had continued to worsen and she had to read to him. These moments had been the anchors of their days and eventually a ritual had developed. They would sit beneath the scriptures from Isaiah carved into the wall and, each time, Miriam would recite the words before she opened one of the scrolls and read from it.

Most Sabbaths and mid-week days, using the donkey to steady them and prevent their falling, they slowly and tediously negotiated their way down the rocky slope to the valley to collect fresh water from the stream in the few jars they had brought and visit other refugees who came for their water. Miriam washed clothes with the women and John Mark visited with the men who were not out hunting and gathering wild fruit and nuts. Soon, the mid-week gathering became a regular practice for all the Christian exiles. It also became an occasion, in addition to their regular Sabbath service, for worship as a group. Even when they had enough water collected from rain showers, John Mark and Miriam would make the effort to attend the gatherings.

The Sabbath service occurred at the cleft in the mountain, directly beneath the cave that held what were believed to be, by some, the revered bones of Thecla. Each time, one of the younger men climbed to the cave that contained bones believed to be those of Thecla, brought one of the bones down, placed it on the ground amid the congregation and, after the service, returned it to the cave.

The practice upset John Mark and Miriam. They contended it was a form of idolatry and they vocalized their views. Thecla devotees defended the ritual. Had not God opened the cleft in the mountain for her when she was pursued by Roman soldiers? Were they not following in her footsteps, in her same situation? But the majority was persuaded by John Mark and Miriam. Was he not the author of the gospel of Christ? Was she not Peter's daughter? In short time, the practice halted, but Thecla's adherents would not be denied. Each Sabbath, they climbed to the cave, those who were able, and worshipped her bones.

Zacharias, John Mark and Miriam's new friend, whom they met when they arrived, served as the leader of the congregation. He had been a presbyter in the ecclesia in Caesarea Philippi. John Mark had been a presbyter at one of the ecclesia in Damascus, but he had been too old to lead. Each service, at their new home, however, he was called upon to recite from the gospel he had written, for word had circulated about the precious scroll.

From copying the scroll numerous times, he knew the entire manuscript from memory. If his memory faltered, which occurred occasionally, Miriam, who also knew the scroll by heart, picked up the thread until he regained the verbal rhythm, then she allowed him to continue. Due to limited bread and wine, communion was held only on the first Sabbath of each month. At one point, water was substituted for wine, not an uncommon practice even in areas where wine was plentiful.

When John Mark and Miriam were not making their way into the valley to get water and to worship, a steady stream of friends, old and new, climbed up to visit them. Upon their arrival, the word had spread quickly that an apostle and the daughter of Peter were among them. People came to get close to Jesus, they said, but also to see the inscription on the wall for there were no others like it in any of the other caves, as though this one had become a shrine because of its inhabitants and the holy word on the wall. John Mark and Miriam welcomed all who came and spent hours answering their questions about Jesus and Peter, and Paul when it became known John Mark had traveled with the famed apostle.

Often, questions about the two scrolls were asked. Was the largest, in fact, a gospel of Christ. What then, was the smallest? When did John Mark begin to write the gospel? Did the work contain Jesus' teachings? What stories were recorded? What miracles? Often, there were requests for them to quote from the gospel. As long as they were alive, the word would live, for they knew the book word for word, could write it again without the original which they often had found themselves doing instead of copying.

As expected, discussions about Jesus and the disciples and their beliefs surfaced. Almost always, questions about the resurrection were involved. None at the cave compound had seen or met anyone who had seen the resurrected Jesus, the Christ. Had they, an apostle and the daughter of Peter, seen him? They had to confess they had not, though they had met and spoken with others who had. John Mark sat back and listened as the discussions took familiar twists and turns. Some believed in the resurrection, and some did not. Those who did not said the words and life of Jesus were all that was necessary. Some indicated they had heard of another document circulating among followers of Jesus that contained only his sayings and nothing of his crucifixion or resurrection. A few from Caesarea Philippi said this scroll had been read to their ecclesia and that many were impressed. Others disagreed with them and clung to the resurrected Jesus and cited a letter from the apostle Paul that said without the resurrection of Jesus their faith was dead; it was nothing. Some among them who, because they believed knowledge was the path of salvation, were called gnostics. They said Jesus was never human and spoke of a spiritual resurrection but not one of flesh and blood, not a physical body risen from the grave.

John Mark and Miriam sat back and listened to these circuitous discussions that eventually wound their way back to them and what they believed. Miriam would turn and defer to her husband, who would always say, "Faith is a personal matter. The question you ask faces you, not me or my wife. What we believe is unimportant. What do you believe?" Some were upset with this deflection. Why did John Mark write a gospel, tidings of good news, if he could not answer the question. "The answer is in your belief," he always responded.

The first major task facing John Mark and Miriam was construction of the permanent home for the scrolls. It was a daunting task. They were old and could not lift heavy rocks. Both had built walls in their youth and knew the mechanics. Rocks, large and small, were plentiful in the area. Clay was also plentiful around the cave's entrance. When it rained, water flowed into the cave, a constant problem. The solution was to dig up the ground in front of the cave creating a runoff slope and channel. They accomplished this by using the flat ends of thin rock slab as shovels. Slowly, little by little, they excavated, creating a mound of gray clay to be used as cement for the rocks they gathered and then later as a form of rough plaster finish so the front and sides flowed naturally with the cave wall.

They needed more water than anticipated. Using their jugs strapped to the donkey, a young lad John Mark met at one of the services, Tomas, brought water up to them daily from the stream. He helped with some of the heavier stones, and they taught him how to use the clay and mud to keep the rocks in place. He would take no pay and was honored to help an apostle and the daughter of Peter, his eyes gleaming with satisfaction and pride.

Aside from the normal chores and weekly services in the valley, they had little to do except work on the enclosure. Day by day, rock by rock, in a month they finished, leaving an opening for the jars before the final rocks were placed and sealed. A plaster was applied over the false wall so it had the rough texture of the cave wall and blended with it. Once their work had set and dried, only on close inspection could one see the seal lines between the rocks.

The day they finished was memorable, but only for them. No one, not even Tomas, knew the real reason of their creation. When others asked, they said it was to make an addition to their new home and smiled. They'd convinced each other they were not being dishonest; it was an addition. No one would know otherwise.

John Mark looked at Miriam and said a prayer. He slid the smaller jar through an orifice on the rear of the enclosure, and rolled it to one side with his hand making room for the larger jar. Miriam helped him with the larger urn. John Mark prayed again, and carefully, inch by inch, their hands moved the vessel through the narrow opening and into its crypt. After they sealed it, they embraced and wept.

"We weep as though we are burying something," Miriam cried.

"We are," John Mark affirmed, dabbing at his own eyes, "but someday, far away in time, it will be resurrected."

"Your words and our timing are fortuitous," she responded.

"I do not understand."

"Surely, you know tomorrow is the Sabbath, not just any Sabbath."

His eyes lit up. "You are right. It has been sixty years."

The completion of the final resting place of the scrolls could not have been more timely. The following morning as they arose to celebrate the day of the Lord's resurrection and looked west, beneath a clear blue sky, their eyes followed the receding shadow of the mountain cast by the rising sun and saw a thin ominous cloud of dust swirling along the shadow's edge. Sitting in their chairs in the entrance of their cave, as they did each morning for devotion, they watched the cloud grow closer, as a storm moves. Then they saw the bobbing head of Tomas scrambling up the rocky slope, exasperated as he arrived.

"The Romans are coming!" he exclaimed and pointed toward the cloud of dust.

"How do you know the disturbance is Romans and not a larger group of exiles?" John Mark inquired.

"Exiles traveling just ahead of them arrived early this morning with the news."

"How many Romans?" Miriam asked.

"About one hundred," the young man reported. "We must leave at once. I came to help you."

"We are grateful to you, Tomas, for warning us," John Mark said sadly, "but we are too old and too tired to leave."

"We will stay," Miriam agreed. "We have each other and will die with each other. As a great woman of our tradition once said when faced with overwhelming odds, 'If I die, I die.'"

"Yes, I know those words," Tomas said, "but Esther had no choice. She could not escape. We can go to the higher mountains and wait until they are gone."

"We are high enough," John Mark said confidently. "Go, help your family. Tell them we are fine. On this day of days, the Lord is with us. We have no fear."

"Yes, my family and I know the meaning of this day," Tomas said. "God bless you. We do not want it to be remembered as a day of death," and he quickly departed toward the valley. He stopped once and looked back to see if they were preparing to follow him, but they had not moved from their chairs and he gave him a final farewell wave.

Throughout the day, they sat and watched the dust cloud expand as it grew nearer. Miriam brought the donkey inside the cave and tied him up. John Mark shoveled dirt into the fire to bank it and smother the smoke lest it identify a place of habitation. They moved everything into the cave. With luck, the small army might be distracted by other things in the valley. Water for their thirsty horses, for there was no other spring within miles. They would see the efforts of irrigation, stop and investigate. They might get so distracted they would not see the needle eye entrance of the siq. If they did, the gorge was narrow. Unless they threaded single file, a small army could not pass through it. Would their commander, a centurion like Jairus of Capernaum, waste time in such an endeavor? John Mark thought not, but Miriam was more cautious. They should leave the cave and trek up the mountain to the other side. He overruled the idea. The scrolls were safe. Their mission on earth was done. They had few years left. "If we die, we die," he repeated to her.

All day, they sat and watched. Late afternoon, the dust column passed behind the mountain that protected them and was no longer visible. They could hear the distant rumble of horses' hooves and then that, too, grew silent.

"They are stopping for the night," John Mark said.

"Yes," she agreed. "They will come in the morning."

In the intimacy of the gathering dark in the cave, the moon visible through its opening, she gazed into his eyes, reached for his hand, and smiled. He observed how, like a child, she was curled up, her right cheek on a dusty cushion, her right arm up towards her face, her hand closed like a fist against her jaw. Her eyebrows shifted, her face was deep in concentration. He watched her chest rise with each heartbeat, listened to her steady regular breathing until he knew she was asleep. He had come to believe she had spiritual powers beyond those even of her father, that she was a saint the world would probably never know, only the extension of her saintliness, her handwriting moved by the Spirit.

He lay awake looking at her, moonlight on her face like skin, remembering how they had met, their years together, all they had accomplished despite the years they had not been together. He thought of what had become of their accomplishments, the spreading of the gospel throughout the empire and beyond. In his mind, he saw the good news spread to a point in time beyond the beyond, when it would be discovered anew and the buried sentences realign the message to its straight and true course, eclipse the substitutes, some worthy and some not, that were sure to follow. Trees would die and sprout, the land would shift and change, empires collapse and new empires rise. But the master's word would remain safe and unchanged and on that thought, he closed his eyes.

CHAPTER TWENTY-SEVEN

Beirut International Airport, November 1, 2011

Their plane was scheduled to leave Beirut at 6:00 a.m. but the flight had been delayed and was now scheduled to depart at 7:50. Chris hoped the early morning scene at the departure curb of the Rafic Hariri Airport would end soon. Muhammed was emotional. He'd grown to love them and hated to see them go. They shared similar sentiments with him, which made the parting more difficult. Kate was fighting back tears. Chris was having trouble restraining his emotions. Despite their protests, Muhammed insisted on carrying their luggage inside with a security guard barking at him to move his car. Once inside, before the Air France ticket counter, the scene repeated. Kate maintained some semblance of composure as Muhammed hugged them one more time and back-pedaled to the door where he was about to receive a citation for being over-parked.

"Except out running and eluding Abdas and the shopkeeper, that's the most difficult thing I've had to do," Chris said.

"I would add not killing Abdas," she managed, still emotionally affected from saying goodbye to Muhammed.

The Beirut airport was renovated in '04, its overall rating in the Mid-East second only to the airport at Dubai. Once inside the spacious foyer ringed by shops and restaurants, they saw the first of many signs plastered everywhere: PASSENGERS COMING TO OR LEAVING THE LEBANESE TERRITORIES MUST DECLARE ANY AND ALL ITEMS IN THEIR POSSESSION.

"We have nothing to declare," he said.

"Absolutely," she confirmed.

They passed through an initial security check point and then followed the signs to ticketing. A Lebanese officer checked their papers.

"The entire airport is under the authority of the Lebanese army," she pointed out. "That's just the first security check. There will be another after ticketing and another before we board. A point in our favor." She pointed at their carry-ons. "They inspect the luggage rapidly and selectively."

Except for the exit tax they had to pay, seventy-five thousand Lebanese pounds each for business class seats and an additional five thousand departure tax, getting their tickets altered was a breeze. Fortunately, Dr. Krekorian had called and secured seats. The clerk behind the counter told them it was a full flight and asked if they wanted to check their luggage. They may have difficulty securing overhead space.

They looked at each other, the obvious message telegraphed. Chris told the clerk he would take his. He could see Kate's wheels turning. If she checked her carry-on it would be subject to random scanning, not the more thorough security check at the gate. The chance of the scroll being detected was significantly reduced, but it was also out of her sight and control. Lost and delayed luggage on Air France were legend. She wavered, looked at the clerk, looked at Chris and then said, "I'll take it with me."

Security was nerve-racking. Several officers checked their tickets and passports three times. Only one of them saw Chris' Israeli stamp, looked him over carefully, and told him to pass on. Chris emptied his pockets and put his bag on the conveyer belt ahead of her, watched it disappear though the black flaps. An officer motioned him to step through the X-ray booth. A bell dinged. He stepped back, removed his belt and passed through cleanly. Another officer conducted a body check. The officer checking the scanner told him he needed to step aside and open his bag. The officer rummaged through and came up with his Swiss knife. He told the officer he'd forgotten about it, and it was confiscated.

So far, so good. Chris looked back at Kate. She was putting her bag on the conveyor belt. This was the critical moment. There would be another check of luggage at customs, but it was selective and often cursory. They wouldn't see the false bottom. This scanner would pick up everything in it but might not detect the partition. Kate had told him she always packed a pair of heels and other clothing items in the false bottom to throw the airport scanners off. "That way they don't see empty space and suspect a hidden compartment," she had said. Kate stepped through the body scanner. Nothing. She was clean.

The bag stayed in the scanning compartment longer than usual. Chris was standing, watching Kate, stiff with fear, digging his fists into his pockets, watching. A security officer told him to move on. Collecting his belongings, he heard them ask for the owner of a bag. It was Kate's. They needed her to open her bag. She was cool and calm. He was just a few feet away and in a cold sweat.

She unzipped the bag and stood back. The security official, who seemed to know what he was looking for and the location, ran his hand down the back side of the interior. Kate stood there, her arms folded. She could have been a cutout poster, she was so still. The official pulled out a tube of toothpaste. Kate apologized and told him it was an oversight on her part, that she should have put it in a Ziploc bag separate from her carry-on. The toothpaste was confiscated. She was told to re-zip her bag and move on.

They collected their belongings. Chris put his shoes and belt back on. She slipped into her boots and put on her earrings.

"You just about caused me to have a coronary," Chris said under his breath.

"And I didn't almost have a seizure and defecate in my pants?" she exclaimed.

"You're a seasoned traveler. The toothpaste is not something you would have forgotten."

"Truly, I did not know it was there," she said. "Rashida was helping me get off this morning. The carry-on was open. She must have dropped it in. What's your excuse about the knife?"

"I made it through coming. I got lax this time and put it in the corner on the bottom."

"That's more serious than toothpaste," she admonished. "Let's hope we make it home."

"Regardless, we will live."

"Hopefully, not in a Lebanese prison," she admonished.

They were approaching the customs area. A sign on a post, in bold letters, read:

IT IS ABSOLUTELY FORBIDDEN TO EXPORT WEAPONS, AMMUNITIONS, NARCOTICS AND ARCHAEOLOGICAL PIECES AND CURRENCY.

She commented, "There are special forms for declaring. You have to jump through multiple hoops, type the items on double papers, get it signed by a customs controller, and have a serial registration number on both copies. Antiquities require an export license."

"Sounds like it takes an act of Congress."

"Oh! Yours acts?" She knocked him on the shoulder.

"Touché. But aren't we breaking a law?"

"Not a Lebanese law. What we have didn't come from Lebanon."

They continued walking down the corridor, and then she stopped.

"My God!" she said, startled.

"What?"

"The official at one of the queues. He's the same one who let us through without a fuss, the one I told we were engaged and getting married at Baalbek."

"Maybe, we're in luck."

"Maybe." She stepped in front of him and turned around. "Just pretend I'm talking to you about something." He looked down and observed her remove the ring from her right hand. "Don't look down." She made the transition to her ring finger then turned the ring around. It had a pearl mounting with two smaller pearls either side. Rotated, the mounting was concealed. Only the band showed. "Now, does that look like we're married?"

He put his arm around her and pulled her to him, "Yes, darling."

She laughed. "That's good. Let him see two love birds."

The customs official recognized them as they approached and motioned them into his queue. He was smiling and asked if they got married. She didn't respond verbally but raised her left hand, her thumb coving the mounting. He smiled and said something else. Chris recognized the word Baalbek and she nodded. The official asked to see their passports. He stamped them, pointed on the second page of Chris's wagging his finger and tut-tutting him about the Israeli stamp, and then wished them well.

One hand pulling their carry-ons, they held hands with the other to the plane's gate.

At the gate, their documents were checked one more time, then they sat and waited. The plane would not depart for another hour and a half. The specter of the Syrian authorities hung over them. Once seated on the plane, their carry-ons stowed overhead, they could still be stopped from leaving the country. Not until the 747 was moving full throttle down the runway and Chris heard the landing gears grind and lock into place could he release a relaxed breath. He leaned toward Kate. "The professor is a prophet," he whispered in her ear.

"I know," she whispered back. "How so today?"

"Remember, at Greyfriars Bobby's he said, 'All Saints Day. It bodes well.'"

She nodded.

Blue. Within minutes, that's all Chris could see from his window; the cloudless sky, the Mediterranean below. Borrowing a delay or, heaven forbid, a malfunction, after a four hour Paris layover they'd arrive in Edinburgh at 4:45 p. m., in the dark.

CHAPTER TWENTY-EIGHT

Edinburgh, November 1, 2011

All night, beneath a single lamp over the center of the long table, with delicate care and millimeter by agonizing millimeter, Kate's surgically gloved hands had been unrolling the scroll. All night, she had carefully plodded, the ancient dry papyrus whispering in her hands, her fingers lightly touching, slowly rotating the scroll, sheet after sheet sliding beneath the bright cone of light from the magnifying visor clamped to her forehead. Often, Chris had found himself more focused on her, the intensity in her eyes, her graceful fingers touching, moving the scroll. the ballet of her hands.

Seated on either side of her, he and the professor had been taking notes, translating, sharing the discoveries. Similarities of the protocol with the protocol of the first draft, had elicited a cheer. Next had come the magical moment of the first words, *The beginning of the gospel of Jesus Christ, the Son of God.* Later, at the point of Peter's confession, a surprise. A sliver of cloth had appeared and Kate had dropped it into a glassine envelope, marked and sealed it for further analysis. The analysis, she had said would date the cloth and its location.

Throughout the lengthy process, the evidence had been mounting. The scroll had appeared to be the result of the aborted draft. Not only were the protocols similar, their dates—66 C.E.—and places of manufacture—Tyre—were the same. The handwriting of the two manuscripts—style, formation and slant of letters—was indistinguishable. Vocabulary, syntax and grammar matched. With minor variants, the text was *verbatim* with the twenty page draft.

But not all had been cause for celebration. It had taken Kate thirty minutes to untie the leather thongs binding the scroll on its rods and another half hour to open the protocol glued to the first page. There had been numerous glitches, times the scroll would stick, its movement halt. Each time, deftly using her manuscript tools—scapulas, tweezers, needles—and applying a combination of techniques, Kate had overcome the obstacles. Each time, she had picked up where she had left off.

In addition to the problems, questions had arisen. What might, or might not, the scroll reveal? Was it a full scroll or another aborted attempt with the real autograph buried somewhere in the caves of Syria? Was it John Mark's work or someone else's? Would the writer leave proof of authorship, initials or a signature? What would the manuscript say about the miracle of all miracles, the resurrection? Looking on as it had unrolled, Chris had imagined how the author must have felt dropping the letters, creating the words, weaving the narrative strands. Did John Mark, if he was the author, have any inkling of the impact of his message upon humanity, any idea he was shaping the destiny of cultures and kingdoms to come? Once the discoveries of the two documents were made public, the impact of Mark's interpretation of the resurrection on Christianity could be explosive. It could cause splits within the church, great schisms, possibly, God forbid, destroy it. In Mark's Gospel, Jesus's tomb, like those of the other evangelists, is empty. But, his treatment of the resurrection could be the equivalent of an un-empty tomb. To Chris, the answer loomed as a terrible weight for the future of the Church as he continued watching the unveiling of the scroll.

As the pages had unrolled, Chris and the professor had conversed about the similarities with the rough draft. At times, the professor had translated aloud from the Greek. The intervals when no one was speaking, the only sound in the room had been the whisper of ancient papyrus unscrolling, its soft scratchy movement, the slight bumps it made over the glued seam lines of the pages.

Until:

The sound was new, a sharp snap, like a twig breaking.

The scroll stopped.

"Rubbish!" Kate cried out.

Everyone cringed. Unable to look, the professor turned away.

"What is it?" Chris asked, seeing the anguish on Kate's face.

"The leather tab!" she said exasperated. "Part of the leather fastener, that caused problems at the beginning, is folded over the edge of the scroll."

"What can you do?" the professor asked, his voice trembling, his eyes alarmed.

"Without causing damage to the page, I'm unsure," she replied.

"Perhaps you should just remove the tab," the professor offered impatiently. "It's not that important. Cut it off."

"With all due respects, Professor," Chris quickly responded, "the tab is a valuable part of the scroll."

For a long time, Kate sat studying the situation. She fogged the magnifying glass with her breath, wiped it on a corner of her sweater sleeve, stood up and assessed the snag from different angles. She picked up a knife-like tool resembling a letter opener, inserted the tip between the tab and the papyrus sheet, gently levered it back and forth, a movement that reminded Chris of someone trying to pry open a sealed envelope. Her brow furrowed, she sat looking at the scroll, tapping the knife on the table. "I could mist it," she said, "but I don't want to compromise the ink, cause any smears. The writing is so clear and unblemished, near perfect."

After several minutes of study, she spotted a possible solution. "The tab covers the margin where there's no print." She picked up a small flask and lightly, carefully, sprayed an olive oil/water mist around the edges of the tab. She waited a few minutes, tried the letter opener, attempted to move the roll. It wouldn't budge.

She looked at Chris. She looked at Professor Stewart. "This may be as far as we get," she said, downcast. "We may have to send it to high-tech, to the British Museum."

The professor groaned. "It would be out of our control. The news would break."

"Sooner or later the news is going to break," Chris reminded him.

"Yes, laddie" the professor agreed, mild irritation in his voice. "You're an archaeologist. You know timing is essential in releasing discoveries to the media. Particularly this one from Syria."

Flipping his palms up, Chris gave an enigmatic shrug.

Kate looked again at the scroll. "We're about seventy-five percent done."

"That's an eternity from the end," the professor murmured dolefully.

Kate had told them it might take hours, depending on setbacks, glitches. They'd been there since six o'clock the evening before. They'd come straight from the plane to the professor's office, phoning ahead to tell him their arrival time and that they had a scroll. Chris had estimated the scroll's length at twenty-five feet and had worked the math. She was probably right. They'd be there throughout the night, probably into early morning before they reached the end of the scroll. Now they were three fourths finished and the early Scottish dawn approaching. Chris checked the time on the clock: 4:15.

Through the tall windows, the brooding misty night had cleared. The wheeling sky, as though turning with the scroll, revealed the horned moon low on the horizon, cocked over the castle turrets like a bright insignia. It was the same moon Chris and Kate had seen in Lebanon and Syria, as if it was riding the dark and following them. Beneath that hopeful omen, they waited.

"Where are we in the narrative, Professor?" Chris asked.

The professor looked again at the page before them. "In Gethsemane, the arrest of Jesus. A young man, presumably our John Mark, is fleeing naked after being stripped of his linen garment."

"How ironic," Kate said sadly, "that we should have to leave it at this point, and because of a fastener."

On *fastener*, they heard a slight pop from the table. The right roll had shifted. Kate reached over and nudged it lightly with a finger. It moved.

"Och aye!" the professor exclaimed, bringing his hands together in a single clap, then steepling them in prayer.

"Your mist worked," Chris said to Kate.

She smiled weakly, snapped on her visor light and continued, scrolled more slowly, deliberately, as though fearing another snag.

Nearing the end, tension grew. Fatigue set in. Fighting sleep, each of them, Chris observed, were moving as though in slow motion through deep water. They'd taken only one coffee break, around midnight. His eyelids grew heavy. Twice he'd almost nodded off. He noticed Kate constantly rubbing her sleep-shot eyes with the heel of her gloved hands. She was becoming more exasperated, less patient. Her hands shook. She jumped at sudden noises—a gust of wind rattling the windows, the professor scooting his chair, the automatic shut off on the coffee pot. Borrowing further surprises, she should finish about seven, near sunrise. But could she endure?

Or the professor? He was having problems seeing the manuscript as it scrolled slowly beneath Kate's bright visor light. His voice was weak and, at times, sounded faraway, his words drawn out more slowly.

They brought Jesus to the place ... called ... Golgotha. The professor's voice shook and halted.

Kate abruptly stopped scrolling.

Chris and Kate looked at their mentor.

"Professor Stewart, are you all right?" Chris asked.

"Yes, yes," he replied and rolled his hand for Kate to continue.

Kate commenced scrolling and the professor resumed translating but the mood in the room had changed. It was as though, at that point, the words on the ancient papyrus sheets breathed, became flesh and blood, took on a life of their own. *They brought Jesus to the place called Golgotha* did not transport them back to a place in time but into that time, as though they were living it, the words infused beneath their skin.

With deep emotion, the professor translated the crucifixion and death of Jesus. Kate had to stop and dab her eyes. Chris found himself wiping away tears. He noticed that Kate's breathing became heavy, at times billowing the scroll sheet from the table.

• • •

Through the tall windows, early morning came like a time of magic, that gray time after first light and before sunrise. Chris recalled Steinbeck had called it, "the hour of the pearl—the interval between day and night when time stops and examines itself." An adage in the Jewish Kabbalah said that wisdom comes half hour before and half hour after sunrise. They were on the brink.

The professor read:

As they entered the tomb, they saw a young man dressed in a white robe sitting on the right side and they were alarmed. "Don't be alarmed," he said. "You are looking for Jesus the Nazarene, who was crucified. He has risen! He is not here. See the place where they laid him. But, go tell his disciples and Peter. He is going ahead of you into Galilee. There you will see him, just as he told you. Trembling and bewildered, the women went out and fled from the tomb. They said nothing to anyone, because they were afraid.

Kate stopped. She looked at the professor then at Chris, a look that said, "Are you ready?"

A shiver passed through Chris. *Am I ready? Is the Church ready?*

Wide-eyed, on the edge of his seat, the professor twirled a finger.

Kate sat gazing at the scroll. After several minutes, she lifted her left hand, held it momentarily as though suspended, then slowly lowered it. Grasping the full roll, fingers deftly turned the right rod.

"Ah," she murmured, the tone between wonder and challenge. Chris and the professor saw it, too, the overlapping double-reinforced page signifying the end of the scroll.

Gravity bolted them to the moment.

"It exists," the professor whispered.

Suddenly, through the windows, the sun laid a band of light across the scroll. Kate's fingers turned again. The last page slid into view.

In that radiant silence, in a somber trembling voice, the professor translated:

> But one of them stopped and halted the others and said to them, "Why are we afraid?" He said, "Don't be alarmed, he has risen go and tell his disciples and Peter." And so the women found the disciples in the upper room where they stayed and told them what they had seen and heard and the disciples did not believe.

Kate was listening but Chris could not wait. He could read *koine* and his eyes moved ahead of the professor's slow translation. He had expected to see a final page. He had expected to see the words *arisen, faith, belief* and *spirit*. But, with astonishment and wonder, he saw words he had not expected to see, read sentences he had not expected to read. He waited for the professor to catch up and observed his eyes wide with surprise, his voice halting on the final words.

After a brief silence, with a faint smile Kate whispered, "Quintessential Mark," and she turned out the visor light.

The professor reread the final sentences then slumped in his chair. His hands fell limp over the arms.

"I guess that's it," Chris sighed dropping his hands to his thighs.

The remark startled the professor and he bolted upright. "Not yet, laddie," he cautioned then he looked at Kate. "Continue!" He nodded at the scroll.

She looked at him questionably as she tucked a strand of hair behind her ear. "But that is the last page."

"I hope against hope, lassie, not the last of this last page," and he nodded again.

Reluctantly, she turned the visor light back on. She lifted a forefinger, rolled it over the scroll a slight turn and there it was, at the bottom edge almost out of view. Not his initials, but his full name. Ἰωάννου Μάρκου.

They sat staring at the page, at the last two words, as though they were eyes staring back at them. Like a blade, the band of sunlight slid diagonally from the page down the table then disappeared, replaced with a great golden light of the fully risen sun.

EPILOGUE

Grand Canyon, Arizona, February 14, 2012

"Something big happened here, Mommy," Kate exclaimed, and raised her glass of champagne.

Chris raised his glass and touched hers.

Dressed casually in blue jeans and flannel shirts and loafers, they lay in lounge chairs on the deck of El Tovar Lodge on the edge of the Grand Canyon's southern rim. Chris had picked her up earlier in the day at the Flagstaff Airport and taken her to see his home, which was on the way. She was taken with the place. She took it all in, observing the little things of his civilization. She kept saying how unique and original the house was with its wall length floor to ceiling windows, spectacular views of the mountains, three bedrooms and baths and two stone fireplaces. He wasn't sure they would ever leave. He shouldn't have told her it was designed by famed architect Edward Jones and that not a single tree was cut during construction, facts which caused another barrage of comments and questions.

"But we shouldn't be here," she said, her tone playfully admonishing.

The comment caught him off guard. He was thinking of the different angles of her beauty. In the bright sunlight her dark red hair turned lighter, her fair skin freckled. Light filled her eyes firing them Irish green. The slant of her Celtic cheekbones added a classical dimension of elegance. "Oh!"

"We should be in Dunbar dining in the manor on my home-cooked food," she said. "The gospel didn't stop at chapter sixteen, verse eight. That was the deal."

He turned and faced her, their bodies mirror images on the chaises. "We are here, dear one, because the issue was not just about a last page but also the resurrection," he retorted gently, his face serious. "The two are intertwined. Yes, there was a last page." He raised a finger. "And, yes, Mark does report a resurrection." He raised a second finger. "But—"

"—But," she interrupted with a teasing smile, "it was not the resurrection you expected."

"That is precisely," choosing that word intentionally, "why we are here and you are not stirring in the manor kitchen at Dunbar. I had thought that the last page would be similar to verses nine through twenty, as we have them in current translations." He paused for a sip of champagne. "I was wrong. I was prepared for the disciples dining at Peter's house. I was prepared for a wind-like phenomenon surrounding them and a voice speaking to them from the wind." He stopped, as if awaiting confirmation of his understanding of the final passage.

She gave him an agreeing nod.

He continued. "But I was *not* prepared for what the voice said: 'The shepherd was struck and his sheep scattered. You were told I had risen and you did not believe. You were told I would go ahead and meet you in Galilee.' Then came the startling statements."

"Not as startling to me," she remarked. "But I understand how they would be to you," and she tipped her glass toward him. "Continue."

"Jesus said, 'I did not say you will see me. Go! Tell others you have been with me, in my presence but not seen me. By faith, I have risen; by faith, we rise.' I remember that sentence. It jumped off the page at me."

"Based upon my memory of the passage," she injected, "the lines following confirmed: 'Many have seen and not believed. Blessed are those who have not seen me and believe I have risen. There is no greater faith.' That was it. And I said, 'Quintessential Mark.' The book ended as abruptly as it began. No introduction or background to Jesus' arrival and none for his departure. That's Mark."

"No description of the resurrected Jesus," he lamented. "I was not ready for that."

"Because the nature of the divine resurrected Christ was indescribable," she added and continued, her face becoming animated. "Think about it. The idea is consistent with Old Testament scribes avoiding description of

Jehovah. In Mark's last page, the disciples do not see Jesus, they hear him. They feel his presence, a key word. There is the voice from the wind, wind a euphemism for spirit. The key concept is presence, one that is indescribable Old Testament again. You even said yourself, on the way to Maaloula, that the oldest New Testament traditions do not have descriptions of the resurrected Christ."

He raised his glass in accord. "I did say that. And I agree with you. Mark treats the resurrection with even greater mystery than his other miracles. He leaves it up to the reader to draw conclusions about the resurrected Christ. You had used the term 'leap of faith.'"

She nodded.

"The resurrection occurred," he said flatly. "But no mention of 'how' or 'what,' no descriptions. In other words," he looked directly into her eyes, 'something big happened.'"

She smiled grandly.

"But how do we interpret that 'something big' for twenty-first century Christians? Do we leave the interpretation as dangling as that last page dangled for two thousand years?"

She peered out over the canyon for several minutes then, with a serious expression on her face, looked at him. "I think the resurrection of Jesus Christ means something new has happened, more than just survival after death. I recall something C. S. Lewis once wrote in connection with the resurrection and I've never forgotten it. He said, 'A totally new mode of being has arisen in the universe. Something new had appeared in the universe: as new as the first coming of organic life.' To me, that's the most profound statement I've ever read or heard about the resurrection of Christ."

"Now, that speaks," he said, raising his glass. "Not only to the twenty-first century, but to centuries before and those to come."

For a long time they lay sipping champagne, watching the changing colors of the canyon in the lateral rays of the sun.

He broke the long stretch of silence. "I've thought a lot about the scrolls, what will be different when the world knows about them."

"That should be soon. And I can tell you, a lot will be different," she predicted. "The news will turn the theological world on its head."

"That's putting it mildly," he agreed. "Why is it taking them so long?"

"Professor Stewart is working with the British Museum on releasing the news and protecting us at the same time." She swung one leg over the other so her foot dangled close to his. "We broke a Syrian law, you know."

"Syrians are breaking Syrian laws," he replied quickly. "Even as we speak, on Valentine's Day, Assad is killing his own—children, the elderly, cripples. There is no law in Syria."

"Regardless, when the dust settles, there may be questions."

Another long silence. He began humming a tune.

"I like that song," she said. "Sinatra was the only one to do it justice. We *were* really strangers when we first met." She looked at him. "When did it turn for you?"

He looked at the vivid sunset display on the canyon walls and thought a while, twirled the golden liquid in his glass, thought a while longer.

"It's taking that long?" she teased and kicked him playfully with her foot.

"No, not the point in time." He turned and faced her. "There were several pivotal moments, but one stands out. It was on the way to Maaloula. I had just told Muhammed to turn and go around Damascus. You were very angry with me, ignored me. I initiated a discussion on Mark's last page and you engaged. You were superb, quoting Kierkegaard, Tennyson, waxing eloquently about faith and doubt versus cynicism. I will never forget it. I was impressed that someone in the British Special Forces knew more of the New Testament than I did with my accumulated years and degrees. Yes, then, during those moments, I saw you differently. My attitude changed." He uncurled a finger from his glass and pointed at her. "Your turn."

"The same time and place," she responded. "It's amazing what can kill anger. You pulled me out of my funk. That discussion loosened things up. I, too, was attracted to your knowledge and reasoning. You made some points, especially about fear, I had never considered. You almost had me doubting my own position."

"That never showed."

"I had wondered if you were a spiritual person or just a rock digger. Your spirituality came through and touched mine. That was a softening point. Then you mentioned the wager. We became playful. In those moments, I began to feel we were on the same page, pun intended."

He laughed. "We are like Mark's blind man in chapter eight, a pivotal point in his gospel. The blind man gradually regained his sight. In the next story, the disciples have been blind and then gradually see Jesus, who he really is."

"It took us a while," she concurred, "But we see."

"Yes," and he looked at her. "We do. C. S. Lewis was right. Resurrections occur in the oddest and strangest of ways." He paused and was still looking at her. "I think we should go back," he suggested with a smile.

"I think not. They're waiting for us in Maaloula."

"Not Maaloula ... Baalbek."

"Is that a proposal?"

"Muhammed could drive us."

"Is that a proposal?" she asked again.

"Maybe even invite the border official."

She reached over and socked him playfully on the arm. "Christopher Jordan, you are not answering my question."

"But I did. You just didn't hear it."

"If I married you," she said astonished, "I would have to move to Arizona. What could I do here?"

"Work with me. Teach at the University of North Arizona. They have a linguistics division in their anthropology and archaeological departments. One of the career paths for students in the graduate program is museum curator. What could be a better fit for you? With your background and credentials, the administrators would be on their knees begging."

She was looking at him, her head cocked to one side as though in a shock of disbelief. Then her face righted. A smile creased it. "I'll say, Chris Jordan, you do drive a hard bargain for this Scottish lass. Have you forgotten I am the lady in charge of a manor? I am a leader in Dunbar. Many people depend upon me. I could not just pull up stakes, *a la* Abraham, and move to Canaan."

"According to our dear professor," he countered lightheartedly, "your main job is in London with the British Museum. You were on loan to him. The loan is over. If you can manage your estate from London, you can manage it from Flagstaff. You could return as needed. I'd be delighted to accompany."

Hiding a smile, she looked away, at the shadows filling up the canyon. He'd observed that she would grind her teeth when in deep thought and could see the muscles rippling in her jaws. She took a drink then faced him, clucked her tongue, jerked her head sideways, and said, "You could always come to Scotland."

"And what would I do there?"

"You could teach at the University. They have a splendid anthropological program. Your archaeological ventures could continue. I daresay they are not all commissioned by the university in Arizona, but many are independent. You would be landed gentry, have a roof over your head, food on your plate, not to mention a dutiful wife as your escort."

"I would have to give up my lovely home here and my job."

"Precisely. And look what you'd gain," she replied resolutely.

They touched glasses again, the sound carrying out over the canyon, its echo returning.

"I accept!" he said.

She leaned over, kissed him and smiled. "Mommy, something big happened here."

THE END

ACKNOWLEDGMENTS

I am indebted, always, to my readers: Dr. Roy H. Ryan, Dr. David N. White, Drs. Gerald and Julie Walton, and Bill Rutledge. Many thanks to editors Carol Killman Rosenberg, Adele Brinkley, and publisher Regan Rothe and his editorial staff at Black Rose Writing.

Frances Henderson of New College at the University of Edinburgh provided helpful updates on the changes since I was there in seminary 1965-66, plus access to recent photos of the campus and buildings.

Leslie Criss and Joe Rutherford of the Northeast Mississippi Daily Journal are credited for birddogging the C. S. Lewis quote.

An abundance of thanks to my parents, William Edward and Joan Ferguson Morris. The research for this book began when I was eight years old and they gave me an *Egermier Bible Story Book* and the questions began. Through seminary, thirty-nine years in the pastorate and now, going into my seventy-eighth year on this earth, the quest continues.

There is no way I could cite and give credit to all of the resources along the way. But several stand out and aided me particularly with the writing of *The Lost Page.* First, and foremost, the New Testament and the Gospel of Mark (NIV Translation). The *Novum Testamentum Graece* edited by Eberhard Nestle and *A Reader's Greek New Testament,* Richard J. Goodrich and Albert L. Lukaszewski helped refresh my *koine* Greek. *A New Eusebius* edited by J. Stevenson, Eusebius' *Ecclesiastical History,* Henry Chadwick's *The Early Church* and Burnett H. Streeter's *The Primitive Church* proved to be excellent resources for the evolution of the New Testament and the Early Church. Additional valuable references include *The New Testament: Its Background, Growth & Content* by Bruce Metzger; *Encountering the Manuxcripts* by Philip Comfort and *The Gospel of Mark* by William Barclay.

A final note of gratitude is in order. This book would never have seen the light of published day without the encouragement and unrelenting support of my wife, Sandi, who also edited the first rough draft.

ABOUT THE AUTHOR

Joe Edd Morris is the author of *Land Where My Fathers Died*, *The Prison* (both awarded Best Fiction by the Mississippi Library Association), *Torched: Summer of '64* and non-fiction works including *Ten Things I Wish Jesus Hadn't Said*. Joe Edd is a psychologist and retired United Methodist minister. He and his wife, Sandi, live in Tupelo, MS where he has a private practice in psychology. He enjoys traveling, gardening, playing the piano and writing.

NOTE FROM THE AUTHOR

Word-of-mouth is crucial for any author to succeed. If you enjoyed *The Lost Page*, please leave a review online—anywhere you are able. Even if it's just a sentence or two. It would make all the difference and would be very much appreciated.

Thanks!
Joe Edd Morris

Other Titles from
Joe Edd Morris

The Prison

In *The Prison*, Shell Ferguson visits his incarcerated grandson Cal with tragic news: his daughter, wife, and grandmother have perished in a fire. Cal must rely on his grandfather to uncover the suspicious circumstances of the blaze, as clues unfold to establish his innocence. Compelling revelations link the fire and Cal's innocence with domestic terrorism. From plots to blow up Mississippi River bridges to threats on their lives, grandfather and grandson take a series of risks, including Cal's daring prison escape, to save the remnants of their family and southern community so disturbingly infiltrated. A surprise addition to their efforts is Cal's six-year-old daughter (thought to have died in the fire), who was kidnapped by the terrorists and escaped from their camp. The trio, in a race against time, help the FBI and Coast Guard thwart the nefarious plot.

Torched: Summer of '64

Torched: Summer of '64 finds Sam Ransom at his first pastoral appointment in Holmes County, Mississippi, in the summer of '64. At a civil rights rally, he is reunited with two friends from his childhood. His decision to join their efforts to rebuild a black church torched by nightriders sets all three on a collision course with the Klan and two grisly murders. The story is about interracial friendship and romance, the ultimate sacrifice, atonement and redemption.

We hope you enjoyed reading this title from:

www.blackrosewriting.com

Subscribe to our mailing list – *The Rosevine* – and receive
FREE books, daily deals, and stay current with news about
upcoming releases and our hottest authors.
Scan the QR code below to sign up.

Already a subscriber? Please accept a sincere thank you for
being a fan of Black Rose Writing authors.

View other Black Rose Writing titles at
www.blackrosewriting.com/books and use promo code
PRINT to receive a **20% discount** when purchasing.

Made in United States
North Haven, CT
12 June 2023

37628098R00155